Smoke filled her lungs

Coughing and choking, Abby reached under the sink for the pail. She could hardly bear to watch as the water ran with agonizing slowness into the bucket. She had to save the family papers!

She threw water into the center of the blaze, and the flames died in a hiss of foul-smelling smoke. But Abby knew better than to think the battle was over. Even as she ran to fetch more water, she could see the flicker of fresh flames burning a yellow path toward the bookshelves. Where was Steve? Why didn't he smell the smoke and come down to the basement to help her?

Her actions were automatic. Scoop water into the pail from the full sink. Run back to the burning cartons. Toss water onto the flames. Over and over again. So much for Steve, probably in the kitchen stirring soup and buttering toast while she saved the house from becoming a blazing inferno.

The lights failed a split second before she reached the sink for the sixth time. The blackness was intense, made worse by the choking smoke. Until tonight, she'd never been afraid of the dark. But then, until tonight, nobody had ever shot at her with intent to kill....

ABOUT THE AUTHOR

Jasmine Cresswell was born in Wales and educated in England. She met her husband in Brazil and, since her marriage, has lived in Australia, Canada and England, as well as in several American cities. She now makes her home in Colorado with her family and a miscellaneous assortment of "badly behaved" pets. Between writing assignments she tries to find time to accompany her jet-setting husband on some of his more exotic overseas trips.

Books by Jasmine Cresswell

HARLEQUIN INTRIGUE
51–UNDERCOVER
77–CHASE THE PAST
105–FREE FALL

HARLEQUIN PRESENTS
913–HUNTER'S PREY

HARLEQUIN HISTORICAL ROMANCE
6–THE MORETON SCANDAL

HARLEQUIN REGENCY ROMANCE
7–TRAITOR'S HEIR

Don't miss any of our special offers. Write to us at the following address for information on our newest releases.

Harlequin Reader Service
901 Fuhrmann Blvd., P.O. Box 1397, Buffalo, NY 14240
Canadian address: P.O. Box 603,
Fort Erie, Ont. L2A 5X3

Charades

Jasmine Cresswell

Harlequin Books

TORONTO • NEW YORK • LONDON
AMSTERDAM • PARIS • SYDNEY • HAMBURG
STOCKHOLM • ATHENS • TOKYO • MILAN

Harlequin Intrigue edition published October 1989

ISBN 0-373-22124-X

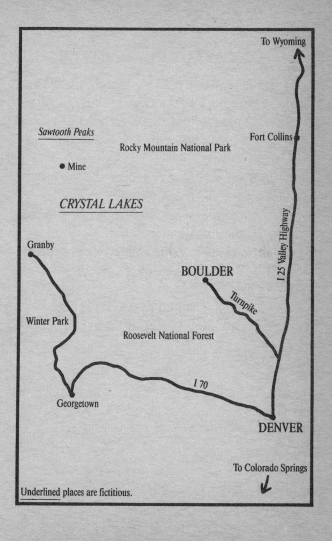

To Wyoming

Fort Collins

Sawtooth Peaks

Rocky Mountain National Park

● Mine

CRYSTAL LAKES

Granby

I 25 Valley Highway

BOULDER

Turnpike

Winter Park

Roosevelt National Forest

I 70

Georgetown

DENVER

To Colorado Springs

Underlined places are fictitious.

CAST OF CHARACTERS

Abigail Deane—Could she match wits with a murderer and save the Deane family fortune?

Steve Kramer—Someone is embezzling money from the bank, and Steve's job is to find out who.

Keith Bovery—Bank president and the pillar of respectability—or is he?

Peter Graymont—An antique dealer who deals in more than just antiques.

Gwen Johnson—Valued bank vice president, who lives only for her job. Or does she have a secret life?

Linda Mendoza—Full of sweetness and charm—is it only a clever mask?

Prologue

Howard Taylor parked his gray Buick LeSabre precisely eighteen inches from the right-hand wall of the garage. He pushed the gear lever gently into Park and set the hand brake. His job at the First Denver Federal Bank required precision, and he had extended his meticulous working habits to his personal life.

Glad to be home at last, Howard collected his briefcase from the passenger seat and uttered a sigh of relief. The mayor's speech had lasted for over an hour, and the Chamber of Commerce dinner seemed to have gone on forever. It would be midnight before he was in bed, and he had another heavy day ahead of him. Something odd—very odd—was going on with the bank's inactive accounts, and Abigail Deane's demand for an immediate appointment was going to make an already busy afternoon almost impossible. But he couldn't afford to cancel the appointment. Miss Deane's input might be just what he needed to convert vague suspicion into a case strong enough to take to his superiors. Howard was an expert with computers and knew how the accounts had been manipulated, but he had no intention of lashing out with wild accusations until he could demonstrate which bank officer had been guilty of the thefts. His suspicions were strong, but cautious people didn't proceed on suspicion alone. Howard was a very cautious man.

Mindful of a recent spate of burglaries in the neighborhood, he locked the car doors and rolled up the windows. No point in making life easy for the thieves and layabouts of the world. He had remarked to his wife only a couple of nights ago that people who got robbed usually deserved it. Howard disapproved of careless home owners almost as much as he disliked thieving layabouts.

With a few swift touches on a pad of electronic buttons, he deactivated his burglar alarm and lowered the garage door. As he stepped across the threshold into the kitchen, Poppy came tearing down the stairs, barking a welcome. Howard smiled and bent down to pat the little cocker spaniel's silky head. He would never have admitted as much to Jill, but he had a soft spot for Poppy and enjoyed taking care of her on the days his wife was away flying for Westway.

"Want to go for a walk, Poppy? You've been shut up a long time today, haven't you?"

The word *walk* had a dramatic effect on the spaniel. She stopped her ecstatic squirming and rushed to the patio doors, pawing at the expensive wooden frames in her eagerness to get out.

"Stop that, Poppy, I've told you before. You're ruining the finish." Howard clucked chidingly as he picked up the dog's leash, but he was smiling as he unfastened the safety bolt and slid open the glass doors. A pool of light spilled out from the kitchen, brightening the pine-scented darkness of the Denver night. The heavy, late-summer foliage stirred in the breeze, rustling a welcome. Howard breathed deeply, relishing the dry, crisp tang of the mountain air. This was a good night to take a walk, a good night to be alive.

True to her usual form, Poppy ran around his feet, barking hysterically as soon as she felt the fresh air under her tail. Without success, Howard tried to convince the overexcited dog to sit still while he slipped on the leash.

"If you'd only stop wriggling, this whole exercise would be finished a lot sooner," he remarked grumpily. "You're worse than ever tonight, Poppy. I'm taking you to obedience class in the fall, and this time I mean it. It's no good sticking your tongue out like that and looking pathetic. You have no manners."

Poppy barely had time to look contrite. Howard heard a whistle of wind, felt a sudden sharp pain and glanced down—to see blood spurting out of a neat hole in the breast pocket of his jacket. A bullet, fired from behind one of the bushes fringing the patio, had hit him square in the chest. He stared in surprise, transfixed by the pulsating gushes of red that were pouring through his fingers.

"I'm shot. My God, I've been shot!" Howard wasn't sure if he spoke aloud. His heart exploded in a burst of agony, and he realized with amazement that he was dying. He fell to his knees, his mouth twisted into a silent scream. The last thing he saw was Poppy, her brown eyes round with fear, her friendly spaniel face contorted into a canine snarl of terror.

Poor Poppy. He hoped somebody would find her before she ran out into the road. She had never shown a lick of sense about traffic.

Howard closed his eyes.

THE FIGURE stepped from the shelter of the bushes, a black shadow against the shadows of the summer night. The murder weapon, a .38 Webley, smelled of burned potassium nitrate and hot metal. The smell brought back vivid memories of Korea, not all of them bad.

Poppy sat beside her dead master and started to howl. The murderer quickly grabbed the leash and led the protesting spaniel back into the house. Once inside, the dog cowered in a corner of the kitchen by the dishwasher, whining quietly. The murderer ignored her.

Howard's leather briefcase sat on the kitchen counter. The murderer flipped open the locks. The papers—those damned incriminating computer printouts—were tucked in the file pocket. With a chuckle of triumph, the intruder removed the papers and gently upended the briefcase. Journals and paper clips and pens tumbled to the floor in a convincing shambles, Howard's wallet resting on the top of the pile. Almost as an afterthought, the murderer reached down and extracted the money from Howard's wallet. Twenty bucks. Hardly worth kneeling for.

Ransacking the kitchen cupboards took no more than two minutes. With quick, quiet steps, the murderer then moved into the study and searched the filing cabinets, tossing papers onto the floor as they were read. Nothing incriminating there, thank God.

Better steal a few more items. The murderer glanced into the nearby family room and hurriedly unplugged the VCR. No need to waste time going up to the second floor. No need to take Jill's jewelry. This chaotic scene was already a convincing imitation of an interrupted burglary.

The murderer cast one final glance at Howard's body and felt a thrill of mingled triumph and excitement. Killing was so easy once you remembered the old techniques. It was astonishing, when you came to think of it, that more people didn't solve their problems this way.

The killer pocketed the gun. Howard was taken care of—very satisfactorily. Now there were only the letters and the certificates to worry about. The letters, the certificates. And Abigail Deane.

Taking care of her was going to be a real pleasure.

Chapter One

Abigail Deane pushed open the heavy outer door of the First Denver Federal Bank. "Mr. Taylor's office please?" she asked the security guard.

"It's way over in back. Turn right by the palm trees. But I don't think you should go through there, miss—"

"Don't worry, I have a four-thirty appointment." Abby cut off the guard's protest with a polite smile and hurried across the bank lobby. Punctuality was the outward sign of a courteous, well-organized mind, and Abby prided herself on being punctual. After all, *somebody* in the Deane family needed to keep their feet firmly on the ground—especially now that her sisters had floated off into the sunset on twin clouds of love and adventure.

Abby gave herself a brisk mental shake. Her life was too well planned for her to feel lonely because Linsey and Kate had gotten married. Love and adventure wouldn't fit too well into her life-style, she thought with rueful humor. She liked a neat life and tidy emotions, and knew from bitter experience that love was rarely tidy. Squaring her shoulders, she rapped firmly on the frosted glass panel inscribed Mr. Howard Taylor, Senior Vice President.

"Yes, what can I do for you?" The plump, middle-aged woman who opened the door sounded curt, despite the soft lilt of her Southern accent. She glanced at Abby from red-rimmed eyes. "If you want the police, the lieutenant's in Mr. Bovery's office."

Police? Abby suppressed a mild curiosity. "No, I don't want the lieutenant, thanks. I'm Abigail Deane. I have a four-thirty appointment with Mr. Howard Taylor."

The plump woman gave an embarrassed gasp. "Miss Deane! Oh Lordie, I meant to phone you right after lunch, but I forgot—"

"Is there some reason why I can't see Mr. Taylor?" Abby tried not to feel irritated by the woman's fluttering manner. "There's a problem with my family's trust account that we need to get cleared up as soon as possible."

"Mr. Taylor's dead," the woman said flatly. "He was shot last night by some crazy burglar. In his own backyard, too. His dog had nearly clawed through the patio door by the time Howard was found. Her paws were covered in blood from trying to scratch the screen open. No wonder people say dogs are more loving than human beings."

Abby shuddered. "Oh, my goodness, how dreadful! How awful! I'm so sorry. I hope nobody else in Mr. Taylor's family was hurt."

"No, thank heavens. His wife's a flight attendant with Westway, and she didn't get home until this morning. She was the one who found him, poor woman, although I guess it's just as well she was out of town. These darn robbers don't care who they shoot."

"I'm so sorry," Abby repeated helplessly, searching in vain for something more comforting to say. Nausea stirred in the pit of her stomach and she swallowed hard, gulping in a deep lungful of air. She'd never met Howard Taylor, but they'd often spoken on the phone, and the violent manner of his death brought back memories that were fresh enough to frighten her. She still had vivid nightmares about her sisters' recent clashes with death and destruction.

The other woman smiled sadly. "Why is it always the good people like Howard who end up dying before their time? Ah, well. By the way, I'm Linda Mendoza, Mr. Bovery's secretary. If you'll step into the office, perhaps I can find somebody to assist you. Personally, I'm afraid I don't understand higher finances, which is a dreadful thing to admit, since I work in a bank."

"Don't worry. I'm sure everyone's busy, and I can come back next week. The computer has been messing up our account for months, so another couple of days won't make much difference."

"Well, that's real nice of you to be so understanding, Miss Deane. I've been trying to sort through Howard's files so that we can share out his work, but my heart isn't in it. And then Lieutenant Knudsen hasn't helped, tramping in and out of these offices for the past two hours, distracting us all."

A chill rippled down Abby's spine. "Lieutenant Knudsen from the Colorado Bureau of Investigation? He's the detective investigating this murder?"

"Yes. You sound as if you know him."

Abby realized her fingers were curled so tightly around the handle of her briefcase that her hands had gone numb. She unclenched her fists and forced herself to answer Linda's question in a normal voice. "Douglas Brady—my half brother—was shot recently. Lieutenant Knudsen was in charge of the case."

"Sometimes Denver seems like a real small town, doesn't it? In good ways and in bad. You meet the same people everywhere." Linda Mendoza tactfully asked nothing further, perhaps because she was already aware of the dramatic circumstances surrounding Douglas's death.

The sound of footsteps in the lobby attracted her attention. "Speak of the devil—here is the lieutenant."

Knudsen stuck his head around the office door. "I'm leaving, Mrs. Mendoza. Sorry for the interruption and all the questions."

"I don't care how many questions you ask, Lieutenant. Just find the brute who killed Howard, that's all I want."

"You and me both, Mrs. Mendoza."

Abigail made some slight, involuntary movement, and the lieutenant stared at her with suddenly narrowed eyes.

"Miss Deane! Abigail Deane!" Knudsen rarely betrayed his emotions, but on this occasion he couldn't conceal his surprise. "What in the world brings you here, Miss Deane?"

"A business appointment. How are you, Lieutenant?"

"Busy, but all the better for seeing you. You've saved me a trip across town, in fact. I have some questions for you about Howard Taylor's murder."

"Questions for me?" Abby controlled a quiver of tension. "I'd be happy to help, Lieutenant, but I'm afraid I don't know anything about Mr. Taylor or his death."

"Perhaps you know more than you think. How well acquainted were you with the deceased?"

"Not at all, except as a voice over the phone. We'd conferred a few times about my account—"

"But your relationship with Mr. Taylor didn't extend in any way outside office hours?"

"Lieutenant, I just explained we barely had a business relationship, much less anything more personal. I was expecting to meet Mr. Taylor this afternoon for the first time. My presence in the bank today is sheer coincidence.''

Knudsen eyed her from beneath bushy red eyebrows. "Is that so, Miss Deane? Well, I'd say it's a real big coincidence, in view of the fact that Mr. Taylor was shot by a bullet from the same gun as shot your brother.''

Linda Mendoza gasped. Abby leaned against the desk, suddenly in urgent need of solid support behind her wobbly knees.

"The same gun that shot Douglas?" she repeated. "Do you mean with the same *type* of gun?"

"No, Miss Deane, I mean the exact same weapon. The lab claims it's a .38 Webley manufactured some time before 1955. There were two different types of bullets in your brother's body, some .45s and a couple of .38s. It was a .45 bullet that actually killed him, and we found the murder weapon, all right. But if you remember, we never did find the Webley that fired the .38s.''

"No, I didn't remember. Precisely what are you suggesting, Lieutenant Knudsen?''

"Nothing at the moment. I'm merely pointing out a couple of odd coincidences. We don't like coincidence in police work.''

A brisk, feminine voice spoke from the office doorway. "Lieutenant, I'm sorry to interrupt, but there's a phone call for you. Urgent. The switchboard has put it through on my line.''

"Thanks, Ms. Johnson, I'll be right there." Lieutenant Knudsen nodded to Abby and Linda Mendoza. "Goodbye, ladies. I'll be in touch if anything comes up.''

It was amazing how such an innocuous parting remark could sound so ominous, Abby reflected. The knowledge that Howard Taylor and her brother had been killed with the same weapon made her flesh creep. Knudsen was right; it was a mighty big coincidence. A horrible coincidence. She was so lost in thought that she jumped when she realized that the second woman had come into the room and that Linda Mendoza was speaking.

"Miss Deane, I'd like you to meet our vice president of customer relations, Gwen Johnson. Gwen worked with Howard on quite a lot of his accounts, and she may be able to help straighten out your problem, if you could give her a few details."

"It's a pleasure to meet you, Miss Deane." Gwen Johnson took Abby's hand in a firm shake. In contrast to Linda's fluttery Southern charm, Gwen's manner was strictly Northern no-nonsense, but her smile was warm. She was taller and more angular than the petite, well-padded Linda, but both women were attractive—walking advertisements for the joys of being female and fifty, Abby reflected.

Gwen Johnson seated herself behind Howard's desk. "I can't imagine why Lieutenant Knudsen's been giving all of us the third degree. Howard's murder was a gruesome waste of a fine man, but the sort of tragedy we have to expect with all the drug-crazed criminals out on our streets. Shocking to think a fine man can die because some junkie needs a quick snort of coke."

"Yes, you don't want to worry, Miss Deane," Linda Mendoza chimed in. "You should put that nasty old coincidence about the gun and your brother right out of your mind."

"It's not an easy coincidence to dismiss," Abigail said. "It's frightening to think that one of the thugs who tried to kill my sister Kate may never have been locked up."

"You're jumping to conclusions," Linda said quickly. "Probably the man who shot your brother threw the gun away before he was arrested. Then some burglar picked the gun out of the ditch or off the roadside, and used it to shoot poor Howard. There's nothing mysterious about that, is there?''

"That's certainly a more likely explanation than some bizarre secret connection between Howard Taylor and Miss Deane's brother," Gwen Johnson agreed. "Now, why don't we put all this grim talk about murder to one side and try to straighten out the problem with the Deane trust account? I don't want to sound heartless, but sometimes routine work is the best way to cope with a tragic loss."

Abigail agreed, and quickly drew a half dozen sheets of paper from her briefcase. "These are my two most recent bank statements. Last week I finally had time to cross-check them against my own records. I discovered that the bond numbers the bank has listed don't agree with the numbers in my personal files, which means our account is missing in excess of ten thousand dollars. Also the income figures for the last quarter seem too low. That could be because of the mix-up with the bonds, of course. Interest payments that should have gone into the Deane accounts have probably gone into another account. Or they may still be lost somewhere in the depths of the computer."

Gwen Johnson glanced swiftly at the statements with obvious expertise. "It was helpful of you to highlight the presumed errors," she said. "If all these bond numbers really have been transposed, some bank employee has been inexcusably careless."

She looked up, her expression half teasing, half admiring. "The bank could do with a few more clients like you, Miss Deane. Most of our customers don't check their statements carefully, and then mistakes go on for months before we discover them through our own internal audits. I've been in banking for nearly thirty years, and I doubt if I've met more than a dozen customers who are sensible enough to keep a fully documented list of their assets.''

Abby flushed with pleasure. Despite all the flak she endured from her scatterbrained family, she took great pride in the meticulous accuracy of her record keeping. "I'm an archivist," she said by way of explanation. "We're trained to keep careful records. Kate always teases me that I could find every document I've ever possessed, from my kindergarten math report on up.''

"And could you?" Linda asked.

"Probably." Abigail's smile was rueful. "My sisters insist I'm a changeling. Nobody else in our family can even balance a checkbook, and here I am with a double entry filing system and a closet with color-coded hangers!''

"Your sisters are lucky to have you," Gwen said. "You've no idea the stories I hear in the customer service department. We have clients who keep thousands of dollars in envelopes behind the furnace, and their citizenship papers hidden 'safely' in a flour sack. And some of the worst offenders are well-educated people.''

Abby laughed. "Remember I'm an archivist, Ms. Johnson. Please don't give me a heart attack!''

"Then I won't tell you about the toddler who flushed his parents' income tax return down the toilet." Gwen Johnson smiled, her blue eyes twinkling. "We'll talk about the problems with your account instead, Abigail. May I call you Abigail?''

"Of course.''

"Thank you. I promise to look into these errors myself, first thing tomorrow, and track down the root cause of the problem. It goes without saying that if the bank has made mistakes, we'll rectify them at our expense. With interest compounded.''

Gwen Johnson was still speaking when a distinguished-looking man with thick white hair and ruddy cheeks poked his head around the door. With a mental groan, Abby recognized Keith Bovery, the bank's president and a longtime friend of her father. This was one encounter she'd hoped to avoid.

Keith Bovery strode into the office without noticing Abby. ''Linda, I've been going through some of Howard's files, and I've found this one marked Investigation—Confidential. But the file's empty. Do you know what Howard was investigating?''

''I've no idea.'' Linda sounded hurt. ''May I see the file, Keith?''

''Certainly, but I don't think it will tell you much.''

Linda examined the empty manila folder with great care. ''I've never seen it before,'' she admitted finally. ''Howard must have made this one himself. That's his writing on the label.'' Her nerves seemed to be on edge after the difficult day, for she teetered on the brink of tears. ''I can't help you, Keith, I'm sorry. I don't know anything about an investigation, although usually Howard confided all the details of his work to me.''

''Perhaps this was something strictly technical,'' Gwen suggested. ''You know you don't understand financial data, Linda.''

''Whatever it is, I ought to have been informed.'' Mr. Bovery sounded cross.

''If Howard was working on something confidential, maybe he took the papers home?'' Gwen suggested. ''If you like, I could make a tactful phone call to Jill Taylor tomorrow and ask her to check through the house for any bank materials he may have left there.''

Mr. Bovery considered her proposal. "No, wait a couple of days," he said eventually. "I doubt if Howard was working on something so vital that we need to bother his poor widow before the funeral. I'll take care of the call myself next week, if nothing's turned up at the office."

He patted Linda's arm. "Look, ladies, it's after five and it's been a rotten day. You should get home and have an early night."

The banker peered over his horn-rimmed glasses as he turned to go, and finally registered Abby's presence. His face broke into a pleased, affectionate smile. "Abigail, my dear, what a nice surprise. It's been too long since I saw you. I hope you're keeping well?"

"Very well, thank you." Keith Bovery had been a friend of the Deane family since he served with Abby's father in the Korean War. He firmly believed that having pushed Abby in her stroller entitled him to make any and every personal remark that flew into his head. Abby smothered an inward sigh and waited for the banker to do his worst. She didn't wait long.

He put one arm around her shoulder, the TV-perfect image of a kindly, softhearted family banker. In reality, Abby knew his heart was about as soft as steel-reinforced concrete, especially where the operations of his precious bank were concerned.

"What are you up to these days, my dear? Still burying yourself in dusty documents over at the Historical Society?"

"Yes, I am." Abby smiled sweetly. "But I try to come up for air every month or so. Just to blow off the dust, you know."

Impervious to sarcasm, Mr. Bovery shook his head. "It's time you followed in your sisters' footsteps and found yourself a husband, Abigail. When I was a young man, we'd have snapped up a pretty girl like you in a minute. Never seen a girl with prettier blond hair than yours."

"I was snapped up," Abby said quietly. "I was twenty-two, and my marriage lasted eight months, if you remember."

Mr. Bovery had the grace to look abashed. "I'd forgotten about Greg," he said. "But not all men are as irresponsible as he was, Abigail. You need to find somebody reliable. Somebody you can trust. You're not getting any younger, you know. You'll need the companionship one day soon, mark my words."

"Right. Here I am, almost twenty-nine. I'd better latch on to somebody hale and hearty while I still have all my own teeth."

Mr. Bovery smiled. "You think I'm an interfering old busybody, Abigail. But your father and I were friends for years, and I'd like to see you happily settled. Believe me, since my dear Helen died last year, I've learned what loneliness means."

Abby suddenly felt tired. Keith Bovery meant well, and she shouldn't be so impatient with him, just because his attitude toward women was stuck in some 1950s time warp. "I'll start looking for a new husband tonight," she said good-naturedly. "Or at least tomorrow. That's a promise, Mr. Bovery."

She shook hands with the two women and walked quickly to the door. "I'm really sorry about Howard Taylor. It seems as if you've all lost a good friend as well as a colleague."

"Sadly, you're right." Keith Bovery's mouth drooped into a smile that didn't seem entirely sincere. "Well, good night, Abigail. And don't you give that mix-up with your account another thought, my dear. First Denver Federated takes pride in its service to its customers. I'm sure this little shortfall has a very simple explanation. I'll take care of sorting everything out personally. Your account will be back in order by the weekend, you have my word on it.''

Abby was halfway back to the parking lot before she realized just why she had found Mr. Bovery's parting remarks so troublesome. During their conversation in Howard Taylor's office, Mr. Bovery had asked Abby about her sisters, her job, and the status of her love life, but he'd never once asked her why she was at the bank. So how come he'd reassured her on parting that the shortfall in her account would be straightened out by the weekend? How did he know about the missing ten thousand dollars in the Deane Trust account? Was it possible that the dignified, pompous Mr. Keith Bovery had taken to creeping down hallways and listening outside his staffers' keyholes? Or did he have some other reason for knowing that money was missing from the account?

Abigail had an archivist's instinct for written records that didn't quite fit the proper pattern, and her professional thumb had been prickling ever since she spotted the errors in the Deane Trust account.

Something very odd was going on at First Denver Federated. But Abigail wasn't at all sure that she wanted to find out what.

Chapter Two

The drive home to her condo in Larimer Square did nothing to improve Abby's mood, which had progressed from puzzlement through minor gloom to full-scale dejection by the time she rode the elevator up to her seventh-floor apartment. For once, the sparkling white paint, silver-gray carpet and gleaming contemporary furniture failed to lift her spirits. She roamed restlessly from living room to bedroom to kitchen before giving a resigned shrug, acknowledging the inevitable. Tonight she was going to need a good stiff dose of Steven Kramer's company, if she hoped to shake off these clinging tentacles of depression. A lot of the time she found Steve's laid-back attitude to life infuriating, but she had to admit that he possessed an uncanny ability to make her relax.

Abby climbed the three flights of stairs to Steve's penthouse apartment, cheered just by the prospect of seeing her old friend. She didn't ask herself whether he'd be home from the office. Steve worked for his uncle's accounting firm, and to the best of her knowledge he'd never put in a moment's overtime in his entire life. Even when she'd first met him as a student at Columbia University, she could never remember actually seeing him study. How he had managed to graduate with a master's degree in finance remained a total mystery to her.

She pressed the buzzer on his front door. "Open up, Steve!" she called. "It's me. I'm throwing myself on your mercy. I need something wonderful to eat for dinner."

Abby would never have invited herself to dinner with anybody else without checking to make sure it was convenient. But Steve Kramer was different. With Steve she felt able to relax in a way that was unique. If he had other plans for dinner, she knew he would say so without embarrassment.

The door swung open, and Steve stood framed in the doorway, all six foot two of muscular body poured casually into faded jeans and a shirt that had lost most of its buttons. His sun-bleached hair was tousled, his skin tanned dark brown from weekends spent climbing in the Rocky Mountains. For a split second Abby's stomach tightened, then Steve grinned and the moment of tension passed.

"I was just hoping some gorgeous woman would walk into my apartment and offer me her body," he said. "And here you are, right on schedule."

Abby returned his grin. "You have to feed me first and ply me with liquor. Then we'll discuss the next part of the deal."

"Honey, you've been promising to discuss the next part of the deal for the last six months. So far I'm out about two dozen gourmet dinners and most of my stock of Bordeaux. But you're not one step closer to discovering what an exciting place my bedroom can be."

"Your kitchen's all the excitement I can stand." Abby followed him through the apartment, sniffing appreciatively. "You shouldn't cook such wonderful meals, then I wouldn't keep coming up here."

"Somehow I think you just missed the point," Steve said wryly. "Again."

Abby detected an unexpected note of frustration in Steve's voice. "What's wrong?" she asked, worried. "Hey, you didn't get fired or anything, did you?"

"I work for the family business. How can I get fired?" He held out a spoonful of aromatic gravy. "Here, taste. Beef burgundy. Does it need more salt?"

She sipped, then closed her eyes in exaggerated ecstasy. "It's perfect, Steve. Heavenly. I've just realized I'm totally, utterly starving. How long before dinner's ready?"

He glanced at her through narrowed eyes, then rumpled her hair in a casual gesture of affection. "Ten minutes, if you help make the salad. You shred and chop, I'll make the dressing."

"Trust you to keep the good job for yourself."

Steve reached into the cupboard and didn't respond for a second or two. "Want to tell me about it, Abby?" he asked quietly, pouring olive oil into a mixing bowl. "You're wound up tighter than a guitar string."

"Is it so obvious?"

"To me it is, yes."

She drew in a deep breath. "I had an appointment at the First Denver Bank today with the VP who handles our family accounts. Howard Taylor. When I arrived there, I learned Mr. Taylor was dead. He was shot last night by a burglar."

Steve put down his whisk, his green eyes darkening. "I heard early this morning that Howard was dead. I didn't know you were scheduled to see him, or I'd have warned you."

"You knew Howard Taylor had been murdered? Was he a friend of yours?"

Steve hesitated. "Kramer and Kramer has done consulting work for the bank from time to time. I'd met him, but I knew his wife better. Jill's a flight attendant with Westway Airlines. We used to date once, a year or two ago, and I've had dinner with her and Howard a couple of times since their wedding."

That was no surprise, Abby thought wryly. Any flight attendant based in Denver was practically guaranteed to be a Steve Kramer girlfriend, and Steve seemed to have a unique capacity for converting his lovers into friends once the sizzle turned to fizzle. Odd, though, that Steve should have known Howard Taylor. Linda Mendoza was right. Denver sometimes seemed like a very small town.

She wiped her fingers on a paper towel. "Here, I've finished cutting and chopping."

"You look more shredded than the lettuce, kiddo. Why is Howard Taylor's murder bothering you so much, when you'd never even met him?"

"It's not only the fact that he was killed…." She leaned against the counter, trying to appear more casual than she felt. She knew her tension was way out of proportion to what had actually happened. "Lieutenant Knudsen was at the bank this afternoon. I don't expect you remember him, but he's the guy from the CBI who investigated my brother's murder."

"I do remember. Seeing him must have revived some unpleasant memories. I'm sorry."

Abby laughed shortly. " 'Unpleasant' isn't exactly the right word. Guess what? The lieutenant said Howard Taylor was killed with the same .38 Webley that shot my brother, Douglas."

For a split second Steve was totally silent. She'd hoped he would dismiss her fears with a witty one-liner, but he didn't. Instead he looked at her searchingly. "What did Knudsen say about that coincidence?"

"That he doesn't like coincidence in police work. He seemed to find my presence in Howard's office highly suspicious." Abby attempted to laugh, but had a feeling that it didn't quite come off. "By the time he'd finished questioning me, I could almost hear the rattle of the handcuffs. God knows what he suspects. Maybe he thinks I'm the leader of the gang terrorizing Howard Taylor's neighborhood."

Steve grasped her shoulders and swung her around to face him. For once, his eyes met hers without a trace of laughter. "Abby, tell me precisely what you were planning to discuss at your meeting with Howard Taylor."

She stared at him in surprise. "Some bond numbers in the Deane Family Trust had been wrongly entered into the bank's computer system. I wanted to alert a bank officer to the problem before our account got into a total mess."

"Did you lose money because of the errors?"

His question was so clipped that it made her uncomfortable. "Yes, some." She cleared her throat. "A lot, actually. Nearly ten thousand dollars. The bank's going to make it right, of course."

"Damn! This is a new twist." Steve released her from his grasp, his expression abstracted. "Sit down, Abby, and I'll get the casserole."

"Oh no, you don't!" She stood in front of the oven, arms crossed aggressively. "You're worse than Knudsen, Steve. What the heck is going on at the bank? Why are you developing this sudden interest in the status of my account? And what do you mean, 'a new twist'?"

For a moment she thought Steve wasn't going to answer. Then he sighed. "I'm breaking my own prime rule about client confidentiality to tell you this, Abby. But the fact is, I'm currently investigating a case of embezzlement at the First Denver Bank. More than half a million dollars has been stolen over the past nine months, and Howard Taylor was our chief suspect.''

Abby sat down on the nearest kitchen chair, almost more startled by the image of Steve Kramer at the heart of an embezzlement investigation than by the possibility that ultrarespectable Howard Taylor might be the embezzler.

"You're investigating an embezzlement?" she muttered. "Good grief, Steve! Somehow I just can't visualize you as a financial supersleuth.''

"That's because I'm not. I'm an accountant. I spend most of my workday running bank ledgers through various computer programs. Hard to imagine anything more boring.''

His reply sounded brisk, dismissive—and oddly competent. Abby looked at him, wondering if she'd ever really seen him in proper focus before. "Why didn't you tell me what you do for a living?''

"You never asked," he said simply. "And a firm like ours works more effectively without too much publicity." He took out the casserole. "The sauce is going to dry up if I let it sit in the oven any longer. Let's continue this over dinner, shall we?''

Abby followed him into the dining alcove and served herself with the tender beef, simmered in burgundy. For once she ate, scarcely noticing the delicious flavor.

"You said Howard Taylor was embezzling money from First Denver Bank?" she asked. "He didn't seem like the type to embezzle a paper clip, let alone half a million dollars.''

"Actually I said that the evidence so far all points to Howard's guilt. Personally, I'm not entirely convinced he was the embezzler. I have a couple more checks I need to run before I'm willing to close the files.''

Abby's mind buzzed with questions. ''Whoever it was, how did he work the embezzlement? Any connection to the mix-up I discovered in our trust account?''

''It's a possibility to consider, although the embezzlements we've discovered so far have all been in the area of sleeper accounts.''

''I don't know what sleeper accounts are,'' Abby admitted.

''Any bank has dozens, sometimes hundreds, of accounts where there's been no activity for several years. For example, a wife opens up a savings account without telling her husband. She makes deposits for years, then she dies. Her husband doesn't know anything about her secret nest egg, and the bank has no way of knowing its client died. Years go by. Interest piles up. The 'little nest egg' becomes a large sum. Most banks have thousands of dollars lying around in accounts nobody will ever claim.''

''And somebody at First Denver decided to help themselves to all the lovely idle cash?''

''Yes. A keen-eyed temporary clerk first noticed the unusual activity and was smart enough to report the flurry of withdrawals directly to Keith Bovery. Fortunately for me, that means the culprit doesn't know the embezzlements have been discovered.''

Abby's eyes twinkled with mischief. ''Unless it's Mr. Bovery himself doing the embezzling.''

Steve grinned. ''Honey, I know you'll never forgive the guy because he's a hopeless chauvinist and once changed your diapers, but he's the soul of integrity and a wealthy man in his own right.''

''Huh! When did being rich ever stop people from wanting to get richer? Mr. Bovery probably has a secret vice that costs millions to support. He framed poor old Howard Taylor and then committed murder to stop his evil deeds from being discovered...."

Abby's voice trailed away; she realized with horror where her flippancy had led her. Even if he was a pompous ass, Keith Bovery didn't deserve to be slandered so outrageously.

Steve tactfully broke her embarrassed silence. "You're falling into the same trap as me, Abby. I always want to tie all the loose ends in my investigations together. But in real life, loose ends tend to dangle. Howard Taylor's death was probably exactly what it seems. A random shooting incident during a burglary that had no connections to the embezzlement at the bank."

She wished she could accept Steve's calm logic. "But doesn't the fact that my half brother and Howard Taylor were shot by the same gun strike you as going a bit beyond coincidence? Especially since Howard was implicated in a criminal situation at the bank? Two major coincidences surrounding one incident. That's not a loose end, it's a gaping hole."

"Okay. Howard Taylor's death strikes me as odd. Very odd. But I can only repeat that the world is an untidy place, Abby. Unreasonable things happen. And in any case, whatever might be going on, I'm sure it's got nothing to do with you or your family."

Abby's smile didn't quite reach her eyes, she knew. "Steve, you've lost your silver tongue. I'm not finding your arguments one bit convincing."

"All right, then. How's this?" Now Steve sounded exasperated. "Some evil psychopath is on the loose, still armed with the Webley he used to murder your half brother. Howard Taylor was shot because he'd uncovered evidence that would reveal the identity of the real embezzler, who'd been working in cahoots with Douglas, both on the embezzlements and to steal the Confederate gold.''

"That certainly ties up all the loose ends," Abby said evenly.

Steve looked at her with sudden intensity. He pushed back his chair, walked quickly around the table and pulled her into his arms. "Abby, for God's sake! I wasn't being serious! Not even halfway serious.''

She stared fixedly at his shirt. "I'm scared, Steve.'' The admission didn't come easy, and she was grateful when he didn't say anything. Instead his hands stroked along her spine, offering silent comfort as she forced herself to shape her fears into words.

"I didn't realize until this afternoon how scared I've been for the past few weeks," she said at last. "My sisters suffered through so much violence this summer that some crazy, superstitious part of me just can't relax. I keep thinking the circle of violence isn't closed yet. The cycle isn't complete. Never two without three." She tried to smile, to mock her own fears. "You name the cliché, I've worried about it.''

Steve framed her face in his hands, his touch gentle. "Abby, what happened with your sisters is over. Their danger ended when you converted the Confederate gold into ordinary currency and stored it in the bank. If the cycle of violence doesn't feel complete to you, that's because your own fear is keeping it open.''

"I'm doing this to myself, huh? I've nothing to fear but fear itself.''

"Something like that." He brushed his thumbs lightly across her cheeks, and his eyes warmed her with the beginnings of a smile. "Sweetheart, let go of the worry. Believe me, there are better things to hug next to your heart.''

Abby stirred uncomfortably in his arms, suddenly aware how closely he was holding her. She was well used to physical contact with him when they climbed, but the sensations she was feeling tonight seemed subtly different. She wasn't accustomed to being held pressed against him, heart beating against heart, thigh nestled intimately against thigh. And the fact that tonight some perverse part of her badly needed his comfort—badly wanted to stay in his arms—made her logical mind all the more anxious to return their relationship to its usual footing.

"Huh," she said. "I know where that advice is coming from, Steve Kramer. You think I should hug *you* next to my heart, that's what it is."

For a split second she felt Steve's resistance to her deliberate change of mood, then the tension seeped out of him, and he responded with a familiar grin. "Honey, that's the smartest suggestion you've made all night. Did you know I come with a certificate of huggability?" His grin changed to an exaggerated leer. "Want to come into my bedroom and check it out?"

"There's no need to check it out," Abby said. "Remember, I'm an archivist. I can spot a fake certificate at twenty paces."

He gave a mock sigh. "Drat! Foiled again." He released her from his arms, squishing her nose flat with one finger as a parting salute. "I'll get us some coffee. Catch me up on the family news. Have you heard anything lately from Kate or Linsey?"

"I had a letter from Linsey yesterday. The honeymoon's obviously over, as far as she's concerned. She only mentions Darren's name twenty-five times."

"How long's the letter?"

"Two pages."

Steve laughed. "What about Kate?"

"She called a couple of days ago, alternately ecstatic and incoherent. The general drift of the conversation seemed to be that RJ is a demanding, stubborn, high-handed Southern brute, and that marriage to him is utter bliss."

"That seems like the Kate I know and love."

"Well, sort of. Would you believe she's actually decided to go back to college and get a graduate degree?"

"I'm glad her husband's given her the confidence to do it. See how beneficial matrimony can be? Partners compensate for each other's deficiencies. If you married me, maybe I'd be able to teach you something wonderful like—"

Abby glowered at him in warning.

"Like how to cook," he continued smoothly.

She laughed. "No danger of that. I'm unteachable!"

Abby and Steve cleared up the dinner dishes together, without making any further reference to Howard Taylor's death. Superficially, their relationship seemed just as it always had been. Going down to her own apartment, however, Abby was aware of some indefinable change. Perhaps it was her own tension; perhaps it was the realization that Steve took his work a great deal more seriously than she'd ever imagined. Whatever the cause, Abby found herself emotionally on edge.

She gave an impatient shrug as she unlocked the door to her apartment. She seemed to be overreacting to everything today, from the weapon used in Howard Taylor's murder to Steve Kramer's sexy body. She'd curl up in bed with the latest copy of the *American Archivist* and regain her sense of perspective. There was nothing like a long article on the effects of creeping damp mold to get an archivist's blood racing.

The phone started to ring as she pushed the front door closed behind her. She hurried across the room and picked up the receiver. 11:00 p.m. Kate's favorite time to call.

"Hello."

"Abigail Deane?" The voice was muffled and somewhat gruff.

"Yes, this is she."

"Miss Deane, there is information you should have about your half brother, Douglas Brady. Vital information that only I can give you."

"What did you say?" Something seemed to be distorting the speaker's voice. Abby was sure she couldn't have heard correctly.

"I have news about your brother, Miss Deane."

Abby's hand was damp with sweat, and she gripped the receiver tightly to prevent it slipping. "My—my brother's dead."

"I have information about his murder, Miss Deane. And about that .38 Webley the police never found."

Dear God, the gun that had killed Howard Taylor! Abby swallowed hard. "I'm listening."

"Not now. I can't talk now. You have to meet me."

"I'm not going to meet you. Do you think I'm crazy? Who are you?"

"That doesn't matter."

"Of course it matters," Abby said sharply, her addled wits beginning to function again, although her body shook with nervous strain. "If you think I'm going to meet some totally unknown person so that we can chat about the gun that killed my half brother, you've picked the wrong victim."

"We can meet in a public place, Miss Deane. You'll be quite safe, I guarantee it. Stapleton Airport, the Westway Airlines check-in counter. Twelve noon. Don't be late. You need to meet me."

The caller hung up.

Chapter Three

Abby knew better than to pay attention to anonymous phone calls. She was also aware of the fact that crank calls could be dangerous, as well as annoying. Being an entirely sensible person, she had no intention of wasting her valuable lunch hour driving all the way to the airport on a wild-goose chase. She gave herself this excellent advice several times before she went to bed. She repeated the lecture as she was eating breakfast, and at hourly intervals during a busy morning at work.

It was, therefore, distinctly annoying when twelve noon rolled around—and Abby found herself pacing up and down alongside the Westway Airlines counter at Stapleton Airport.

What in the world are you doing here? she asked herself angrily, glancing around the bustling concourse in search of—she had no idea what. Some nasty little man in a shabby raincoat? A suave, mysterious stranger in sunglasses? The airport teemed with purposeful businessmen, harassed mothers and crying babies. Lurking informants seemed in short supply.

Abby stared up at the computerized information screen above her head. The clock flipped to 12:07, a one-minute advance on what it had shown the last time she looked.

Five more minutes, Abby muttered beneath her breath. Her lunch hour was already shot, so she might as well give the crank caller five more minutes.

At that moment she spotted a familiar figure trotting through the concourse. With a smothered groan she cowered behind a pillar, but to no avail. She might have guessed this was a day when Murphy's Law would be in full operation. Mr. Bovery saw her at once, and puffed over to greet her.

"Abigail my dear, what a pleasant surprise! Now I've seen you twice in two days." Mr. Bovery was a firm believer in stating the obvious.

"Hello, Mr. Bovery. Are you off to catch a plane?"

"Not today. Actually, I'm meeting a consultant who's flying in from Berkeley."

Abby smiled. "Goodness, I didn't know bank presidents consorted with freethinking radicals from Berkeley."

Mr. Bovery didn't appreciate the joke. He nodded in worried agreement. "I feel the same way myself. But I've been assured this man's an expert—the best person for the job, and the bank certainly needs the expertise." He stopped short, clearing his throat uncomfortably. "Well, I must be on my way. The plane lands in ten minutes. Don't forget now, Abigail! Say hello to those lovely sisters of yours."

"Pompous old fellow, isn't he?" intoned a voice close behind her. Abby spun around, nerves jangling.

"Peter Graymont!" she exclaimed, recognizing the attorney cum antique dealer. "Good grief, you nearly gave me a heart attack! When did you learn to sneak up on people like that?"

"This summer, chasing Southern antiques with your sister." Peter Graymont smiled.

"Where are you off to, Peter? Somewhere exciting?"

"I'm meeting an art dealer from Chicago. He's bringing me a dozen porcelain vases that the Chinese government just agreed to release for export. I'm more excited than if I were going off on a trip."

From the corner of her eye, Abby glimpsed Steve Kramer running toward a set of escalators. Probably he was late for a heavy date with a flight attendant, Abby thought, surprised by the sudden twinge of jealousy the thought inspired. She knew Steve wasn't the sort to expend that much energy running for a business appointment.

"I should come here more often," she remarked to Peter, dragging her gaze away from Steve Kramer's disappearing back. "If I stand on this corner much longer, it seems like I'll see everyone I know in Denver."

He laughed. "That's what they say about the Via Veneto in Rome. Personally, if I had to stand on a corner, I'd choose Rome rather than Stapleton Airport."

"I didn't exactly choose this spot, Peter. It was thrust upon me."

Peter's gaze focused somewhere over her left shoulder, and he seemed to lose interest in what she was saying. He patted her arm in a vague gesture. "I'll leave you to your celebrity spotting, Abigail. Must run. I have to get to Concourse E before Jack arrives."

"That's right at the other end of the terminal."

"I know. I parked my car without thinking. Let's hope Jack doesn't mind a brisk walk. Let's have lunch soon."

Peter strode off, debonair and purposeful in his dark blue suit. Abby took another look at the clock. 12:20. Way past the five minutes she'd promised herself to wait and definitely time to go.

On the other hand, if the mysterious caller wanted to talk to her alone, her chats with Peter and Mr. Bovery would have presented major obstacles. Perhaps she ought to allow just a couple of minutes more. After all, if somebody had important information to reveal about Douglas Brady or the gun that killed him, she owed it to the family to find out precisely what. Abby deeply regretted the fact that her half brother had been killed before she or her sisters had had a real chance to know him. If the anonymous phone caller could fill in some of the gaps in Douglas's life story, it was worth a few minutes' wait.

Two tense minutes stretched to five and then to ten. When the computer screen clock showed 12:30, Abby stopped pacing her stretch of floor and tucked her purse firmly beneath her arm. Furious with herself for having hung around so idiotically, she strode toward the main exit. In addition to being angry, she felt more than a little ashamed. There was no excuse for her foolishness. If Kate had responded to a similar crank call, Abby knew she would have delivered a long lecture on her sister's total lack of common sense. Abby ruefully acknowledged that her wasted lunch hour was no more than she deserved.

Halfway between the Westway counter and the exit, her progress was halted by a crowd waiting for some electric carts to go by. The last cart was just driving past with its load of passengers, when Abby felt a sharp blow to her back. It was followed by a hefty shove that sent her stumbling and flailing off balance into the row of people in front of her.

Abby screamed with all the force of her lungs, then realized belatedly that her nerves had been strung taut ever since yesterday. When another scream tore its way out of her throat, she knew she was close to hysterics. She swallowed hard, fighting for calm. Good grief, why had she lost control like that?

The people standing closest to her moved slightly away, distancing themselves from an obvious weirdo. She felt her cheeks flame scarlet with humiliation.

"Somebody pushed me from behind," she said in explanation, reaching up to smooth her hair in a reflex gesture—and suddenly realizing that her hands were empty.

"My purse is gone!" Abby felt hysteria rise again, and determinedly pushed it down. "My purse has been stolen," she repeated in a cool, flat voice. "Somebody pushed me and then snatched my purse."

"Did you see who did it?" asked a young woman, who appeared a little more sympathetic than the rest of the bystanders.

"You should report it to airport security right away," a middle-aged woman suggested. "Their office is downstairs by the baggage claim, I think."

"Hold on a minute, missy. Is this yours?" An elderly man with a slight European accent held out a gray leather shoulder bag, its flap hanging open, but its shoulder strap undamaged.

"Oh, yes, thank you, that's mine!" Abby took the purse, acute embarrassment mingled with her relief. "I'm so grateful to you. Where did you find it?"

"You must have dropped it on the floor when you were pushed. It was right under everyone's feet, only a couple of yards from where you're standing. Better check to see nothing's lost, yes?"

The crowd thinned rapidly, since there was nothing particularly interesting in the sight of an overwrought woman who had dropped her purse. No longer the cynosure of a dozen doubtful eyes, Abby nevertheless felt all fingers and thumbs as she unzipped the inner compartment. "My wallet and change purse are here," she said, checking quickly. "Everything's safe."

Abby turned with renewed gratitude to the elderly man. "Thank you again. I hate to think how many hours and how many phone calls it would have taken to replace everything." Feeling the need to offer some justification for her screams, she added, "I really was pushed hard, you know."

"I believe you, missy." The old man smiled kindly. "Everybody was getting a bit impatient in that crowd, and there was a lot of jostling. You know what it's like at airports. We're all running on tight schedules, yes? Now, are you sure you've got everything? Your credit cards? Your keys?"

Her rescuer obviously felt that Abby was a person who needed help in the simplest everyday tasks, and right at this moment, Abby almost agreed with him. Her bunch of keys was indeed missing. She felt for them in every nook and cranny of the purse without success, but this time refused to get flustered. She'd made enough of a spectacle of herself for one day, without coming unglued over a lost set of keys.

"Darn it, my car keys are gone," she said as casually as she could. "Looks as if I'll have to take a cab back to the office. At least I have the money to do that, thanks to you. I guess I'm lucky. One smashed pocket mirror and a missing set of keys isn't the end of the world."

"Glad everything turned out more or less okay, missy. I am sorry, but I have to run. My plane's waiting." The man pointed. "I found your purse right over there. You might look to see if the keys fell out anywhere nearby, yes?"

"Yes, I will. Goodbye, and thanks again."

"My pleasure, missy."

Abby walked slowly toward the place the man had indicated. The glossy tile floor was now relatively clear of tromping feet, and she spotted her keys on their distinctive brass chain almost at once. They lay nestled against the base of a trash can, where they must have fallen or been kicked by passing travelers. She knelt down and retrieved the keys. They were all there: office key, front door key, apartment building key, car keys.

The back of her neck prickled, and a tiny bead of sweat rolled down her spine, intensifying the uncomfortable sensation that she was being watched. Abby swung around, eyes narrowed in suspicion. She saw nothing out of the ordinary for a busy airport, nothing to justify her creeping case of paranoia. No men in dirty raincoats. No suave strangers in sunglasses. This time, not even anyone she knew.

But however sternly she lectured herself, Abby couldn't quite shake the conviction that she had been set up. Somebody had tricked her into visiting the airport for a specific purpose. But what had that purpose been? To snatch her purse? The idea made no sense. Why would anybody steal a purse and then toss it onto the ground, without removing so much as a dollar bill? The thief couldn't have feared discovery. In the crush of people surrounding Abby, any thief would have been out of sight twenty seconds before her first scream.

She had just started to backtrack toward the exit, when a pair of arms slid around her waist in a playful squeeze.

"This must be my lucky day," a husky voice murmured into her ear. "You've followed me to the airport, hoping for a little lunchtime R and R. Sweetheart, what a great idea!"

She recognized Steve Kramer's voice immediately, but she still jumped as his hands splayed out against her rib cage. "Hey, what is this?" he asked softly. "Usually you don't even notice when I touch you. Now you're twitching like a scalded cat."

"It must be all the years of repressed sexual desire finally catching up with me," Abby said caustically. "Or else, of course, it could just be that you startled me."

"Nah," he said, pretending to consider the matter. "It's definitely repressed sex. Abby, my sweet, if you'd only let go of all your inhibitions, you'd discover that you've been madly in love with me for years."

"Right. Since college, in fact."

"At least since then. Maybe even in one of our former lives."

"You Anthony, me Cleopatra? Somehow it doesn't ring any bells in my heart."

"That's because you're being sexist, sweetheart. It was probably the other way around. You were Anthony, and I was Cleopatra, pining for you aboard my golden barge, while you strode off to conquer the world."

She laughed. "I can't visualize you with black ringlets."

"How about with a snake pressed to my maidenly bosom?" Steve took Abby's hand and tucked it under his arm, propelling her away from the exit and toward the row of restaurants and coffee shops. "In compensation for your two-thousand-year-old neglect, will you keep me company while I drown my sorrows in a Coke?"

She was already so late for the office that another twenty minutes would scarcely matter. "Make that an iced tea and you have a deal," Abby said. "What particular sorrows are you drowning today? The flight attendant of your choice didn't make her connection in Chicago?"

Steve didn't answer for a moment, then he spoke without any trace of his usual flippancy. "You have a false impression about my sex life, Abby."

"I know. You're really a monk in disguise, working on a secret mission for the CIA. The women you escort all over town come to you for spiritual advice."

"The women I escort all over town are either friends or business acquaintances. I haven't dated anyone in six months. Not since I moved into the apartment above yours, in fact." Having dropped his bombshell, Steve stopped outside a bakery. "Want to go in here? Those croissants look almost edible for an airport coffee shop."

Abby cleared her throat. "Here's fine," she said, although what she really wanted to ask was why he hadn't dated for six months. Steve Kramer, celibate? The image was about as likely as Steve Kramer, workaholic.

"So what are you doing at the airport in the middle of the day?" Steve asked, as they unloaded their tray at a table by the window.

Abby stirred her tea, avoiding Steve's clear, blue-eyed gaze. "I think I'm too embarrassed to tell you."

"We've been friends for a long time, Abby. You ought to know by now that you can trust old Uncle Steve."

Abby glanced up, struck by the startling realization that although she had known Steve for over ten years, in actual fact she knew very little about his innermost hopes and dreams. Their relationship, she saw with sudden and uncomfortable clarity, was entirely one-sided. With most people, Abby was the strong partner. With Steve, she was always the person who received.

"The situation must be worse than I thought," Steve said with mock solemnity. "You're not talking and you're not eating. Abigail Deane is in company with Steven Kramer and doing nothing but staring deep into his eyes.

Sweetheart, are you coming down with something? Flu, maybe? Or a dose of bubonic plague?"

"I had an anonymous phone call last night," Abby admitted abruptly. "After I left you. As I walked into my apartment, the phone was ringing. When I picked it up, a voice at the other end told me they had some important information about my brother."

"About Douglas Brady?"

"Yes." Abby drew in a deep breath. "The caller said there was something important I needed to know about the gun that shot Douglas. The .38 Webley."

"So you called the police, right? And spoke to Knudsen."

Abby felt her cheeks redden. "No," she confessed. "The caller said I was to meet him at the Westway Airlines counter today at noon. So I came."

"Without telling *anyone*? Are you trying to get yourself killed?" Steve's voice tightened with anger. "What is this, Abby? Some sort of perverted guilt trip because both your sisters have been shot at and you haven't? You're an intelligent woman. You know better than to respond to that sort of a call."

"You needn't yell," Abby said, surprised by the vehemence of Steve's reaction. She had never before seen him waste energy by losing his temper. "Nothing happened. Nobody came."

"How do you know nothing happened?" he demanded. "All you know is that nobody approached you. How do you know some crazy person wasn't watching you from behind a pillar, gloating over the fact that you responded to his call?"

The image Steve summoned up was horrifying, but Abby forced herself not to overreact. She'd had enough of that for one day. "Even if some crazy was watching me, it won't do him any good."

"Why not? Maybe he wanted to identify you. Maybe he didn't know what you looked like before, and now he does."

"But if he already knew my name, presumably he knew what I looked like—"

"Abby, when Linsey found that wagon load of Confederate gold, there was enough media attention to bring every lunatic in the entire Rocky Mountain region crawling out from under their rocks. By the time Kate recovered the gold from those gangsters, there wasn't a newspaper or TV station in the country that hadn't mentioned the 'three lovely Deane sisters' at least half a dozen times. I expect every weirdo between Cheyenne and Santa Fe knows your name. Half of them probably have fantasies about kidnapping you and acquiring the gold for themselves."

"Steve, the gold has all been converted into stocks and bonds, and half of my share's been given to charity..."

"I know that. Any rational person knows that. But we're talking about crazies, Abby. About people who make anonymous phone calls in the middle of the night."

"If I promise to report any more crank calls to the police, could you please stop shouting at me?" Abby asked meekly.

Steve looked taken aback. He ran his hand through his thick blond hair and leaned back in his chair. "I'm sorry," he said, his expression rueful. "I think I lost my famous Kramer cool there for a moment."

She risked a tiny smile. "Only for a moment."

"Do me a favor, Abby." Steve reached out and covered her hand. "The next time a disembodied voice invites you to chat about your long-lost half brother, decline the invitation. Call the police. And if you still want something exciting to do, come upstairs to my apartment, and we'll make mad, passionate love.''

"It's a deal," she said, draining her iced tea. "And in the meantime, Steve, I'd better get back to work. The Art Museum's mounting an exhibition of Gardner Alleyn's work, and I'm sorting through all his personal papers so that they can hang biographical notes alongside every picture. The curator's going to tear out his hair if I don't send over some meaningful material this afternoon.''

"God forbid. The curator can't afford to lose a single hair. He only has twelve.''

"You always exaggerate, Steve. The poor man has at least twenty-four.'' Chatting amicably, their relationship back on its familiar footing, Steve and Abby walked quickly to the parking lot, parting with a friendly goodbye and no mention of when they would next meet.

It was nearly two o'clock when Abby sat down at her desk. Putting the unsettling events of her lunch hour out of her mind, she buried herself in the boxes of Gardner Alleyn papers. He was a Western artist, and his subjects were limited to cowboys and horses, but his correspondence revealed both a passionate interest in women and a witty style of writing. Abby was engrossed in a love letter written to the wife of a neighboring rancher when the phone rang. Her attention still focused on Gardner Alleyn's purple prose, she spoke abstractedly. "Hello, this is Abigail Deane.''

A hoarse, muffled voice replied. "Hello, Abigail. You don't mind if I call you that, do you? I feel like we're becoming friends. It's nice to talk to you again. I've been waiting all day for the pleasure.''

Abby's stomach lurched. "Who is this?''

"I told you, Abigail, a friend. A buddy of your father's from way back when."

The statement didn't reassure her. Feeling slightly sick, she spat out the next question. "What's your name?"

"That would be telling, wouldn't it? But it was an interesting meeting we had at the airport today, Abigail. I sure appreciate your cooperation."

"What do you mean? I didn't cooperate with you. We didn't meet at the airport. *Who are you?*"

A hoarse cackle of laughter grated into the phone. "Are you sure we didn't meet, Abigail? Are you absolutely certain I'm not one of the people you talked to this afternoon?"

"Of course I'm sure—"

"Maybe I was one of the people in the crowd when you dropped your purse." Again the eerie cackle of laughter. "Think about it, little *missy*. Worry about it. I like you to worry."

The caller hung up.

The dial tone buzzed for several seconds before, fingers shaking, Abby cleared the line and dialed Lieutenant Knudsen.

Chapter Four

Abby was making coffee and trying not to think about the anonymous phone caller, when Steve knocked on the door of her apartment that evening.

"Want to come rock climbing with me this weekend?" he asked, following her into the kitchen. "We haven't climbed together for over a month, and the way this week's gone, I feel like doing something extremely physical."

Pitting her frustrations against the side of a mountain seemed like the best idea Abby had heard in several days. Clinging to the sheer face of a precipice seemed considerably less dangerous than hanging around in Denver, taking messages from demented phone callers.

"Sounds wonderful. Why don't we make a weekend of it?" she suggested. "We could go to the Flatirons. I've been promising Linsey and Kate for weeks that I'd go through our old family home in Boulder and decide what stuff we need to keep. The basement's piled high with three generations of junk. We could sort through the junk tomorrow, spend the night at the house, and climb on Sunday."

Steve rolled his eyes. "Boy, how in the world did I get so lucky? A whole day of chasing spiders and heaving boxes. That's a proposition to make the heart of any red-blooded male pound with excitement!''

Abby grinned and poured out the coffee. "It must be those devastating blue eyes of yours, Steve. They'll lead a girl to ruin every time."

"I didn't realize your ruin was thrown in as part of the deal. In that case I'll come. Shall we leave tonight and get straight to the ruining part?"

"Tomorrow morning would be better. Mr. Bovery at the bank has some papers he wants me to sign. His secretary called this afternoon and asked me to stop by. It shouldn't take more than fifteen minutes, so we could leave here at nine and still be in Boulder soon after ten."

"Anything that keeps me away from those darn boxes is welcome." Steve perched on the stool next to hers and sipped his coffee. "So what's been happening in your life since lunchtime, Abby?"

"I had another anonymous phone call," she admitted. "It came this afternoon at the office. It was...frightening. More frightening than the first one, for some reason. He sounded ... The caller sounded—"

"Crazy?"

"Yes, but more than that. Vindictive. He sounded as if he hated me."

Steve swore beneath his breath. "But the person who called was the same as before?"

She nodded. "I'm pretty sure of that."

"What did he say?"

"He said he liked making me worried." Abby became excessively interested in washing a spoon. "He also said that he'd enjoyed meeting me at the airport."

Steve swore long and fluently. "So much for your claim that you didn't meet anybody at the airport."

"I said I didn't meet any *crazies*. But I saw a couple of people I knew. Keith Bovery from the bank, and Peter Graymont. And then I met you."

The kitchen suddenly became deathly quiet. "If that's a question, I have no idea how to answer it," Steve said at last. "If you need me to tell you that I didn't make those anonymous phone calls, then there's something desperately wrong with our relationship. God knows, whatever else we're not, I thought at least we were friends. Good friends."

She heard the pain beneath the flatly spoken words, and reached out to touch him. Beneath her fingertips his arm felt hard and strong, and a glow of heat ignited somewhere deep inside her body.

"It wasn't a question, Steve," she said quietly.

The look he gave her was long and searching. Whatever he read in her eyes seemed to reassure him. He took her hand and raised it to his face, brushing her knuckles lightly across his cheek.

"Did you talk to anybody else at Stapleton?" he asked. "An airline employee? A porter? A security guard?"

"Just an elderly man who picked up my purse when I dropped it near one of the exit doors. He seemed nice enough at the time, except—"

"Except what?"

"He called me *missy*. Not just once, but several times. He sounded as if he was from Europe, and the way he said it didn't strike me as offensive, just friendly. But the person on the phone this afternoon deliberately called me *missy*. And he made the word sound . . . scary."

Steve's mouth tightened, but the hand cradling hers remained gentle. "You called the police, and told them all this, right? Like you promised me you would."

"Yes, I called the police." Abby shivered, despite the late-evening sun streaming in through the kitchen window. "I managed to get through to Knudsen. He was very helpful, although in practical terms there's not much he can do."

"Did he arrange a wiretap with the phone company?"

"Yes, it should be operational by tomorrow morning. But for technical reasons they can only put a tap on my personal phone, and the call this afternoon came through at my office."

"Did Knudsen have any reaction to that piece of information? That the call came to your office, I mean."

Abby pushed her coffee to the far side of the counter. The smell suddenly made her feel sick. "He thinks it's odd that I should start getting anonymous calls, right after Howard Taylor was murdered with the same gun that pumped bullets into my brother. Especially in view of the fact that the caller mentioned Douglas's name as a lure to get me to the airport. Knudsen's going to run an intensive background check on my brother and on Howard Taylor, to see if he can come up with some link between the two of them."

"You sound frightened," Steve said quietly.

"I am, a little. But logically, I know there's no reason for this guy to call again. He set up some sort of a sick joke, but now he's had his fun, and the game's over."

"How did Knudsen respond to that theory?"

"He agreed the calls might stop as irrationally as they began. He also pointed out that harassing phone calls are far more likely to be made by disgruntled colleagues and ex-spouses than they are by criminals."

"Would you recognize Greg's voice, if he'd been the caller?"

She grimaced. "Probably not. He hasn't contacted me in the six years since our divorce, and the caller obviously disguised his voice with a handkerchief or something. But Greg has no reason to harass me. He was even more relieved to be out of our marriage than I was. The last I heard of him, he was sailing off into the Mexican sunset, with a divorcée who'd had diamonds surgically stapled onto her nipples. Greg wasn't feeling revengeful. He was in hog heaven."

Steve looked amused. "The guy never did have any discrimination. Personally I'd prefer rubies. Much more suggestive."

"But less valuable," Abby explained succinctly. "This baby wanted everyone to see at a glance how hard she'd worked for her money."

Steve laughed. "Well, if Greg has no cause to harass you, have you offended any of your colleagues lately? Apart from the curator of the Art Museum, that is?"

She managed a wan smile at the picture of the chubby, good-natured curator hunched over his phone, making threatening phone calls. "I can't come up with a single name. Archivists are a mild bunch of people, and we're an especially peaceful lot at the Historical Society. Darn it, Steve, the people I work with are friends as well as colleagues. None of them would do this to me."

Steve carried his coffee mug over to the sink without comment. "I have some work I need to finish tonight," he said finally. "Some papers I must check. But I could bring my files down here, if you'd like the company. I could put a sleeping bag on the bed in the spare room and answer your phone, if it rings."

Abby looked intently at Steve, overcome once again by the feeling that she'd been seeing him with blinders on for the past six months. This morning he'd told her he hadn't dated since he moved into her apartment building. Now he was talking about doing work at home. Late at night. On a Friday. Her old image of a carefree, hedonistic Steve was blurred beyond recognition, but the new image wouldn't come into focus.

"What was that amazing statement you just made, Steve?" The laugh she gave sounded forced, even to her own ears.

"I'll go upstairs and get my sleeping bag—"

"No, the other one. About papers to go through. Whatever happened to the famous Steven Kramer three-hour workdays?"

"They vanished about a week after college ended," he said wryly. "If they ever existed. Right now, I'm lucky to get through my workload in a ten-hour day."

"But you're always home by four!"

He shrugged. "I work better late at night. So I take a break in the early evening."

Abby shook her head. "You're shattering all my illusions, Steve. I thought you were America's last holdout against the perils of yuppiedom."

"No, Abby. You didn't think any such thing. You simply assumed that since Greg and I were roommates in college, we had to be cut from the same type of cloth." Steve looked at her, his gaze ice cool. "I'm not Greg, Abby. One day you're going to have to face up to that."

The painful truth was that she'd always known—all too well—that Greg and Steve weren't the same man. Her marriage to Greg had been a costly experiment in pretending. But that was an emotional can of worms she didn't want to open tonight.

"Are you still coming to Boulder?" Abby asked in a small voice.

"How could I miss the thrills and chills of a day in your basement?" he asked. "And you never answered my question. Do you want me to sleep here tonight?"

She wanted to answer yes, but for some reason shook her head in denial. "I'll be fine, Steve, really I will. Thanks for the offer, though."

"You're welcome. See you tomorrow, Abby. Good night."

"Good night."

She bolted the door behind him then flopped onto her pristine white sofa and stared aimlessly at her pristine white sneakers. One way or another, Abby decided, this had been a hell of a day.

HOWARD TAYLOR'S MURDERER walked up to Abigail Deane's apartment building, smiling cheerfully. Saturday afternoon, and little Miss Deane was safely on her way to Boulder. The coast was clear, her apartment empty. One way or another, this was shaping up to be a damn good day. The sun shone with the startling brilliance typical of Colorado in September, but a nip in the air hinted pleasantly at cool nights and snowy days ahead. The weather alone was enough to lift the deepest depression, but Abigail's visit to the bank this morning had been the event that put the crowning touch on a wonderfully successful two days.

Abigail had signed a stack of documents, never realizing—despite her years of fancy education—that the signatures were unnecessary, a simple ruse to get her into the bank. In fact, summoning her to the bank had been even easier than luring her to the airport. And she'd chatted so amiably about her plans for the weekend, including her intention to sort through the basement of the Deane family home in Boulder.

"I'm expecting to unearth a fortune in junk," Abigail had joked. "My grandfather's stamp collection must be down there, and my grandmother's old recipe books. Not to mention all the stuff my father brought back from Korea. Who knows what scandalous family secrets I'll uncover?" She'd smiled, showing perfect white teeth. All the Deane girls were pretty, *damn them*.

"I guess that's what attracts me to working as an archivist," she had added. "It's exciting to think that we can reconstruct a person's entire life from the paper trail he leaves behind."

Gwen Johnson and Linda Mendoza had both agreed that there was a fortune to be made in junk. "I just sold my father's baseball card collection for five hundred dollars," Gwen had said.

"And I have a set of my daughter's Barbie dolls that I'm going to sell one of these days," Linda remarked.

Keith Bovery hadn't said much at all. He'd seemed to have other things on his mind. Weighty things. These days he was always frowning.

Abigail had signed the last paper with a flourish. "Let me know what happens about those errors in our account, won't you?" she'd said, addressing her question to the bank president.

"Oh...er...certainly." Keith Bovery had pulled himself back from an abstracted examination of the parking lot. "We'll be in touch shortly, my dear. You can count on it."

"Thanks. Well, I must run. The basement is calling out to me! Not to mention the friend I left eating ice cream in the car."

Abigail had taken herself off with a final cheery goodbye, never realizing that out of her own mouth she'd just signed confirmation of her death warrant.

Howard Taylor's murderer pulled out a shiny new key, letting it dangle from its red plastic key chain, letting it gleam in the golden sunlight. Getting the keys had been fun. Fooling Abigail Deane had been fun. Calling her— frightening her—had been risky. But fun.

In the end, getting the keys to Abigail's apartment had been so easy. A phone call about Douglas, the lure to the airport, and then the quick, efficient snatch of her purse. Ten seconds to take a wax impression of her front-door key, and then the careful, silent disappearance into the crowd. It helped to look ordinary. The murderer had discovered years ago that the world judged people strictly according to the way they looked. Kindly eyes and conservative clothes could conceal a multitude of sins.

The outer door swung open, granting admittance to the lobby, which fortunately was deserted. This was a nice apartment building. Fancy. Expensive. But why wouldn't it be? Ronald Deane had left his daughters with more money than they could possibly need. And then, to add insult to injury, those silly girls Kate and Linsey had found the Confederate gold and claimed it for their own. Oh yes! It was about time somebody served the Deanes a bit of the bad luck lesser mortals had to contend with all of their lives.

The murderer stopped outside Apartment 704. Abigail Deane's apartment. Another shiny new key fitted noiselessly into the lock. The murderer gave a gentle twist. The door swung open. Unable to conceal a little crow of triumph, the murderer stepped into the black-tiled apartment foyer. Very nice. Very classy. Very Deane family.

A soundless shadow, the intruder glided through Abigail's neat apartment. Gloved hands pulled open drawers, cupboards and cabinets, calmly searching. No need to hurry. The fool was safely stashed away in the basement of Ronald Deane's house. Waiting, if only she knew the truth, for her killer to join her. She was bound to step out into the yard sometime.

The intruder searched every inch of the living room and the spare bedroom before finally coming across the three big file cabinets in Abigail's room. They stood neatly against the wall, pale gray to match the carpet, four drawers in each. The task of completing the search would have been daunting, if Abigail hadn't been so well organized. But her filing system was excellent: simple, logical and complete. She was no doubt an excellent archivist, if this was a sample of her work.

It took less than five minutes to locate the letters in a series of files marked Ronald Deane—Personal Correspondence—1950-1955. The intruder quickly scanned the three letters. They should never have been written, of course, but fortunately their significance would not be apparent to the casual reader. Even in those days, the murderer had known better than to threaten blackmail in terms that were too explicit. In fact, reading the letters again, it was impressive to see how potent a threat had been contained in such seemingly innocuous language. With all the papers Abigail Deane had had to organize following her father's death, it seemed safe to assume that she wouldn't remember specific details from these particular letters.

Unfortunately, that was a risk the murderer couldn't take, particularly with Abigail rooting around at the old family home in Boulder. Pity Abigail was so damned persnickety in her personal record keeping. The way she had picked up the transposed bond numbers had been chilling. If only ditzy little Kate had been in charge of selling the family home, or even Linsey, there would have been no problem, no need for more killing. The murderer felt a flash of irritation. Life really was unfair. Some people had to plan and scrounge and fight for every red cent, for every scrap of affection, while other people—like the Deane sisters—just sat back and waited for life's blessings to shower over them in a hail of glory.

But this wasn't the moment to rail against fate. This was the moment for action, the moment to carry out the most important part of today's activities. Where were the certificates? Somewhere in these three cabinets there had to be copies of the all-important birth and death certificates for Christopher Deane Renquist. Those two simple documents could rip apart thirty-five years of delicately woven subterfuge.

A patient survey of the middle cabinet revealed the desired papers. With a muffled exclamation of triumph, the intruder removed a birth certificate for the baby boy, born in Arapahoe County in the State of Colorado on May 15, 1954. Silently the intruder examined the death certificate, issued for the same infant a scant six weeks later. With a sudden vicious energy, the intruder ripped the certificates apart again and again before pocketing the pieces. Too late now for mourning thirty-five-year old wrongs.

With a faint smile of satisfaction, the intruder returned every file and paper to its appointed place. Within ten minutes there was no sign that anybody had ever been near the filing cabinets. No reason remained for anyone to suspect that documents were missing. Now that Ronald Deane was dead, only the intruder understood the importance of the certificates. And soon, no one except the intruder would even know of their existence.

Leaving the bedroom, the interloper's eye was caught by a framed photograph that stood in a position of honor on Abigail's chest of drawers. The photograph showed a handsome man in pilot's uniform, receiving a medal from his commanding officer. The interloper returned to the bedroom, drawn by an irresistible force to the picture. Picking it up, the interloper stared in taut silence at Ronald Deane's handsome features, then returned the photo to the bureau with such a jerk that a bottle of perfume was disturbed and fell onto its side.

The stopper couldn't have been properly inserted into the bottle. Cursing, the interloper reached for a tissue, but it was quickly obvious that tissues were too flimsy to do the job. Striding impatiently into the kitchen, the interloper grabbed paper towels from the wrought-iron holder and returned to mop up the spilled perfume. Infuriatingly, a little chunk of glass had been chipped off the crystal stopper. What to do? Probably it would be best to remove the entire bottle from the apartment. Next problem. What to do with the soiled towels? Carrying a bundle of sopping wet towels and stinking of perfume, it wouldn't be very smart to run into some nosy neighbor.

The interloper's gaze ran quickly over the bedroom: a solitary, used manila envelope poked invitingly out of the wastebasket. The interloper scooped the towels into the envelope, added the chipped perfume bottle, then heaved a sigh of relief. Despite the minor mishap all was well. The cloying, spicy smell of Opium remained strong, but it would soon dissipate, and in any event, Abigail Deane would never come back to her apartment to discover that one of her bottles of perfume was missing. The murderer exhaled another contented sigh. Yes, indeed. All was finally well.

Now there was nothing left to betray the truth about Douglas—or about little baby Christopher. Now it was time to finish an old story that had begun thirty-five years ago in Korea.

Now it was time to kill Abigail Deane.

Chapter Five

"Ta-da!" Steve declaimed, throwing his arms wide in exaggerated triumph. "The last bag of trash has just been deposited at the end of the driveway. Start cracking open the champagne."

Abby peered up at him through a dusty tangle of hair, blowing a stray wisp away from her nose. "What? Did you say something, Steve?"

"Nothing earth-shattering," he answered wryly. "The trash has been taken out, that's all. What have you found in that box, Abby? It must be fascinating. You haven't stirred in nearly an hour."

"It's mostly old photographs, and a few letters. If I'd known they were here, I'd have organized them years ago. They're an absolute treasure trove of family history. See this photo? It's my great-grandmother on her wedding day. Don't you think she's a lot like Linsey? Same hair, same nose, same everything."

Steve glanced at the fading, sepia-toned picture. "Yes, they're very alike. Petite and delicate, but with an underlying hint of steel. You should have a copy made and send it to Darren and Linsey. They'd like it."

"Good idea. I'll do that," Abby replied absentmindedly. Her attention had already returned to the precious cardboard carton. She reached in and extracted another photo, this one tucked inside a flimsy envelope along with a yellowing letter. With infinite care she extracted the thin pages and spread them open, revealing a photo of a reed-slim woman holding a tiny baby.

"Who's she?" Steve asked, peering over Abby's shoulder. "Your grandmother?"

"No, I'd recognize Gran. Besides, it's too modern. The dress looks nineteen-fiftyish." Forgetting Steve's presence in the excitement of discovery, Abby curled up against a floor cushion and started reading the letter.

Steve gazed down at her, his expression hovering between affection and exasperation. Looking at the jumble of two hundred or so photographs still remaining in the box, he sighed—loudly. Abby gave no sign that she'd heard him. After five patient minutes, he risked speaking.

"Abby, my sweet, I know that as far as you're concerned a carton of discarded family papers is more compelling than fine wine and chocolate truffles combined, but have you noticed that it's five o'clock and we neither of us took a lunch break?"

"What? Did you want something, Steve?" Abby pushed a hank of hair behind her ear, leaving a streak of dirt from nose to jaw. Her vision cleared of hair strands, she returned to reading the letter as if neither of them had spoken.

Steve reached out and gently ran his finger across the smudge of greasy dirt. "Barbecued steak," he murmured, leaning close. "Baked potato with sour cream. Fresh corn, dripping with butter. A glass of fine burgundy."

At these magic words Abby blinked, visibly jolting herself back into the everyday world. "Heavens, is it dinnertime?" she asked. "I just realized I'm starving."

Steve's eyes darkened with wry laughter. "I thought the mention of food might do the trick, when all else failed. Inside that slender body of yours throbs the appetite of a three-hundred-pound stevedore. Yes, Abby, my love, it's dinnertime."

"Three hundred pounds, huh?" Abby got to her feet, smoothing her hands over her slender thighs with deliberate provocation. She twirled around, wriggling her hips. "Look at this perfect body and weep, Steven Kramer."

"Sweetheart, the sight of your body definitely doesn't make me want to weep."

She blushed, and he grinned. "Come on, hand over that letter before you get engrossed again. Have you ever considered taking counseling for your addiction to tattered old pieces of paper?"

"This isn't just any old piece of paper," Abby said, her smile fading. "It's a letter to my father from a woman called Lynn, sending a picture of her newborn son. I remember seeing some correspondence from her before, although I didn't realize then who she was. I can't imagine why this letter got separated out from the other stuff she wrote, except maybe because of the photo."

Steve looked at the solemn-faced woman and the shawl-wrapped baby. "For a new mother, poor Lynn doesn't seem all that happy. Who is she?"

Abby grimaced. "I think she must have been my father's mistress. You know, the nurse Dad fell in love with when he was in Korea."

"Douglas Brady's birth mother, in other words."

"Yes. Which means this may be the only surviving photo of Douglas and his mother before he was adopted."

"What's her name? Apart from Lynn, I mean."

Abby flipped over the envelope and peered at the two-line return address. "I can't read anything, except 'Alabama.' The ink's all blotched from water or something." She paused. "Maybe tears."

Steve squeezed her shoulder. "And if you can't pin a precise identity onto your father's ex-mistress, maybe it's just as well. Take the advice of someone who's survived a couple of hair-raising family battles: usually it's better to let the past stay safely buried."

"That may be great advice, but our past isn't safely buried. Douglas brought the past violently into the present when he came looking for me and my sisters."

"But Douglas is dead now, Abby, and it's time to let him go. When you get right down to it, he and Lynn were part of your father's life, not part of yours."

Abby stared down at the picture of the sad-eyed Lynn, and her heart constricted in empathy for what the woman must have endured as a single mother in the straitlaced fifties.

"I understand how in wartime emotions run high and relationships get messed up," she said. "Reading this letter, though, all I can think of is how badly my father behaved. Having an affair with an army nurse when he was already married to my mother, and then refusing to acknowledge the existence of his own child. He cut Lynn and her son out of his life so completely that nobody in our family even knew her name until I found this letter."

Steve spoke quietly. "Try not to judge him, Abby. God knows, we all screw up our relationships when we're young. Look at the two of us. We're prime examples. You married the wrong man. I sure as hell married the wrong woman—and made her utterly miserable in the process. If you heard my ex-wife's version of our marriage, I doubt if you'd want to sit in the same room with me. She genuinely believes slime mold is nicer to have around.''

"But neither of us created an illegitimate child whose existence we refused to acknowledge for thirty-five years."

"True. But then neither of us flew combat missions into enemy territory, either. Your father was risking his life on a daily basis when he met Lynn. Do you blame him for snatching a little comfort where he happened to find it?"

"If we were talking about anybody else's father, I'd understand perfectly," Abby admitted. "But this is my dad we're discussing. It's kind of tough for me to accept that the man I idolized was just a regular guy, with all the failings of any other regular guy."

"And all the strengths, too," Steve reminded her. "He isn't here to give us his side of the story, Abby, so don't toss him too far off his pedestal."

"You're right." She got up, forcing a smile, although deep inside she remained unconvinced. "Let's concentrate on really crucial issues for a while. Who's cooking tonight?"

"That depends, I guess. Do you want to eat charbroiled cinders? Or would you prefer flaky potato, juicy ears of corn and tender pink steak?"

"Gee, that's a hard choice. But since I bought the food, I probably should let you earn your keep by cooking it. I don't want you to feel neglected or useless or anything."

"You're all heart." Steve saw her gaze stray back to the carton of photos and took her firmly by the hand. "Come on, Abby, it's shower time. If we don't hurry, it'll be too cold to eat outside."

Abby reluctantly returned the letter and picture to the carton. "I'll just take this upstairs to my room—"

"Oh no, you don't!" Swiftly Steve removed the box from her grasp. "I'm going to hide this, or I'll come up to your room in an hour's time and you'll be sitting on the floor reading, your hair still buried in cobwebs.''

"I don't have cobwebs in my hair," Abby denied indignantly. "I'm notorious for my immaculate appearance."

Steve chuckled. "Take a look in your bedroom mirror, my sweet. You not only have cobwebs in your hair, you have smut on your nose, grease on your cheek, and a smear of ink on your forehead."

Abby pulled a rude face. "How do you keep from ravishing me when I'm so glamorous?"

"I don't know," he said. "It's a severe strain on my self-control, that's for sure."

Despite his casual tone, Abby found her gaze locked with his. Steve's eyes appeared very green and oddly intent. Heat flamed in her cheeks, and her mussed appearance no longer seemed a joking matter. She was filled with the craziest desire to look exotic, bewitching, glamorous. For Steve Kramer, of all people! She walked hurriedly toward the stairs. Too many hours in the basement had obviously caused incipient brain damage.

"See you in a little bit," she said, her voice husky.

"I'll light the grill." Steve reached for a box of matches and tossed them casually from hand to hand. "Sizzled steaks will be on the table one hour from now. Don't be late, kiddo."

Their conversation could hardly have been more mundane, but Abby found herself shaking as she stripped off her clothes and stepped into the shower. For the first time in all the years since she left college, she was wondering what it would feel like to be ravished by Steven Kramer.

Devastating and *wonderful* were the two words that sprang into her mind.

STEVE WAS PUTTING leaf-wrapped ears of corn onto the grill, when Abby walked out onto the patio forty minutes later. He glanced up from his task and gave her a quick smile of welcome. "You look great, kid. The no-cobweb look suits you."

He returned to his cooking, and Abby scowled at his back. *Kid? No-cobweb look?* For this she had put on brand-new jeans and spent fifteen minutes in front of the bathroom mirror, fussing with her makeup? Restless, she paced the patio for several moments before plopping onto a lounger and staring up at the evening sky. The September night was crisp with the promise of fall, but the high elevation lent the stars a brilliance and gave the air a crystal clarity that made eating outside well worth the addition of an extra sweater.

Steve handed her a glass of burgundy, then drew a chair close to hers. "A friend of mine recommended a new route for our climb tomorrow," he said, sitting down. "Up the west face of the Flatirons. He says it's pretty challenging, so it should be an interesting day, if you're game."

Abby flexed her arms. "I'm ready. More than ready. Bet I'll beat you to the top."

"What're you betting?" Steve asked, his voice lazy.

"Five bucks."

"Huh! Try again."

"Dinner on me?"

He grinned. "As long as it's not home-cooked, sweetheart, you've got yourself a deal."

She glared at him. "One of these days I'm going to learn how to cook, just to frustrate you."

There was a small silence. "You already frustrate me, Abby. You don't have to add to the problem." Steve got to his feet and walked over to the barbecue grill. Abby scrambled after him.

"Steve, what in the world do you mean? Does it bother you so much that I can't cook? What's happened to you these past few days, anyway? What's happened to us? You've been saying the craziest things."

His laughter contained little mirth. "For an intelligent woman, Abby, you are sometimes incredibly dumb."

To her total and utter amazement, Abby found herself grabbing Steve's arm, rage consuming her. "Dumb? How am I dumb? I have two graduate degrees, for heaven's sake."

"That, my sweet, is exactly what I mean."

"Will you stop turning those damn steaks and look at me!"

Steve's muscles tensed beneath her touch. "My pleasure, Abby," he muttered, flinging the tongs onto the grill. "Okay, I'm looking." His gaze ran over her with cool appraisal. "That's a great sweater, kid. Two inches tighter and you could get yourself arrested."

Hands on hips, heart pounding and eyes blazing, she confronted him. "Stop calling me kid! I'm twenty-eight years old! And you still haven't explained why I'm dumb."

Steve slammed the lid of the grill. "Because any woman with the brains of a flea ought to know how badly I want to do this," he said, pulling her into his arms and slanting his mouth hard across hers.

His kiss was hungry, passionate, demanding, and yet incredibly tender. His tongue slid into her mouth, and Abby felt her entire body melt in response. He must have felt her tremble, for his hold tightened until they were wedged together, thigh thrust against thigh, breast against chest. Abby would have cried out her pleasure, but Steve left her no breath. He swallowed her little moan into their kiss, grinding his lips against hers with a need that felt close to desperation.

The darkness of the night sky wrapped itself around Abby, leaving her blind and deaf to the world. Only Steve existed, Steve and the feelings he was miraculously arousing deep inside her soul. She wanted their kiss to last forever. She wanted it to stop right now this second, before her body flew apart at the seams.

"Steve, please, no," she murmured.

As soon as he lifted his mouth from hers, she realized that she hadn't really wanted the kiss to end. She felt bereft and insubstantial without his arms around her. Without his lips touching hers, she felt less than fully alive.

"I smell burning steak," he murmured, avoiding her eyes. "Time to eat, I guess."

"Yes, something smells a bit smoky," Abby lied. At that moment, she doubted if she'd have noticed the smoke from a three-alarm fire. Her senses were numb to everything except Steve.

"I'll get some more wine," he said. "The plates are on the wooden table by the grill. Why don't you serve the food?"

Abby nodded dazedly. She walked over to the table Steve had indicated, picked up two heavy pottery plates, then stared blankly into the middle distance. She was supposed to be doing something, but couldn't remember what. If she followed Steve to the other side of the patio, would he kiss her again? If he did, this time she sure as heck wouldn't be crazy enough to call a halt.

Her reverie lasted about fifteen seconds. She put down the plates and turned toward him, just as his anguished shout shattered the evening calm.

"Abby, get down! For God's sake!"

He yelled the command at the same instant as he launched himself toward her in a flying tackle. His body hurtled through the space that separated them, and Abby had a blurred impression of a muffled explosion. She ducked, and they landed on the brick-paved patio with a thud that knocked every scrap of air from her lungs. Steve lay spread-eagled on top of her. Through her layers of clothing she could feel that his body was hot, hard—and shaking violently.

She lay immobile, trying to draw breath into her aching lungs. The crash of feet running through the undergrowth surrounding the yard assailed her ears. She stirred in reflex reaction to the sound.

"Keep down," Steve ordered tersely, rolling off her body and crouching beside her. "I lost count of the shots, so he might have a couple more bullets."

A couple more bullets? Abby was so shocked that she almost forgot to be frightened. Dear God, the explosions she heard had been gunshots! Someone had taken aim at her in her own backyard, and now that somebody was getting away! She sprang to her feet, unreasoning in the wildness of her anger, but Steve grabbed her waist and dragged her back behind the picnic table.

"For heaven's sake, Abby, play the heroine some other time, okay?"

"But he's escaping!"

"And you're still alive. Let's keep it that way."

She collapsed against the picnic bench, her teeth suddenly chattering. Someone had shot at her! "Did you see him?"

"Yes, I happened to turn around just as he stood up to take aim. That's why I yelled at you to get down. Somebody medium tall, medium build and wearing a black ski mask.''

"Gee, a sharp description like that should help to set the police right on him! There can't be more than fifty thousand people in Boulder County who fit that description perfectly."

Steve heard the panic bubbling beneath her sarcasm. He took her into his arms and stroked her back in a gesture that was comforting and entirely asexual. "Let's go inside," he suggested gently. "We'll be safe there, even if by some insane chance he decides to come back."

She didn't protest, partly because her teeth were chattering too hard to allow her to form coherent words. Steve guided her inside, and they sat down on the sofa.

"D-dinner will be ruined," Abby said finally.

"And I dropped the bottle of burgundy." Steve kept his arm around her shoulders. "Looks like we're going to eat canned soup washed down with milk for our dinner. Sound tempting?"

Abby shuddered, "No, but I'm not very hungry right now."

Steve got up and returned moments later, carrying a glass. "Here, try this. Maybe it'll spark your appetite."

"What is it?"

"Brandy. I found a bottle in the cupboard earlier on, when I was looking for salt. Why don't you take a few sips, while I call the police?"

"The emergency number's pinned up next to the phone." Abby took the brandy gratefully. Her hands shook so badly that she needed both of them to hold the glass steady. The realization of how close she had come to death was beginning to sink in with painful force. Somebody had hidden in the overgrown bushes surrounding the backyard, then shot at her from the concealing darkness.

Somebody had tried to kill her. Somebody wanted her dead. It was impossible, but true.

"The police are sending out a squad car right away." Steve returned from his phone call. He sat down beside her, one hand resting on her knee. "You know, it might have been nothing more than a hunter. Accidents can happen, and amateur hunters do crazy, dangerous things."

With weary effort, Abby pulled herself upright on the sofa. "Don't try to placate me, Steve, I'm not that fragile, or that scared. We both know hunters don't creep around in suburban backyards wearing ski masks. Somebody shot at me with intent to kill. They'd have succeeded, if you hadn't shouted a warning."

His hand tightened over hers, his grip warm and comforting. "Just part of the friendly Kramer service."

She cleared her throat. "Did I . . . um . . . did I remember to say thank you?"

"No, but that's okay. I'll hold you in my debt until the right moment, and then I'll demand some exorbitant repayment."

Abby drew in a deep breath. "I'll pay willingly. I owe you one, Steve."

He hesitated for a moment, then reached out and pulled her into his arms. She went without resistance, and he stroked the tangled mass of her hair with gentle fingers.

"Why did someone try to shoot me, Steve? What have I done to make someone hate me so much?"

"I don't know. Yet. Abby, are you sure that darn Confederate gold has all been converted into stocks and bonds? Or something else equally inaccessible to stray thugs and kooky treasure hunters?"

"I'm sure."

"You and your sisters don't have a little nest egg of gold bars buried in the backyard for sentimental reasons?"

"Steve, we don't have so much as a single gold flake, let alone a secret stash of ingots. Linsey, Kate and I all felt the gold cost far too many lives and we didn't want any part of it. That's why we gave so much of the proceeds to charity. We're all sick to death of hearing about that wretched Confederate treasure wagon. I truly wish my father had never found it."

Steve nodded agreement. "Anyway, even if you did have a stack of gold bars buried under the rosebushes, there would be no reason to kill you for them. Much easier to come here when the house is empty and dig them up."

"But you think there's some connection between my sisters finding that gold earlier this year and now this attack on me, don't you?"

"Logically that seems unlikely—"

"But what other reason is there for anyone to try to kill me? Steve, I'm an archivist working for the State Historical Society, not an international spy or a billionaire, or even some glamorous sex symbol with a string of discarded, jealous lovers."

"Maybe the gunman didn't have a logical reason for shooting at you." Steve took a sip of her brandy and savored it reflectively. "Maybe—somehow—you've attracted the attention of a genuine loony. After all, you and your sisters were media stars for almost a whole week."

"Like the person who made those anonymous phone calls, you mean?"

"Could be a possibility, don't you think? And a deranged person might have reasons for taking potshots at you that would seem totally irrational to us, but quite sensible to him. Like Brian Hinkley shooting the President of the United States in order to gain Jodi Foster's attention."

"Is it better to be pursued by a lunatic or a run-of-the-mill criminal?" Abby's laughter was shaky. "Gee whiz, there's a delightful choice to ponder while we wait for the police."

Steve made no answer, and his expression was grim as he got up and switched on the outside lights. The patio sprang to life against a dark fringe of surrounding trees and bushes. Clouds of smoke belched from the barbecue, and the coals hissed with burning fat.

"I'd better turn off the grill and dump what's left of the food," Steve commented. "Otherwise we'll need the services of the fire department as well as the police."

Abby's fingers tightened around his wrist. "Don't go outside until the police get here," she whispered.

He paused long enough to brush a fleeting kiss against her forehead. "Sweetheart, there's no risk to either of us anymore. The gunman's long gone. He may be crazy, but he's not a fool."

Abby dashed her hand across her eyes, rubbing away unwanted tears. "You know what makes me angriest about this? It's that some perverted lunatic with a gun has the power to make me feel unsafe in my own home. I hate him for that."

Steve stroked his thumbs against the wetness on her cheeks. "We'll find him, Abby. I promise you we'll find him."

Just for a moment, while Steve held her close, she believed him.

THE POLICE TEAM, consisting of a young uniformed officer and a detective wearing jeans, arrived while Steve was dousing the barbecue flames. The uniformed officer scoured the bushes with a powerful portable floodlight, while the detective asked dozens of questions. They were both polite, concerned, and pessimistic about their chances of ever capturing the gunman.

"Are you absolutely certain you have no enemies, Miss Deane?" The detective repeated his question for the second time. "Most shooting incidents occur during the commission of a crime—a home invasion or a car robbery, for example. Nearly all other shooting incidents are perpetrated by people who know their victims. A jealous ex-spouse, maybe, or a disgruntled colleague."

"My husband and I parted with extreme mutual relief, and I don't have disgruntled colleagues." Abby felt as if she'd made the same denial a dozen times in the past couple of days, but the detective's comment—so similar to the remarks made by Lieutenant Knudsen—underlined the possibility that the anonymous phone caller and the backyard gunman might be one and the same person. She hesitated, wondering whether to draw police attention to a link she barely wanted to acknowledge.

The detective was a perceptive man. "I hear a *but* in your voice, Miss Deane."

"I guess there is one thing," she admitted. "Although I can't really believe it's connected."

"Why don't you let me decide on that?"

Abby thrust her hands deep into her jean pockets. "I received two harassing phone calls last week," she said finally. "Anonymous ones. When I reported the calls to the police, Lieutenant Knudsen remarked that anonymous phone calls are usually made by ex-spouses or angry colleagues. You said almost the same thing."

"Hmm, I see." The detective scribbled busily in his notebook. "Did somebody talk with the phone company to arrange for a wiretap?"

"Yes, it's already in place."

"Which officer did you say you talked to in Denver?"

"Lieutenant Knudsen of the CBI."

The detective's pen stopped in midair. He looked up from his notebook and stared at Abby in surprise. "Knudsen from the CBI? Why is the Colorado Bureau of Investigations involved in a simple phone harassment case?"

"It's not all that simple," Steve interjected, making virtually his only contribution to the interview thus far. "Abby's half brother was killed last July in a shoot-out in Denver. Abby and her sisters inherited a wagon load of long-lost Confederate gold from their father."

The detective glanced up with quickened interest. "I remember reading about the case. It generated a lot of media attention."

"Far too much from my point of view," Abby acknowledged ruefully.

"All that publicity might explain the anonymous phone calls, though. You've attracted the attention of some treasure-hunt freak, Miss Deane. Or some other variety of media nut case. We have quite a few celebrities living in this area, and you'd never believe the harassing phone calls they receive, unless you'd actually heard them."

Abby agreed almost eagerly. "That's what I thought—"

"Except the phone calls aren't the whole story," Steve interrupted again. "Three days ago, a vice president at the First Denver Federal Bank was shot in his home during a burglary. The .38 Webley that killed the bank officer was the same gun that pumped bullets into Abby's brother the night he was killed. What's more, Abby had an appointment to meet Mr. Taylor, scheduled for the day after his death to discuss certain irregularities in her accounts. And to cap it all, the anonymous phone calls started coming right after Mr. Taylor's murder.''

The detective allowed himself a low whistle of astonishment. Abby didn't blame him. Condensed by Steve into the bare factual bones, she saw just how extraordinary the events of the past few days had actually been. She wasn't surprised when the detective turned to stare at her with frowning speculation. She could almost see his opinion of her changing, his suspicions beginning to build. Law-abiding citizens weren't supposed to get shot at in their own backyards. And they certainly weren't supposed to have half brothers who got killed in blazing shoot-outs with guns that later murdered a bank officer.

"You seem to have been skirting some dangerous activities these past few months, Miss Deane." The detective's voice was carefully neutral.

"Really it seems much more dramatic than it is." Even to Abby's ears, her excuse sounded lame. She hurried into an explanation. "It was my sisters who were in danger searching for the gold, not me. I was out of town and had no idea what was going on most of the time. And anyway, the whole situation with the Confederate treasure is entirely over now. The gold has been converted into regular currency, and my half brother is dead—"

"You're quite sure of that?"

"Absolutely sure. But Lieutenant Knudsen can give you the official police autopsy report, if you want to check. My brother's body was riddled with bullets from three different guns. He had at least five wounds severe enough to kill him."

"And the Webley was never found?"

"No. The pathologist designated a .45 as the bullet that actually killed my brother, so the Webley wasn't a murder weapon. I'm sure the police looked for it, but they didn't actually need the gun to make their case... You know how it is. Nobody gave that gun much thought until Howard Taylor was shot with the same weapon."

"Humph." The detective wrote copious notes, then called over his shoulder to the uniformed officer. "You managed to get those bullets out of the wall yet, Gerry?"

The policeman came into the living room, and held out three bullets sealed in a plastic bag.

"Looks like rifle shot," the detective said.

The policeman nodded in agreement. "Standard catalog variety, at a guess."

"They definitely couldn't have been fired from a .38 Webley?" Abby asked. Despite having had a keen hunter for a father, she disliked guns and knew little about them.

"No, Miss Deane, they definitely couldn't have been fired from any .38 caliber weapon." The detective's reply left no room for doubt.

"You don't find many .38 Webleys around in this country," the young policeman commented, trying to be helpful. "Not nowadays, at least. They were mostly made for the British army in World War II. The British used them in Korea, too. They're easier to handle than a .45, but just as lethal."

Abby slumped against Steve, overwhelmed by an unexpected wave of relief. She wasn't sure why it felt so much better to know that she had been shot at with a hunting rifle, rather than the same gun that killed Howard Taylor and Douglas Brady. A rifle bullet would have done the job equally well. But somehow, the feeling that this shooting incident wasn't directly connected to her half brother's death, or to the death of Howard Taylor, was almost exhilarating.

"Maybe it was a hunter, after all," she suggested. *Please say yes,* she silently begged the detective.

He didn't oblige. "In a ski mask in your backyard? What was he hunting, Miss Deane? Field mice?"

"But nobody has any reason to want me dead! Damn it, I'm efficient and organized and...and boring! Not exactly prime murder victim material."

"I'd think about that some more, Miss Deane. In police work we soon learn that people attempt murder for a very limited number of reasons. Sex, money, revenge. Fear that some secret will be uncovered or a crime revealed. That's about the sum of it. If I were you, I'd make a list of all the men you've turned down recently, and another list of who inherits your money when you die. And if you happen to have inside information about any juicy scandals, share that information with me or Lieutenant Knudsen. Share it pretty darn quick. Your gunman won't kill to protect a secret that's already public knowledge."

"I don't know any secrets," Abby said despairingly. "At least not recent ones. The scandals I work with at the Historical Society are all at least fifty years old. Nobody's going to shoot me because I discovered that the public works director in 1930 was taking bribes."

"You'd be surprised," the detective remarked. "Sometimes fifty-year-old secrets pack a potent punch. They've had a long time to ferment in the darkness. Think about it, Miss Deane, and make a list." He shook hands in brisk farewell.

"Lock all your doors and windows tonight, and don't stand silhouetted against flimsy curtains," he added. "I'll call you in Denver if we come up with any information, or if I think of any more questions. The lab might be able to give us a lead when they take a look at those bullets." He sounded considerably less than hopeful. "Good night,

Miss Deane—'' he nodded toward Steve ''—Mr. Kramer.''

The living room felt unnaturally quiet after the two policemen had left. Steve paced restlessly for a few seconds, then swung around to confront Abby.

"The detective was right," he said curtly. "You know something threatening, Abby. Something dangerous. And somebody is prepared to kill to stop you passing on that information."

"Steve, all the work I do at the Historical Society is a matter of public record. Killing me wouldn't keep a single fact secret. My successor would just—"

"I'm not talking about the Historical Society, I'm talking about here and now. Your personal life. Your family."

"You mean Douglas," Abby said with a sigh of resignation. "You want me to try to find some mysterious secret link between my half brother and Howard Taylor. Damn it, Steve, there isn't one!"

"So you keep telling me." Steve frowned, then his face lighted with a sudden blaze of enlightenment. "We already know the link between them," he said slowly. "My God, Abby! We already know the link." With the air of a magician pulling an entire family of rabbits from the hat, he exclaimed, "How could we have missed it? *The .38 Webley that shot them both.*"

Abby didn't attempt to hide her exasperation. "Good grief, Steve, how is that piece of information dangerous to anybody? Nobody would try to kill me over a fact every law enforcement agency in Colorado already knows."

"They know the same gun was used," Steve said. "They don't know who pulled the trigger."

Her exasperation increased. "Two different people. A thug from Las Vegas shot at Douglas. A burglar killed Howard Taylor."

"What if that's not true? What if the same person pulled the trigger in both incidents—?"

"You spent hours the other night convincing me it was mere coincidence that the same gun was used twice," Abby protested.

"That was before somebody tried to kill you." Steve's mouth clamped into a grim line. He took her hands and held them tightly in his grasp. "Abby, if the same person pulled the trigger both times, then that person probably isn't a small time neighborhood burglar. It's a person with lots to hide. Secrets about his past and his present, Abby. Secrets waiting to be uncovered by you."

She wanted to find a rebuttal, but Steve drove home his point relentlessly.

"Somehow, Abby, you have the power to uncover a secret that will direct suspicion straight at a murderer. A man who has already killed at least twice."

"I don't know anything!" she protested. "However much you and the police nag, I can't tell secrets I don't know."

"Then you'd better start working on the secrets you don't remember," Steve said harshly. "Think what they might be, Abby, for God's sake. Your life could depend on making the right connection."

Chapter Six

Abby wanted to laugh, but somehow the laughter stuck in her throat, refusing to come out. Her voice was heavy with sarcasm when she finally spoke.

"Right, I'm sure there's some deadly secret hidden in those family papers I'm going through. Dad probably left us a warning note. 'Dear Daughters: Watch out for evil Mr. X. He's planning to murder you all, in order to gain control of the family inheritance....'"

Steve didn't answer except with a look, and Abby felt the blood drain from her cheeks. "Good grief, Steve, I was joking!"

"Were you?" he asked quietly. "Think about what you said, Abby."

She sat down on the sofa with a bump. Had her subconscious forced her to speak a truth that her conscious mind wanted to suppress? She certainly had the skills and the professional training to uncover any remaining family secrets. But how could a Deane disgrace, however terrible, threaten an outsider? *For heaven's sake, what did she know?*

She faced Steve with a rueful shrug. "I guess in view of all the colorful family history we've uncovered since Dad died, it would be irrational of me to insist that there's nothing possible left to discover."

"And you're never irrational," Steve said with a slight grin. "I distinctly remember you telling me how orderly and logical you are. Unlike me, of course."

She glared at him. "The problem is, where do I start looking for this deep, dark secret? Linsey stumbled over the truth about our half brother and Dad's past affair quite by accident. She didn't deliberately go searching for secrets."

"What would you do if this were a routine research problem at the Historical Society?"

"I'd define the most likely area to produce results, and search outward from there."

Steve grimaced. "And I guess that's why we have a problem. We don't know which area is most likely to produce results."

Abby didn't reply. She stared at him abstractedly, feeling the first faint glimmerings of an idea. A little sunburst of excitement exploded deep inside her. "Wait, let me work this through step-by-step." She held up her hand and counted off on her fingers.

"First. Somebody at the bank is embezzling funds. We know that for an absolute fact, right? Second. You believe Howard Taylor was murdered because he was about to expose this embezzler. Third. Somebody tried to kill me tonight because I'm a danger to them. Fourth, the person I'm a danger to is the same person who murdered Howard Taylor. Who is also the bank embezzler." She quirked an eyebrow in Steve's direction. "How am I doing so far?"

"Great. Terrific. Now all you have to do is identify the embezzler, and we've caught ourselves a murderer."

"No problem," Abby said airily. "Give me another thirty seconds or so, and I'll toss his name right off." She stared at the ceiling, until the frustration simmering at the edges of her mind boiled over and blanked out thought. She hunched forward, resting her head on her hands. "This is hopeless, Steve. I'm chasing my own tail and getting dizzy in the process. The embezzler is a bank employee, and I don't know a soul at the bank except Keith Bovery."

The words had no sooner left her mouth than she sprang up from the sofa, energized as if she'd been jolted by an electric prod. She and Steve stared at one another in mutual astonishment.

"My God!" Steve exclaimed. "Keith Bovery!"

"Keith Bovery," Abby repeated in a whisper. "And this time I'm not joking. Steve, he has a lifetime of connections to our family. My father could have known a dozen secrets about his past."

"Plus he's the only person at the bank who knew the embezzlements had been discovered," Steve reminded her.

"Which means he's the only person with a solid motive for murdering Howard Taylor."

Abby grabbed Steve's arm. "The basement!" she said. "Those boxes of Dad's mementos. I'd bet the family trust fund we'll find something incriminating in them. Good grief, I even told Mr. Bovery this morning that I was coming to Boulder to sort through Dad's war mementos! I handed him a motive to kill me. On a silver platter, no less!"

"I can't imagine why he'd want to kill your half brother, though."

"Maybe Douglas was blackmailing him," Abby suggested. "Steve, it's all beginning to make sense at last! Keith Bovery is the only person at the bank that I might be a threat to. He must be scared out of his mind about what I'm going to reveal."

Steve frowned. "You know, Abby, I've spent hours with Keith over the past couple of weeks. He just doesn't strike me as a man who feels cornered and desperate. Frustrated about the embezzlements, maybe, but not personally frightened."

Abby didn't want to listen. Somehow she wanted to keep this discussion as a game of Hunt the Murderer, not a serious assessment of whether an old family friend was trying to kill her.

"Maybe Keith committed bigamy," she said, ignoring Steve's comments. "A lot of our servicemen married girls in Korea and then abandoned them when their tour of duty was over. Most of Keith's money comes from his wife's family, you know. He'd be in big trouble if his marriage to Helen wasn't really legal. His wealth would vanish overnight."

"His salary at the bank is hardly chicken feed," Steve pointed out.

"It would be, if he's grown accustomed to living on his wife's family fortune. What's a hundred thousand a year when you once had a million?" Abby felt almost light-headed with the sense of impending discovery. "Come on, Steve, let's go down to the basement and start our search. We have a bunch of letters and photos still to get through."

"I'll willingly search all night. But first I'm going to heat us a can of soup."

"I'm not hungry."

"Five minutes, Abby. Be reasonable, you can wait five minutes. We've neither of us eaten all day, and those boxes aren't going to run away."

In Abby's current mood, five minutes sounded like a lifetime. Adrenaline coursed through her veins, leaving no room for hunger. "I can't hang around doing nothing. Bring my soup downstairs when it's hot. Please?"

She bounded toward the basement stairs without waiting for Steve's reply and wrenched open the heavy door. The smell of smoke was strong enough to make her cough.

"Yuk," she muttered. "Burned corn always makes the worst smell. One of the basement windows must be open." Looking over her shoulder, she called to Steve. "Are you sure you turned off the barbecue grill?"

His reply came faintly from the pantry. "I'm sure. Do you prefer mushroom or tomato soup?"

"Mushroom." The basement door swung closed behind her. Abby flipped on the light and ran quick-footed down the steep wooden stairs. She stopped, transfixed with horror, as she rounded a supporting pillar and looked toward the corner that housed her father's collection of memorabilia. Acrid smoke billowed in gray clouds from the neat stack of cartons. Hungry tongues of orange flame already lapped at the edge of the bottom few boxes and, even as she watched, an extralong lick of flame flared out, reaching greedily for the nearby bookshelves. The shelves, thank God, were imitation wood, less flammable than the real thing, and they resisted the encroaching fire. At least for the moment.

Her legs regained the power of movement. "Steve!" she yelled, cursing the heavy door that so effectively cut off sound between floors. She ran toward the old-fashioned stone sink that stood in an alcove next to the washing machine and dryer. "Steve!" she yelled again as loudly as she could. "Oh, God, Steve, get down here!"

Smoke filled her lungs. Coughing and choking, she reached under the sink for the plastic pail. She tossed out a collection of cleaning rags and stuck the pail under the taps, praying it wouldn't leak. Hopping from one foot to the other with impatience, she could hardly bear to watch as the water ran with agonizing slowness into the bucket. At this rate she was never going to put out the fire! Oh God, she had to save those papers!

She thrust a stopper into the sink, leaving the water running as she carried the heavy bucket over to the smoldering cartons. The smoke had lessened, but the flames were edging higher, and she could feel the heat of the blaze when she was still five feet away. She threw water into the center of the blaze, and the flames died in a hiss of foulsmelling smoke.

Abby knew better than to think the battle was over. Even as she turned around to run back to the sink for more water, she could see the flicker of fresh flame burning a yellow path toward the bookshelves. How long did it take to heat a can of soup, for God's sake? *Steve, don't get any fancy gourmet ideas,* she prayed. *Just get the heck downstairs.* If she could keep the flames under control for another couple of minutes, surely Steve would be here to help.

Her actions went into automatic. Scoop water into the pail from the full sink. Run back to the burning cartons. Toss water onto the flames. Another hiss. Another billow of black smoke. Return to the sink. Scoop more water. Toss it onto the dying flames. Run back to the sink. The linoleum floor was soaked, flecked with charred paper and slippery beneath her feet, but at least her efforts were meeting with success. The water had already doused most of the flames. Abby's panic lessened. Hah! So much for Steve, stirring his darn soup and buttering toast while she saved the house from becoming a blazing inferno.

The lights failed a split second before she reached the sink for the sixth time. The blackness was intense, made worse by the choking smoke. The heat had obviously melted an electrical wire somewhere, and the circuit had clicked off. The creak of a soggy carton shifting position sounded loud—almost frightening—in the darkness. Abby shivered. The basement, she reminded herself, hadn't changed because of the dark. It was still the familiar room of happy childhood memories and winter games. At this moment, however, it seemed filled with menace. A living, breathing, *watching* menace. Until tonight she'd never been afraid of the dark. But then, until tonight nobody had ever shot at her with intent to kill....

One more pailful, Abby decided, clenching her teeth, willing herself to ignore the debilitating fear. She couldn't risk going upstairs until the fire was totally out. Thank God she'd come downstairs when she did; she ought to feel more cheerful. Unfortunately, although she had put out a dangerous fire, she'd ruined her father's mementos. The few water-soaked remnants weren't going to be legible enough to reveal secrets about anybody.

Feeling her way gingerly across the treacherous floor, she toted the heavy pail back to the smouldering embers. Sadly she poured water onto the pulpy, charred mass of paper and cardboard. A final, feeble tongue of flame flickered, then died. Smoke belched. The darkness became total.

The crash of books falling from the shelves echoed through the basement like an explosion. Pain detonated inside in her head, sharp and all-enveloping. An ornament. She'd been hit by a falling knickknack. Abby gagged, trying to control the sickness that welled up from the pit of her stomach. She drew in a deep breath, hoping to conquer the nausea. Instead, the sickness increased as she inhaled lungfuls of the awful, stinking smoke. She doubled over, clutching her stomach, dizzy with pain.

A ray of light pierced the blackness. "Abby?" *Steve's voice.* "Abby, what the hell's going on down there?"

"Steve." She wasn't sure if she spoke his name out loud. Pain exploded behind her left ear. She'd been hit a second time, Abby realized. Deliberately hit? She tried to turn around to confront her invisible attacker, but her knees buckled.

Steve. In her mind she screamed the warning. In reality, her voice produced no more than a whimper. Oh God, she couldn't die. Not now. Not when Steve was so close.

Her body crumpled. She keeled over, her face sank into the sodden remains of her father's papers, and her breathing stopped.

Darkness claimed her for its own.

THE NIGHT had not lived up to the bright promise of the morning. It sure as hell hadn't.

The murderer drove along the Boulder Turnpike at a steady fifty, keeping to the inside lane. No point in attracting the attention of an overeager cop, although the rifle had been tossed into a garbage Dumpster twenty minutes ago, along with the ski mask and the glove liners. In Colorado, ski masks and glove liners were a dime a dozen. Thank God for winter sports enthusiasts. Thank God for hunting enthusiasts and the gun lobby. No danger that the rifle would be traced. No danger that the murderer might be identified.

Still, there was no denying the grim fact that Abigail Deane was alive. Not dead. And she should have been dead. It was always better to face truth head-on. That way it couldn't creep up and scare you from behind, when you least expected it.

There were consolations. Tonight hadn't been a total waste of effort. Ronald Deane's Korean relics had all been destroyed—the fire had taken care of that. Now there was no need to worry that some long-forgotten photo or letter might turn up. And, of course, the really crucial documents had been stolen from Abigail's apartment this morning.

The murderer leaned back in the driver's seat and relished the warm glow of satisfaction that the morning's work evoked. The neatly executed robbery had been a total success. But the stark fact remained that if Abigail had ever read those letters and noted those certificates—especially that damned death certificate—then the murderer would never be safe. Abigail was an archivist, and unfortunately archivists were trained to have retentive memories for odd, incongruous bits of paper.

Yes, whichever way you looked at it, Abigail Deane should have been dead by now. Stretched out cold on her backyard patio. Like Howard Taylor. The murderer pounded the steering wheel. Damn Steven Kramer for the interfering busybody that he was!

In fact, come to think of it, Steven Kramer ought to die, too. He deserved to die. Not because of his investigation at the bank. No, that investigation had been cleverly stymied and posed no threats. Steven Kramer had a dazzling reputation as an investigator, but even his keen eyes would never uncover the truth of who was behind those embezzlements. All the crucial computer entries had been made using Howard Taylor's confidential access code, and the first trail stopped dead with good old Howard. Stopped dead. That was a nice choice of words. Good old *dead* Howard, who couldn't protest his innocence. Nothing was left to refurbish Howard's reputation except a file labeled *Investigation—Confidential*. Such a shame that nobody would ever find the contents of the file!

And if by any amazing chance Steven Kramer insisted on digging a little deeper—well, that had been taken care of as well. If Kramer didn't accept that Howard Taylor was the embezzler, then he had thoughtfully been provided with a trail of clues leading to another villain. A double frame. A brilliant, subtle double frame.

The murderer smiled. Yes, Operation Howard had been a success, a total success. And Operation Abigail Deane would soon be a success. Next time. A double success, because Steven Kramer would die with her, slowly and painfully. A fitting punishment for thwarting the murderer's efforts not once, but twice.

The murderer glanced into the rearview mirror and switched lanes, picking up a little speed. Not a cop in sight. Excitement warred with caution. Excitement won. The murderer pressed down the accelerator. Sixty. Seventy. Eighty miles an hour. The speed felt good. Wonderful. This was how it would feel when Abigail Deane and Steven Kramer died. Crack! Bang! Adrenaline would surge. High. Flying beyond the stars. Eat your heart out, Ronald Deane. *I've killed one of your children, and maybe later I'll kill the other two as well.* Not because Kate and Linsey know anything. As punishment. As retribution for what you did to me.

Ninety miles an hour. The thrill was incredible. But foolish. Too foolish to continue. People didn't get on in life by being foolish. The murderer eased up on the accelerator and carefully reduced speed to the prescribed fifty-five sedate miles an hour.

Still not a police car in sight. Squad cars never seemed to be in the right place at the right time. Breaking the law was easy. The murderer had taken advantage of that fact for years.

The murderer gave a small, satisfied sigh. Killing was easy, too. As easy as any other crime, when you had a brilliant brain planning the method of death. Tonight's setback was only temporary. Tonight was just a hiccup on the march to victory.

Watch out, Abigail Deane. Watch out, Steven Kramer. And to hell with you, Ronald Deane. *If you aren't already there.*

ABBY KNEW she was alive because she felt so totally god-awful and wretched. She was cold, wet, and stank of smoke. Her head pounded, her eyes throbbed, her throat rasped, and her stomach couldn't decide whether to sink into her toes or tie itself in knots around her rib cage. While making up its mind, it lurched around like a roller coaster. The only only good thing about her situation was the strong, broad, masculine chest that she was leaning against. Steve's. She nuzzled her cheek against his sweater. Yes, unmistakably Steve's.

With considerable effort, Abby forced her eyelids open, and was rewarded with a wave of nausea so powerful that she literally gagged. She closed her eyes again. When the sickness finally subsided, memory returned. Somebody had hit her over the head! She wanted to murder the person who had caused her to feel this rotten. Abby would have laughed if her ribs hadn't hurt so badly. She wanted to murder her would-be murderer.

She struggled upright. Had her attacker gotten away again? She tried to ask Steve. Unfortunately, her smoke-charred throat managed to do no more than emit a sound somewhere between a squeak and a groan.

Steve greeted her grunt with flattering enthusiasm. He smiled at her rapturously, and lifted a damp hank of hair away from her forehead with gentle fingers. "Hi, beautiful."

"Gromph," *Hi, yourself.*

"Abby, my sweet, don't try to talk. Rest for another moment. Can you understand what I'm saying, sweetheart?"

"Gromph." *Yes, of course.*

"You did a fantastic job of putting out the fire, Abby. Congratulations, sweetheart."

"Gromph, oomph." *Dad's papers are all destroyed.*

"You don't seem to have any broken bones, but there's a lump behind your ear. Something must have fallen on you when the bookshelves collapsed."

Her tongue managed to shape a coherent word at last. "No." She shook her head, which was a serious mistake. She waited till the pounding in her skull subsided, then tried again. "Hit. Someone hit me."

"*What?* You mean you were attacked? The bump on your head wasn't an accident?"

Abby winced at the decibel level of Steve's bellow. "You didn't see the guy who did it?" she croaked.

"No, I didn't see anybody, not even a glimpse. I never suspected anybody had been down there with you. The basement window was open, the wind was blowing in the right direction, and I just assumed a spark from the barbecue coals started the fire." Steve grasped her hands. "Abby, can you be sure somebody hit you? That it wasn't an accident?"

She thought for a long minute. "No," she admitted. "I can't be absolutely sure."

Steve jumped to his feet. "We need to call the police."

Abby leaned back against the sofa pillow. "Better to call Bovery first," she rasped. "See if he's home."

"For a person who's just been hit on the head, that's a damn good idea." Steve tucked the afghan across her knees. "Don't get up while I'm gone, sweetheart."

He had to be joking! Twitching her little finger required more strength than she possessed. Abby watched Steve walk over to the phone and, through the hammering of a hundred men pounding nails into her skull, listened to him dial. As soon as she heard him say, "Oh, Keith, I'm glad to have found you home," she closed her eyes and stopped listening. The hundred hammering men reduced themselves to a mere fifty or so.

"Keith Bovery says he's been home all afternoon." Steve returned to the living room. "Says he was catching up on his reading and hasn't seen anybody since he left the bank at lunchtime. He thought this was a mighty strange hour for me to be calling to set up a Monday meeting."

"Could he have reached Denver this quickly if he'd . . . been up here?" She couldn't bring herself to say *if he attacked me in the basement*.

Steve glanced at his watch. "Eleven o'clock. If there was no traffic on the turnpike and he speeded a bit, I think he could have swung it."

"So we're no further forward." Sickness stirred in Abby's stomach, and this time it had little to do with her physical state. Was she seriously considering the possibility that Keith Bovery had tried to kill her? Did she really believe that a respected man, who had figured in her life from the time she was a toddler, had suddenly acquired homicidal tendencies? She shuddered, revolted by the image, clamping her teeth together to stop them chattering.

Steve cradled her in his arms, and the shivering gradually stopped. "I called Knudsen," he said. "Of course, he wasn't available. But the switchboard operator said he'd collect his messages tonight."

"Cops are never around when you need 'em." Her stomach had started swooping again with serious intent.

Steve's brows knotted in worry. "Abby, sweetheart, I hate to say this, but you look awful. If you don't stop turning from gray to green and back again, I'll have to take you to the emergency room."

"Make me a cup of tea instead." She managed a small smile. "I'm too sick to cope with a hospital right now."

Abby's mind floated in limbo until Steve returned with a steaming pot of tea. She grimaced when she tasted the spoonfuls of sugar he had added, but drank two full cups. Her body slowly began to feel human again. As the pain lessened, her thoughts became more coherent. The tea had worked equal wonders on her throat and her brain.

"The most frustrating thing about this whole mess is that Dad's papers have all been burned or drowned." She stared disconsolately at her empty cup. "We're never going to find out Mr. Bovery's secrets now."

"I have a piece of good news for you."

She looked up, and Steve smiled. "That box you were so excited about—the one with all your dad's photos and letters—it didn't burn with all the others, because it wasn't in the basement."

"Where was it?"

"I took it upstairs to my room before dinner."

Her aches vanished in a surge of relief. "Steve, that's wonderful! Terrific! How lucky we are!" She frowned. "Incredibly lucky, in fact. Why in the world did you suddenly decide to heave that box all the way up two flights of stairs?"

"Because I expected you to go racing back down to the basement to find it, the moment my back was turned. And I had other plans for the evening." He grinned. "Mind you, I'd never admit this, if you weren't too weak to wreak vengeance."

"I'm feeling stronger by the minute."

He ruffled her damp, stringy hair, his gaze catching hers in a rueful smile as flakes of charred paper detached themselves from her scalp and stuck to his hand. "Do you feel strong enough to take a shower, maybe?"

"Sounds heavenly."

He swept her off the sofa and into his arms before she had even struggled into a sitting position. "Steve, you can't," she protested. "I'm too heavy."

"Abby, my sweet, leave my shattered masculine ego some scrap of pride, could you? So far tonight, I've watched while a gunman took potshots at you. Then I ambled around the kitchen making tea and toast, while you single-handedly extinguished a blazing fire. And when I finally made it down to the basement, I missed spotting the gunman for a second time." He took the stairs to the second floor at a run and arrived not even panting. He grinned as he deposited her gently alongside the shower. "At least let me show off my lung capacity and flex my biceps, sweetheart. It's all I have left to boast about."

"You're supposed to say, 'Abby, you're light as a feather.'"

He pulled back the shower curtain and turned on the faucet, adjusting the temperature. "How about 'Abby, would you like me to help you get undressed?'"

Her cheeks stopped turning from gray to green and settled on scarlet. "I think . . . I think I can manage just fine by myself."

"Pity," he said huskily. His hands lingered for a tantalizing moment at the buttons of her damp and filthy shirt, then he straightened and headed for the bathroom door. "Leave this open," he instructed. "Yell if you need me. I'll be waiting in the bedroom."

Abby stripped off her clothes and stepped into the shower. Need him? Dear God, she needed him! But was she ready to risk losing her best friend on the off chance that she might gain a lover? Somehow a night when she'd been shot at, choked by smoke and banged on the head didn't seem the right time to be answering such an important question.

"Steve," she whispered, lathering her singed hair and letting the warm water cascade over her aching body. "Steve, I need you. To take me into your arms. To hold me close. To show me that making love needn't be the disaster it always was with Greg. *I need you.*"

Fortunately—unfortunately?—Steve didn't hear.

Chapter Seven

By nine o'clock the next morning they had examined every photo and read every scrap of paper in the box of mementos that Steve had rescued from the basement. When they had read and discarded the final newspaper clipping, Abby gestured wearily to the two small piles of photographs she and Steve had set aside.

"That's it, I guess. The sum total of our information about Mr. Bovery. No incriminating letters. No tantalizing postcards. No revealing newspaper clippings. Just a few photos from Korea. How many did we find, Steve?"

He counted quickly. "Five of Keith himself. And about twenty more in this other pile that show your father and his various military buddies, but don't include Keith."

Abby fanned out the five photographs and stared at them fixedly. "There's nothing," she said at last, her frustration mounting to boiling point. "Absolutely nothing that even hints at a secret. They're just a bunch of young guys in uniform, smiling at the camera."

"Nothing special about the backgrounds?" Steve peered over her shoulder.

"They're posed next to their tents or their airplanes." She held a snapshot out to him. "In this one they're standing in front of their clothesline. If wet T-shirts and droopy boxers are incriminating, Keith Bovery could be in big trouble. Otherwise he's home free."

"Wait." Steve shuffled through the second pile of pictures. "Do you think the person who's half cut off in this snapshot is Keith Bovery? He's got his arm around a woman, but her features are too blurred to identify."

Abby perked up. "Hey, maybe he really did get married in Korea."

"So that his marriage to rich Helen was bigamous?" Steve flipped over the photo. "Unfortunately it doesn't say anything except the date. 1953. Not even a month."

Abby reached behind her for a magnifying glass and studied the blurred snapshot. The excitement drained out of her in a long sigh. "It's Keith, all right, but the woman with him isn't going to provide us with any dazzling new insights. Look, it's Lynn. Dad's mistress. Compare her with the photo we found yesterday."

Steve examined the two pictures. "You're right, darn it. So much for Keith Bovery and his bigamous marriage." He stood up and dusted off his jeans. "Well, kiddo, I don't know about you, but I'm just about done in. Want to head back to Denver?"

"You don't want to go climbing?"

"Not unless you're wildly enthusiastic. I'd like to call my investigating team and see how their background check on Keith is coming along. Since we've had no luck rummaging around in your dad's mementos, let's try and tackle this from another angle."

"And we could call Knudsen again."

"I don't think there's any great rush," Steve said wryly. "I'm afraid the lieutenant isn't going to take action against the president of a major bank simply on the grounds that the man once served with your dad in Korea.

And in cold, hard fact, that's all we have against Keith at the moment."

"I suppose you're right," Abby acknowledged. With a rueful smile she added, "Can you think of some socially gracious way I could call Keith up and ask him if he's trying to murder me?"

"That one might stump even Miss Manners." He reached out and pulled her to her feet. "Come on, Abby, let's get out of here."

They spent the journey back to Denver hashing over the same stale set of facts, and arrived back there tired and dispirited. "We should have gone climbing," Abby said morosely, lifting her bag from the rear seat of the car. "It would have been a more useful way to spend the morning than poring over those dumb family papers."

Steve feigned astonishment. "Can this be the Abigail Deane I know and love, referring to a collection of precious family mementos as 'dumb papers'?"

Abby couldn't summon a smile. She stirred restlessly as they waited for the elevator. "It's crazy, Steve. Yesterday somebody tried to kill me. At least once, and maybe twice. And today, less than twenty-four hours later, I can't think of anything better to do than tell myself to stop worrying about the situation and wait for Knudsen to call. That's more than crazy. It's bizarre. Fantastic."

"No, it's sensible," Steve said. "Abby, we tried solving this ourselves by delving around in your father's past, and that didn't work. Now we should concentrate on the present. Which is my department. Mine and the professional detectives'. I'm pretty damn good at my job, hard as you may find that to believe, and my professional reputation is on the line. I'm going to discover who embezzled funds from the First Denver Bank, and then we'll have a whole new perspective on who might have been trying to kill you."

"I guess." Abby remained unconvinced. The elevator reached the seventh floor and they walked quickly to her apartment. Steve held her bag while she fished inside her jacket pocket for the front-door key.

The door swung open on well-oiled hinges and the neat, polished cleanliness of her living room reached out to greet her. Abby felt a wave of gladness to be home, strengthened because Steve was with her. His friendly presence, combined with the familiar tidy atmosphere of her apartment, provided a sense of safety that had rarely seemed so welcome. She realized with an ache of bitter regret that her childhood home in Boulder no longer represented a refuge from the hustle of everyday life. It would be a long time before she ever again felt at ease in her old family home. The rifle shots and the fire last night had blasted away far more than her immediate physical security.

"Hey, kid." Steve's voice interrupted her sad thoughts. "This box weighs a ton. Where do you want it?"

"The bedroom, please. We can stand it on top of the filing cabinets. Wait, I'll go first and open the door."

She stepped across the threshold of her bedroom—and stopped so abruptly that Steve banged into her.

"Sorry." She spoke absently, aware that her heart was beginning to pound with a nameless, formless dread. She moved out of Steve's way, sniffing the slightly stale air as she walked across the room to her dresser. She checked quickly. Her glamorous black and gold bottle of Fendi, a gift from Kate, stood in its usual place. The distinctive, squat brown bottle of Opium had vanished, and was nowhere to be seen.

For a split second, fear turned her mouth dry. She realized, with a detached flash of astonishment, that she felt more afraid at this moment than she had the previous evening when bullets first started to fly. Bullets were brutal, but they were also concrete and comprehensible. People fired them when they wanted to wound or kill. A missing bottle of perfume, like purposeless trips to the airport, was terrifying in its irrationality.

"Steve." Her throat rasped so badly that the word was scarcely more than a whisper. But he heard her, and turned around at once.

"What is it? Abby, you're white as a sheet. What's happened?"

She couldn't disguise her panic. "My bottle of Opium perfume is missing. I smelled scent in the air as soon as I came into the bedroom. I came over here to check. The bottle's gone."

He didn't laugh at her, thank God. "You're sure you didn't put the bottle somewhere else before you left for Boulder? The bathroom, maybe. The drawer beside your bed?"

She shook her head. "I only wear Opium for special occasions. It's too heavy for everyday use. I haven't touched the bottle in two weeks, except to dust." Nevertheless, she crossed over to the bathroom and ran her gaze quickly along the counter. A box of talcum powder, translucent face soap in a dish, toothbrush, toothpaste, four lipsticks and a comb in a small crystal tray. No perfume.

She pulled open the mirrored door of the cabinet above the sink. Toilet articles, a box of aspirin, Band-Aids, more makeup. No perfume. Suddenly frantic, she pulled open the double doors under the sink and grabbed a plastic travel bag, unzipping the top and shaking out the contents all over her counter. Tissues, suntan lotion, hair spray. Another comb. No perfume.

Abby walked back into the bedroom, arms clutched across her stomach. When someone had shot at her last night, she hadn't shed a tear. When her father's papers went up in flames, she had thought only about extinguishing the blaze. Now—absurdly—she felt distraught, overset. Sobs welled up in her throat.

"Steve, it's gone. Somebody's been in my apartment and taken a bottle of Opium perfume. For God's sake, who would do something so crazy? Why would they do it?"

Steve put an arm around her waist. His body felt warm and solid against her side, restoring a sense of balance to her world. He spoke quietly, reassuringly. "If the perfume was stolen, Abby, the thief surely must have taken something else, something that makes more sense. Shall we walk through your apartment together and see if we can spot what's missing?"

She nodded, her hand sliding into his, welcoming the warmth of his grasp. She felt chilled and shaken to the bone. "I'm sorry, Steve," she muttered. "I know I'm overreacting, but I feel I'm standing at the center of something crazy. And the craziness is moving closer to me all the time."

"You're not overreacting, kiddo. You've had some terrifying experiences over the past few days. Imagining a stranger inside your apartment, pawing through your belongings, is the final straw. Let's start in the kitchen, and see what else has been disturbed."

They searched with meticulous care, but Abby couldn't detect anything out of place in the small kitchen or the adjoining dining area. In the living room she had the impression that the magazines on the coffee table might have been moved, but she couldn't swear to it, and nothing else appeared out of place.

The perfume thief clearly wasn't interested in ordinary valuables. Two small pre-Colombian statues, each valued at several hundred dollars, glared down from their special shelf beside the fireplace. Her state-of-the-art stereo equipment and collection of CDs didn't appear to have been touched, and not even a teaspoon was missing from the chest of antique silver she'd inherited from her grandmother.

"What about jewelry?" Steve asked as they returned to the bedroom.

"I don't have anything really valuable. My mother's pearls, a heavy gold bracelet Dad gave me on my twenty-first birthday, that's about it." Abby opened the drawer in her nightstand and pulled out a flat leather case. "The pearls and bracelet are both here," she said.

She returned the jewelry case to the drawer and sat down on the bed. To her embarrassment, tears trickled down her cheeks, refusing to stop. "Steve, I'm not crazy. I swear to you that a bottle of Opium perfume was standing on my dresser top when we left for the bank on Saturday morning."

"I believe you, Abby." Steve frowned, staring at the dresser. "I have an idea," he said. "Maybe the thief didn't steal the perfume. Maybe he spilled it and then removed the bottle, in the hope that nobody would know he'd ever been here."

Abby's tears stopped. A tiny ray of light broke through the miasma of gloom and craziness. "Oh yes! You might be right, Steve. If he spilled the perfume, that would explain the strong smell. Opium lingers for ages." She jumped up from the bed. "And if the thief thought we wouldn't notice he'd been here, he must have taken something quite small, something I might not realize was missing.''

She peered at the top of her dresser, trying to see it with the eyes of a thief. ''What could have interested him on my dresser? Here's a newsletter from my aerobics group with a paperweight on top of it. A tiny silver tray that used to be my mother's. A fancy box of tissues. The remaining bottle of perfume is on the left-hand side. And right behind that, a picture of my father with his commanding officer in Korea....'' The words trailed away, and she looked at Steve in silent question.

''Yes, you're right,'' he said, his voice husky. ''Anybody who picked up that picture to have a closer look would be in danger of knocking over your perfume.''

Abby's mouth tightened into a grim line. ''Do you have the impression that we keep stumbling over little bumps in the ground that all lead back to the same massive tree root? *Korea*. Something happened in Korea.''

She pulled a tissue from the boutique box and blew her nose. Korea was the key to everything, she was sure of it. When she spoke with Lieutenant Knudsen she was going to tell him her suspicions about Keith Bovery, no matter what. And yet, in her heart of hearts, could she really visualize Mr. Bovery—dapper, ruddy-cheeked Mr. Bovery—firing rifle shots from the backyard, then sneaking around her basement and setting fires, before racing back to Denver to gaze at a picture of her father? Of course she couldn't. Oh God! Nothing made sense.

She dropped her tissue into the wastebasket and stared absently into its depths. A frisson of something between fear and hysteria ran down her spine.

''Steve,'' she said, choking back a gurgle of laughter. 'I've just discovered something else the thief stole.''

''What?''

"An empty manila envelope, torn at one end." She pointed to the wastebasket. "It was the only thing in the trash on Saturday morning, and now it's gone."

For a moment Steve's face reflected the same blank incredulity as she felt, then his expression brightened. "That's not so hard to explain. The thief used the envelope to carry away the spilled perfume bottle. If he didn't want you to know he'd been here, he'd need to mop up the spill. He wasn't to know you'd have such an accurate memory for tiny details."

"Perfume isn't a tiny detail to a woman," Abby said flatly. "You're probably half right. He didn't want anybody else to know the apartment had been robbed. But he wasn't worried about me. He didn't expect me to come back. He expected me to be dead." Abby was surprised how calmly she managed to give voice to her fears.

Steve didn't deny the possibility. "I agree. And everything we know suggests the person we're dealing with is cunning, not crazy—"

"And so?"

"And so presumably he didn't break into your apartment for the sole purpose of admiring one of your dad's old photographs. I'm more convinced than ever that something else has been stolen. How about a document from your file cabinets—?"

"Wait a minute!" she interrupted. "My God, Steve, it's not some thief who's crazy, it's us! We keep talking about somebody *breaking into* the apartment. But nobody's broken in anywhere! You saw me open the front door. The lock hadn't been jimmied. No windows are smashed and besides, we're seven floors up and the balcony doesn't connect to anywhere. If somebody's been in my apartment, that person came in the front door with a key!" She laughed, grabbing Steve in her relief. "Good grief, you great investigator, how come you never noticed those trivial facts? I haven't been invaded. That shooting last night, coupled with the fire, has given us both an oversize case of the jitters.''

She hadn't realized Steve had been as tense as she was herself until she saw him relax. He grinned. ''Okay, so here's just the teensiest layer of tarnish on my Supersleuth image. Who do you think has been here? One of your sisters?''

Her laughter faded. ''No, they'd leave a note. Besides, Kate has never visited my apartment in her life without forgetting a scarf or a slipper or a book she was reading. And Linsey's in Canada. Apart from which, she could no more come calling without bringing a basket of muffins or a jar of cookies than she would fly.''

''Then who else has a key?''

''The superintendent has a master key in case of emergencies. You know that. But nobody else. The super must have been up here to do some routine maintenance.'' Energized by the thought that the visitor to her apartment had been entirely legitimate, Abby bounded over to the phone and dialed the superintendent's number.

Bill was home and indignantly denied the possibility that he would have entered Miss Deane's apartment without asking permission or leaving notification that he had done so.

''Ain't nobody been in your apartment this weekend that I seen, Miss Deane, and I been watching out pretty good. Me and the security guards both.''

''George and Lenny both showed up on time?''

''Of course.'' Bill sounded outraged. ''Somebody was on that entrance door from sundown to sunup, same as always. And I kep' an eye on the door the rest of the time, just like always. Been quiet as the grave around this place.

Everybody away for the weekend, makin' the most of the sunshine, I reckon.''

''I thought you might have needed to make a check on the plumbing or something. Bill, I think somebody was in my apartment this weekend.''

''Not unless they got a key, they weren't. I didn't see or hear no alarms on my panel, and the new electronic security system works real good. George or Lenny's always on duty after dark, and you need a key to get through them outer doors during the day, Miss Deane. We got real fine security in this building. Ain't been no trouble from burglars or vandals or nothin' for more'n three years. And that's how long I bin workin' here.'' Almost without pause, he added, ''But if you're worried, you're worried. You want me to call the police?''

''Oh, no.'' She hesitated. ''Thanks, Bill, but I don't think there's any reason to call the police.''

She hung up the phone, wiping palms that were suddenly sweaty against the side of her jeans.

''No luck?'' Steve said.

''I'm not sure,'' she answered slowly. ''I think I just had a great insight. You know those anonymous phone calls?—I have an idea why the caller needed me to visit Stapleton airport.''

''*What?*'' Steve was rigid with surprise. ''The super sure must have told you something I didn't hear!''

''He told me nobody could have gotten into this apartment over the weekend without keys to the main entrance door as well as to this apartment. I believe him. So the logical conclusion is that somebody has acquired themselves a duplicate set of my keys. When did they do that? When *could* they have done it?''

Steve exhaled in a quiet whistle. ''Two days ago, when your purse was snatched at Stapleton. My God! *You were called to the airport so that somebody could take an impression of your keys.''*

''It seems logical, don't you think? There are always people waiting in tight-packed clusters at Stapleton. One way or another, the thief could count on getting access to my purse.''

''He'd only need the keys for a second or two,'' Steve agreed. ''Any kid who's ever read *The Hardy Boys* would know how to make the necessary impressions.''

''I'll get my purse from the living room,'' Abby said. ''Maybe we can find some trace of wax on the keys.''

They examined the keys with a magnifying glass, under a strong reading light. The car keys were clean, but on each of her house and office keys they spotted minute traces of clear wax.

Abby shivered. ''I'm changing my locks first thing tomorrow morning. Steve, somebody must have been desperate to take such a huge risk.''

''I'm not sure it was all that risky. I'd say the guy's biggest danger was that you'd decide to change the locks on your apartment door just as a precaution.''

''The keys were only missing a couple of minutes. It never occurred to me.'' Abby paled. ''Keith Bovery was at the airport, Steve.''

''Yes.'' Steve frowned. ''But he didn't have much time for stealing your keys, Abby. He was with me and the consultant from Berkeley almost until the moment you and I met up.''

''He didn't need more than ten minutes.''

''And he probably had that much time. *Damn.* It's like the drive back from Boulder to Denver. Bovery scarcely had enough time to make it, but with a lot of luck he could just have been home to answer my phone call.''

Abby walked back to the dresser and stared at the picture of her father. "What did he want from my apartment, Steve?"

"Nothing obviously valuable. Bovery, or whoever the thief is, went to a lot of trouble to get in and out of here without leaving any trace of his presence. That means he took something he could reasonably expect wouldn't be missed. Some sort of document is the logical choice." Steve's face suddenly lighted up. "Of course! Your banking records. Maybe there's something in them that would nail the embezzler."

Abby felt her cheeks flush with excitement. Everything was beginning to fall into place again! She ran to the filing cabinets and pulled open the drawers.

The files looked untouched. The half dozen folders that contained financial documents took no more than ten minutes to search. Nothing was missing, nothing looked disturbed. She examined the documents relating to the Crystal Mine and the Confederate gold with particular care, but everything was just as she had organized it, right down to the maps and surveys in her father's own handwriting. Abby resisted the impulse to burst into tears. She'd be darned if she was going to let this thief cause her any more tears.

"We keep having these great ideas that go nowhere," Steve said, looking as frustrated as she felt. "Damn it! I thought I was about to unmask my embezzler."

"Instead we're right back where we started." Abby's temper exploded. Muttering swear words she hadn't even realized she knew, she stood up and slammed the file drawer shut with an angry kick. The drawer responded by refusing to close. The corner of a folder poked out, wedging the drawer open.

"I'm going to leave you sticking out like that, you stupid file," she muttered through gritted teeth. She turned away with a flounce, but seven years of training got the better of her temper. With a sigh of resignation, she turned around again and squatted in front of the cabinet, adjusting the folders one by one until the offending file returned to perfect alignment. In the process, a square of heavy paper fluttered to the floor. She picked it up, thinking ruefully that it was no more than she deserved if she'd damaged some important document in her childish display of anger.

She sat cross-legged on the floor and examined the piece of paper, trying to determine where it belonged. The words *Patricia Day Trien, Registrar* appeared on one line, and above it, partially obscured by the torn edge, ...*pher Deane Renquist.*

The scrap of paper had fallen out from between two folders, one holding outdated family records, such as her parents' wedding certificate, and another containing the few pieces of family correspondence that had survived from the early days of their marriage. She pulled both files from the drawer and opened them.

"Have you found something, after all?" Steve asked.

She held out the scrap of paper. For some reason her fingers were trembling. "This was loose in the file drawer. I'm trying to see where it came from, but there don't seem to be any torn documents in either of these folders."

"Can you tell if anything has been taken?"

She shook her head. "Not by looking, but I have a separate record, of course. In my alphabetized index to the file system."

"Of course." Despite the tension of the moment, there was affectionate laughter in Steve's voice. "I wonder why

I'm not surprised to hear you have an alphabetical index of your personal files?''

"All archivists keep a separate index of any documents they store," Abby said. She took a three-ring binder from the triangular desk that occupied one corner of her bedroom. "How else are people supposed to know what they have inside their filing cabinets?''

"I think most of us just hope we'll remember," Steve suggested.

"Very inefficient," Abby said disapprovingly, her professional instincts taking over from her previous outbursts of emotion. She opened the binder and turned its pages with an almost intimidating briskness. "Here's the contents list for the file we want to know about.'' She turned from binder to file a couple of times, then looked up at Steve, her brow wrinkled.

"Two documents are missing," she said. "A birth and death certificate for a little boy called Christopher Deane Renquist. They were both issued in Arapahoe County in 1954, but that's all the information I recorded in the index. This scrap of paper is obviously from one of the certificates.''

She closed the binder with a snap, then clenched her hands tightly together. Panic washed over her in a consuming wave. The sensation of drowning in a sea of someone else's madness overwhelmed her. Could someone really have gone to such tremendous trouble in order to steal thirty-five-year-old birth and death certificates? Why was it that each time she and Steve concocted some halfway sensible explanation of what was happening, the picture shattered, disassembling into chaos?

"Damn it," she murmured despairingly. "Why didn't he steal my bank records?''

Steve took her into his arms. "Nineteen fifty-four could be a significant year," he said. "It's the year your father came home from Korea."

She stared at him in horror. "You mean, you think this might be *another* illegitimate child my father produced?" Abby felt her stomach rise in rebellion. "Oh, good Lord. Surely he didn't have another affair the minute he came home from Korea?"

"I wasn't suggesting that," Steve said. "I was pointing out that you were right earlier, when you said that everything seems to tie back to something that happened in Korea."

Abby pulled herself out of Steve's arms and walked into the bathroom. She ran the water until it was very hot, lathered soap all over her hands and scrubbed fiercely at her face and arms. "I'm not going to think about this stuff any more until Knudsen calls," she said through a mouthful of bubbles. "We're just going in circles. We'd be more usefully employed if we sat down and watched *Wheel of Fortune* on TV. Oh blast! Now I've got soap in my eyes."

"Have a towel," Steve said, handing her one. "You can curl up with Vanna in a minute, if you insist. First you have to check the other file. Just in case anything else is missing."

Abby had rarely approached her filing system with such an intense feeling of distaste. She opened the three-ring binder and flipped crossly to the appropriate page.

"Family correspondence," she muttered. "There's a bunch of stuff here." Her eye ran expertly down the list. Her heart suddenly lurched. "Lynn Renquist. July, 1954. August, 1954. September 1954." Her heart hammered painfully within her chest. She looked up at Steve.

"Lynn Renquist," she repeated. "Lynn. Dad's lover from Korea. Her last name is Renquist."

"Christopher Deane Renquist," Steve said. "Born the year Lynn would have returned from Korea. Do you think he's Lynn's son?"

Silence blanketed the room. "But this baby died when he was just an infant," she said at last.

"Yes, he did, didn't he? Which makes me wonder how he could have been adopted and grown up to become Douglas Brady, your long-lost half brother."

"Our long-lost half brother whose existence—strangely enough—was never mentioned while Dad lived."

"But who turned up so conveniently when there was a five-million-dollar inheritance in gold waiting to be claimed by your father's heirs."

"Except, of course, that he had to find the gold before he could claim it—"

"Which he couldn't do without the help of you or your sisters."

"Who wouldn't have helped him, unless they believed he was their half brother with a rightful claim to some of Dad's money."

"Abby, my love, I have the feeling that we're both suggesting the same thing." Steve spoke very softly.

"We are." Abby nodded. She drew in a deep breath. "I don't think the late Douglas Brady was our half brother. I think... I think Douglas Brady was an impostor, whose only purpose in contacting my sisters was to steal the Confederate gold."

"At least we know why somebody went to so much trouble to gain access to your apartment."

"Yes," Abby agreed. "They wanted to steal the only documents that would have proved Douglas Brady was a fraud."

The buzz of the phone cut into the maelstrom of Abby's thoughts. "Let's hope it's Knudsen," she muttered to Steve. "Boy, do we have stuff to tell him." She picked up the phone.

"The fun and games are over, Abigail." The hoarse, muffled voice she had begun to hate spoke into the phone without salutation. "You were lucky last night, but luck doesn't hold for ever, Abigail. Your family's had a long run of luck, and now it's my turn. Your father's going to start paying what he owes. And you're the first installment on the debt. You, and then your sisters. I've decided I want you all. The three lovely Deane sisters." Angry laughter cackled over the wire. "Mine. Do you hear, Ronald? They're all going to be mine."

Chapter Eight

After half an hour of agonized debate with Steve, Abby called her sisters and told them about the latest anonymous phone call and all the events that had led up to it.

She spent an hour on the phone with each sister, trying to strike the correct balance between warning them that this caller meant business, and assuring them that they didn't have to catch the next available plane to Denver in order to prevent her from being murdered.

Both Kate and Linsey disputed Abby's suggestion that Douglas Brady might not have been their half brother. "Everything he said about himself tied in with what we know," Linsey pointed out. "And he had that letter of introduction from Dad, remember."

"Which you yourself said might have been a forgery," Abby countered. "You know how shaky Dad's handwriting got toward the end of his illness."

"But Douglas died to save my life!" Kate protested a few minutes later. "He *felt* like my brother. Besides, he had exactly the same color eyes as us. You know that shade of Dresden blue is a family trademark."

"We don't have an exclusive patent," Abby said dryly. "There are other human beings out there with blue eyes."

"But ours are a really unusual shade," Kate insisted.

Unusual, but not unique, Abby thought. There were probably several thousand American men of the right age with Dresden-blue eyes. Somebody who knew the Deane family well could easily have chosen Douglas for the impersonation, precisely because his eye color was so strikingly similar to that of the Deane sisters.

Kate, ever trusting, was almost equally outraged by the suggestion that Keith Bovery might have secrets worth killing to protect. "Mr. Bovery is a nice man," she protested. "He always gave us huge chocolate Santas at Christmas when we were kids. And creme eggs at Easter. If he hates us because of some silly old feud with Dad, why has he always been so friendly? He sent RJ and me his wife's favorite painting of Colorado for a wedding gift, in case I got homesick for the mountains. Besides, Abby, he's so respectable! Exactly your kind of guy. How can you suspect him of having dreadful secrets?"

"*Because* he's so respectable!" Abby exclaimed, exasperated.

"But you're respectable, and you don't have any dreadful secrets," Kate pointed out, with unexpected logic. "You're just as prim and proper inside as you are on the outside."

"Am I?" Abby demanded, annoyed beyond caution. "If I'm so darn prim and proper, why have I fallen in love with—?" Appalled, she stopped just in time. Good grief, how did Kate always manage to reduce conversations to her own level of indiscretion?

Kate was ecstatic. "RJ! Come here quickly and listen! Abby's fallen in love! Who with, Abby? Do we know him, and when are you getting married?"

"With whom," Abby corrected, trying to ignore the sudden pounding of her heart. "Kate, I have to go. Talk to you soon. Give RJ my best wishes." She dropped the receiver back into the cradle as if it were scalding her fingers.

"Kate doesn't think Mr. Bovery wants to kill anybody, especially us," she told Steve hurriedly, before he had a chance to comment on the rather odd ending to her conversation.

"Why not?"

"Mr. Bovery always gave us chocolate Santas for Christmas."

"Conclusive," Steve said with a grin. "At least if you're Kate." His smile fading, he added, "Abby, I've had nothing to do but sit here and think while you were talking to your sisters."

Had he heard her admit she'd fallen in love?

"And I've come up with a problem," he continued. "If Douglas was an impostor, why did he never worry about his supposed birth mother? Why was he so sure Lynn Renquist wouldn't turn up and say, 'This guy is a fraud. My baby died thirty-five years ago'?"

"Most likely Douglas knew Lynn Renquist was dead. Or living thousands of miles away on a desert island."

"But if Lynn's on a desert island, where did Douglas get all his information? And how did the thief know about those letters Lynn wrote to your father? Come to that, how did he know that your father had kept the birth and death certificates of the real Christopher Deane? Those strike me as the sort of thing only Lynn Renquist herself might know."

Abby's mouth went dry. She swallowed hard. "Are you suggesting Keith Bovery and Lynn Renquist are in this together?"

"They could be, you know. Remember that picture we found in Boulder? The one with Keith half chopped off, and Lynn all blurred? That photo proves the two of them knew each other in Korea. Maybe Keith hated your father all these years, because he himself was secretly in love with Lynn.''

Abby paced restlessly around the living room. "It just doesn't seem believable," she said. "Why would Lynn agree to defraud the daughters of the man she once loved?"

"For money. Enough money will tempt most people." Steve paused. "Maybe for revenge."

"Revenge doesn't last thirty-five years," Abby said with conviction. "Not in the real world. I study family papers all the time in my work, Steve, and the most remarkable thing is the way life moves on. Old wounds heal. New opportunities present themselves. I can't believe Lynn Renquist brooded for thirty-five years about how much she loved my father. What's more, I can't believe Keith Bovery harbored thirty-five years of frustrated love for a nurse he met in Korea." Shaking her head, she added, "Besides, a couple of days ago you were trying to convince me Mr. Bovery was in love with Linda Mendoza."

"I could have been wrong. It's never happened before, of course, but there's always a first time...." Steve's teasing smile died away. "My God! *Linda.*"

"Linda." Abby breathed the word on a note of wonder. "*Linda, nickname Lynn.* Gosh, Steve, it's possible, don't you think? And she's been divorced so her name could have been Linda Renquist before she hitched up with Mr. Mendoza."

"It sure could. Tomorrow at the bank I can access a computerized list of all First Denver employees. I can check to see if the record shows Linda Mendoza's maiden name. She's probably had the smarts to delete it, of course. But one way or another I'll track it down."

Abby thrust her hands into the pocket of her slacks, shaking her head in instinctive denial. "Steve, we're building a sixty-foot castle on top of two-inch foundations. Five minutes ago, Linda Mendoza was just a secretary at the bank, without the slightest breath of suspicion against her. Now she's suddenly my father's ex-mistress, with a bent for computer fraud and homicidal tendencies."

She walked across to the kitchen, frustration in every step, and thrust the kettle under the hot-water faucet. "I'm going to make some tea and think about something else. I'm tired of suspecting the whole world of embezzlement, mayhem and murder."

"Want to go to a movie?"

"No, thanks. I wish Knudsen would get here," she muttered, grimacing when she realized that her resolution hadn't even lasted ten seconds. "Doesn't anyone in the police department care that an anonymous caller just threatened to wipe out my entire family?"

As if hearing her complaint, the lieutenant arrived a few minutes later, armed not only with a tape of the threatening phone call, but also with a preliminary report from the Boulder police.

"A kid working for Burger King found a rifle in the Dumpster outside the restaurant, with a mask and gloves sitting on top of it," Knudsen told them. "Unfortunately, the rifle is K-Mart's most popular model, and the mask is like ten thousand others. The gloves are those metallic thread ski liners. Men's size Small. So we know the guy who shot at you isn't a giant. But we knew that already from Mr. Kramer's description. No fingerprints on anything, of course."

The detective considered the voice tape of the anonymous caller a more promising lead. He listened intently, both to Abby's suspicions of Keith Bovery and to Steve's unwillingness to accept Howard Taylor's guilt in the bank embezzlements.

"The trail's too obvious," Steve explained. "Howard used the bank's computers every day. He had plenty of time to discover all the system's weaknesses. Why was he careless enough to leave his electronic calling card everywhere he went?"

Knudsen shrugged. "Probably planned to fly the coop, so he didn't care. That's what embezzlers usually do. Pull the big one, and take off for Brazil."

"Except that nobody at First Denver pulled a big one. If Howard was the thief, and he planned to make a run for South America, why didn't he steal ten million and to hell with it? The way this money was stolen—two thousand here, five thousand there—it looks to me like a thief who's supporting some sort of expensive habit. Gambling. Fancy women. An obsession with collecting antique cars."

"Why not drugs?" Abby asked.

"If he'd spent half a million on getting high, the effects on his health ought to have shown up by now. We checked pretty carefully, and I'm sure none of the employees is a serious addict."

"I think we have legitimate cause to ask the FBI lab to compare Mr. Bovery's voice with the one on this anonymous phone call tape," Knudsen said. "They have the equipment, and experts who can correlate voice patterns, even when the speaker has disguised his voice. We'll send this tape to Washington tonight, express. We could get a preliminary reading back in three days."

"Where will you get a tape of Mr. Bovery's normal voice?" Abby asked.

"I'll go over to his house right now and ask a couple of routine questions," Knudsen said. "I'll tell him I need to record his answers for the DA's office. He won't object. People never do." He smiled tightly. "Especially white-collar criminals with something to hide. They like to think they can outsmart you while they pretend to cooperate."

The lieutenant rose to his feet. "I'm glad you called your sisters, Miss Deane. You want to take that last threatening phone call seriously. Ninety percent of harassing phone calls never go beyond harassment. But your caller looks like he's one of the remaining ten percent. And I wouldn't count on his psychological stability, if I were you. The voice on this tape sounds to me like someone who's hovering right on the edge."

He held out a card. "Here's the name of a reliable locksmith. He works on twenty-four-hour call. Don't sleep alone tonight, Miss Deane, and don't walk down any dark alleys. You might want to consider taking an out-of-town vacation. I hear the West Coast's having some beautiful weather."

"I won't run away because of some crazy lunatic, who may not even mean what he says. Besides, I have too much work—"

"You won't get through much work if you're dead, will you, Miss Deane?"

Abby's cheeks whitened, and Knudsen gave her a grim smile, clearly satisfied at having made his point. "Personally, I recommend Oregon. Great state for a vacation." He walked to the door and was out in the corridor before he turned back.

"One last warning, Miss Deane. Keith Bovery may be a villain. But then again he may not. Don't assume Bovery is the anonymous phone caller. Or the killer. It might be the last assumption you ever make."

"Cheerful soul, isn't he?" Steve remarked into the silence that followed the detective's departure.

Abby cleared her throat. "Yes." The single word was all she could manage.

"He's right about one thing. You should start packing for a long trip to somewhere else. Anywhere that isn't Colorado. There's no point sitting around here, taunting the killer to come and get you."

"And suppose I run now?" Abby asked tiredly. "What happens in six months' time, when the killer decides I'm still a threat to him? Am I going to pick up and run again? And again three months later? And next year?"

"In six months' time the killer may be behind bars. He probably will be behind bars."

"If we're lucky. If he doesn't turn his attention to Linsey and Kate instead. And I can't let that happen. Linsey's pregnant. Kate's finally getting her life in shape after twenty-six years. Neither of them needs to spend the next few weeks being stalked by a homicidal maniac."

"So you plan to offer yourself up as the sacrificial lamb?"

She hoped her smile didn't look as wavery as it felt. "That's not quite the simile I'd have chosen. I prefer to think of myself as the lure. The juicy, fat worm dangling on the end of a hook that's going to bring this killer to justice."

"Very noble. But the survival rate of bait worms isn't anything to make a man sleep easy." Steve turned away and stared out of her window at the distant park. He spoke without looking at her, his voice flat, tightly controlled.

"I'm frightened by the thought of you staying in Denver," he said harshly. "Hell, what do I mean, frightened? I'm scared out of my mind. I don't want to lose you, Abby. You're much too important to me.''

The intensity of his admission made her pulses race and the blood thrum in her ears. Part of her wanted to respond by moving closer to him, acknowledging that she needed him, too. Most of her wanted to run. To run far and fast. To retreat into the comfortable pattern of their old relationship. To protect herself from the danger of betrayal, and from the pain of intimacy.

A flippant remark hovered on her lips, but she bit it back just in time. In a moment of self-revelation, she became aware that she'd been retreating from Steve for months, frustrating all his attempts to put their relationship on a more serious footing. Strange that it should have taken an argument about physically running away to show her what she'd been doing to herself emotionally. She wasn't afraid to stay in Denver and face a murderer. Surely she wasn't too scared to face the truth of her feelings for Steve?

She wanted him as her lover. Abby let the words sink into her mind, accepting their inevitability.

She took a step forward, then another. *This won't hurt, unless you start hoping for a long-term commitment,* she told herself. She took the final step that brought her beside Steve. They stood together, not touching. Neither of them spoke. They looked down at the parkway.

''The aspen trees are beautiful,'' Steve said at last. ''Each fall, I think I've never seen such a perfect yellow.''

Once again he was offering her the chance to retreat from intimacy. How many times had he offered her similar escape routes? Abby wondered. And how many times had she callously seized them without any regard for Steve's feelings?

She slipped her hand through his arm. "This view's okay," she said casually. "But there's a much better one from my bedroom. Want to come and see it?"

He turned around to look at her, his green eyes guarded, his entire stance wary, almost vulnerable. *Good Lord,* she thought in amazement. *He doesn't know what to say next.* Her confidence grew slightly at the thought that Steve, the mighty sexual conqueror, wasn't treating his seduction of her as entirely routine. Maybe he, like her, wanted them to stay friends when the affair was over. Which wasn't going to be easy for either of them.

She grasped her courage in both hands. "Do you know something?" she murmured. "The very best view of all is right from my bed."

"Your bed . . ." Steve's voice thickened. He cleared his throat. "Your bed is nowhere near the window."

She gazed up at him, blue eyes limpid. "I know."

He framed her face with hands that shook just a little. "Abby?" he asked hoarsely.

She put her arms around his neck and pulled his mouth down to hers. "Yes," she whispered against his lips. "Make love to me, Steve. Please."

His eyes blazed with all the passion he had been careful to keep hidden for so long, then closed as he sought blindly for her mouth. His lips touched hers, and her entire body trembled in response. He deepened the kiss, gradually teasing her mouth open to welcome the thrust of his tongue. Fire leaped along her veins, spark after spark of excitement feeding the flames until she burned with pleasure.

"I think I've waited a lifetime to hold you in my arms like this," Steve murmured. His hands stroked down her spine, cradling her against his thighs. "I want you, Abby."

A bubble of laughter formed somewhere in the seething cauldron of her emotions. She glanced up at him, eyes dancing. "I know," she said, moving her hips provocatively. "Quite a lot, I think."

"Brazen hussy. Have you no shame?" He returned her smile. Then he slowly opened the buttons of her blouse and brushed his thumbs lightly across her nipples. "Mmm..." he said. "Something tells me the wanting's quite mutual." His smile faded, and his eyes darkened to an intense, smoky green. "Abby, tell me that you want me."

"I want you, Steve. I need you." *I love you.*

He slipped her blouse from her shoulders; it fell silently to the floor. A few seconds later, her bra followed. Steve's hands buried themselves deep into her thick blond hair and he drew her closer. "Abby, my sweet," he said huskily, his eyes gleaming. "Have you ever been kissed senseless before?"

"No, never. Is that what you're planning to do?"

He bent his head slowly toward her mouth. "Sweetheart, I'm sure as hell gonna give it a try."

She chuckled, glad that they could still share the warmth of laughter, even in passion. She started to tell him how much she liked him, how much she enjoyed having him as her friend, but his hands found the zipper of her jeans, and suddenly she was naked in his arms.

Her laughter died in a quiver of desire unlike anything she had ever felt before. Her breath caught in her throat, choking off meaningless words. The pounding of her heart grew louder, drowning out all sound, muffling her senses until it seemed as if no world existed outside the magic circle of Steve's arms. She could taste her own desire in his kiss, feel her own driving need in the heated urgency of his touch.

She sighed in restless, eager anticipation as Steve lowered her to the ground, tossing a pillow from the sofa behind her head. For a fleeting moment she thought how strange it was that in all her twenty-eight years this was the first time she had ever made love without lying on a bed in a bedroom. Then Steve's body straddled hers—thigh to thigh, hand to hand, heart to heart. All thought ceased. And when he finally claimed her, Abby's world exploded in a sunburst of love and happiness.

AT WORK the next morning, Abby fully expected her colleagues to demand an explanation for the dramatic change in her looks. One glance in the mirror Monday morning had been sufficient to show her that when a woman spent all night making mad, passionate love with Steven Kramer, their activities had an astounding effect on that woman's appearance. Sleeplessness, Abby decided with a self-satisfied smirk, had never been so flattering.

Her colleagues, however, proved to be an imperceptive lot, more interested in discussing the stars of the weekend football game than the ones in Abby's eyes. Settling into her small office, she was soon absorbed in final research for the Art Museum exhibit, humming quietly as she riffled through files and folders. Her humming stopped abruptly when the phone buzzed. An outside line. She picked up the receiver.

"Abigail Deane." Annoyingly, her voice quavered.

"Hello, Abigail. This is Peter Graymont."

Her hands stopped shaking, and the fog of fear cleared from her brain. Peter was inviting her to a lunch-hour reception at his antique store, in honor of his new Chinese vases. "French champagne," he promised. "And excellent sandwiches. No rabbit food."

She was on the point of making a polite excuse, when she suddenly remembered that in addition to being an antique expert of some note, Peter was also a consulting attorney for the state of Colorado. Just the person she needed, Abby thought with a little flare of excitement. The ideal person to advise her on how to track down the official record of those missing birth and death certificates. Something about those certificates nagged at her, refusing to leave her alone. If only she could read the complete, original documents, she was sure light would be shed on—something.

"I'll be with you at twelve-thirty on the dot," she said. "Thank you, Peter, for the invitation. And could we try to find ten minutes to talk privately? I have a favor to ask of you."

"Any time, Abigail. You know it's always my pleasure to be of assistance to you. You're exactly the sort of woman I most admire."

Which sort of woman was that? Abby wondered, hanging up the phone with a tiny smile. The woman who lay on her own living-room floor in abandoned ecstasy? Or the one who clung to the bed, arching her body beneath Steve's tantalizing caresses? She blushed at the erotic trend of her thoughts.

"You're looking good this morning, Abby." The senior archivist, a motherly woman of fifty, strolled past. "New dress?"

"No, actually it's quite an old one."

"Well, you look different. Must be this incredible weather we're having. Never known everyone to appear so darn cheerful on a Monday morning." With a wave, the director disappeared into the microfiche room.

PETER'S ANTIQUE STORE, Golden Treasures, was crowded, despite the fact that Monday midday struck Abby as a somewhat odd hour to display valuable Chinese porcelain to prospective buyers. Grabbing a sandwich and a plastic flute of champagne, she bypassed a cluster of assorted businessmen, edged past a pair of hard-eyed matrons discussing the potential social prestige that would come from possessing a Chinese vase from the Ching period—Ming was so much more chic, but cost three times as much, and really those gold and green colors would fit in so well with the carpet—and finally tracked down Peter Graymont at the back of the store.

He stood by a tastefully arranged collection of small Ching bowls, chatting to two middle-aged women. Abby's stomach performed a back flip of surprise when she recognized one of the women as Linda Mendoza. And surely the other one was Gwen Johnson, also from First Denver Bank.

Peter glanced up and saw her. He smiled and came forward to shake her hand. "Abigail, I'm so glad you could make it. Let me introduce these two lovely ladies to you. Linda Mendoza and Gwen Johnson. They're from the First Denver Bank, and they're here to consider the purchase of one of my lovely vases for the bank lobby."

"We've already met." The three women spoke at once, then fell into a rather awkward silence. Linda Mendoza was the first to speak again.

"This is certainly a happier occasion than the last time we met, Abigail."

"Yes, it is. I hope Mrs. Taylor is managing all right?"

"She's being very brave, I hear."

Another uncomfortable pause. "Are you interested in Chinese antiques, Abigail?" Gwen Johnson changed the subject, to everyone's relief.

"My father loved Native American pottery, and I've become fascinated by pre-Colombian sculpture. But I'm afraid I don't know anything about Chinese or Far Eastern art."

Gwen smiled. "Then we're in the same boat, you and I. The entrance lobby at First Denver is due for a decorative face-lift, and Keith Bovery thought an Eastern theme might be appropriate. Colorado is doing so much trade with China these days, you know. Unfortunately, I can't tell a priceless antique from a second-rate imitation, but bank decor comes under my job description, so here I am." Gwen nodded toward her colleague. "Linda kindly volunteered to come along and give me her advice, since she's an expert."

"You're an expert on Chinese porcelain?" Abby asked Linda Mendoza, trying to sound natural. It was amazingly difficult to behave normally, when half her mind was trying to visualize Linda as her father's long-ago mistress, and the other half was occupied with nightmare visions of Linda and Keith Bovery as present-day conspirators and killers.

How ridiculous social conventions are, she reflected silently. The truth about Linda's past may be literally a matter of life and death for me, and here I stand, talking to her about a set of two-hundred-year-old vases.

"Eastern art is my hobby," Linda confessed shyly. *Was she really shy? And was there any rule that said shy people couldn't be murderers?* "I have an interior decorator's license, as well. One of these days, when I manage to scrape a few thousand dollars together, I hope to set up my own design consulting business."

"And in the meantime she squanders her artistic talents, working at the bank," Gwen said. She glanced at her watch. "Peter, I have an exceptionally busy afternoon.

Would it be very rude of me to ask if you could leave Linda and me alone for a few minutes, so that we can discuss this privately?''

''Not at all.'' Peter was clearly at his most gracious. ''I'm absolutely thrilled by how much interest there's been in my little shipment of vases. I do believe I could sell them three or four times over. Actually, I know Abigail wanted to talk to me in private about something, so this will be the perfect opportunity for us. Shall we go into my office, Abigail?''

She followed him into the opulent, gilded room, which served as his office, wondering how he ever managed to work in such cluttered, baroque surroundings.

He gestured her to a silk-upholstered Louis XVI chair. ''Your glass is empty, my dear. Let me fill it from my personal supply.'' Peter took an open champagne bottle from the ice bucket on his desk and topped off her glass. Abby took a sip, then put the glass down. She had too much work to finish this afternoon to risk feeling sleepy.

''Peter, I'll get straight to the point. I find myself in the midst of a most bizarre situation.''

He raised his eyebrow. ''You are? Are you sure we aren't talking about Kate?''

She smiled, then quickly sobered as she went on to give him a concise, selective account of the events of the past few days, omitting any reference to her suspicions of Keith Bovery. ''I've no idea why those birth and death certificates were stolen,'' she said, realizing that she spoke less than the whole truth. It suddenly seemed to her quite obvious that they had been stolen to conceal the fact that Douglas was an impostor. Somebody would be deeply threatened by the revelation that Christopher Deane Renquist had died in infancy. But who? Damn it, she felt wrung tight with frustration at the need to see those certificates.

"Anyway, they must have been stolen for a reason." She hurried on. "Nobody would go to the risk of robbing my apartment unless those certificates were very important."

"That's true. A robbery is a serious matter, Abigail. Very serious. I certainly hope you've had the lock changed on your front door?"

"The locksmith came at six o'clock this morning."

"Well, Abigail, I'm dreadfully sorry about all that's been going on. It sounds like an absolute nightmare for you. But I'm not quite sure how I can help. Would you like to move into my town house until things quiet down?"

"Thanks, but Steve Kramer lives in my apartment building, and I can stay with him if necessary. What I really need, Peter, is to see a copy of those missing certificates. But I can't, because records in this state are closed. As you know."

"You can apply to the secretary of state's office for special permission," Peter suggested. "Why don't you contact your family lawyer and see if he can expedite things for you?"

"Have you ever met Mr. Tubbs?" Abby groaned. "His definition of speedy action means before the end of the next decade. Besides, I'd have to show reasonable cause." As an archivist, Abby was all too familiar with the rules about access to state records, which in Colorado were exceptionally rigid. "And how can I 'show cause' when I haven't the faintest idea who Christopher Deane Renquist was? Plus there's another problem. I can't give an exact date for either certificate, which means the records have to be searched for the whole year of 1954. And the records from 1954 aren't computerized. I'm not even sure they've been put onto microfiche. So to find these two certificates, somebody is going to have to search page by page through the original files in the Arapahoe County Registrar's office.''

Peter looked wary but resigned. ''I have a horrible suspicion I know what you're about to ask.''

''Can you get me into that office, Peter?''

''Kate has infected you with her bad habits. My dear, it's *illegal* for you to search those records.''

''I'm asking you as a friend, Peter. You must have met the registrar and the county clerk a hundred times. Could you call in a favor on my behalf?''

''Yes, I expect I could. But Abigail, shouldn't you be asking the police to make these inquiries through the proper channels?''

''The police *are* making inquiries through the proper channels. That's the problem. Proper channels take days, maybe weeks. You know that as well as I do, Peter. We both work with state bureaucracies. And in the meantime, by the time the 'proper authorities' get their acts in gear, I may be dead.''

Peter's expression softened into sympathy. ''My dear, I'm sure we can count on Lieutenant Knudsen not to allow that to happen. But as for tracing these certificates... Well, I suppose sometimes we have to forget the technicalities of the law and do what we know is right. The county clerk is a friend of mine, as you guessed. Let me give her a call and see what I can do.''

''Thank you, Peter. Thank you!'' Abigail astonished herself, and probably Peter as well, by jumping up and dropping a quick kiss onto his cheek. Good Lord, she thought in amusement. Peter must be right. Kate has infected me. I've caught the lovebug.

Peter rose slowly to his feet. "You haven't finished your champagne. Can't you stay another couple of minutes? Where are you dashing off to, Abigail?"

"Work. Where else?" She picked up her purse. "Give me a call as soon as you fix something up with the county clerk, won't you? I'm sorry to sound so pushy, but this is important."

Peter opened his office door and glanced warningly toward Gwen Johnson and Linda Mendoza, who still stood nearby in earnest discussion. "Abigail," he murmured in reproof. Raising his voice, he added, "I'll be in touch as soon as I've found what you're looking for. Thank you for stopping by."

"Thank *you*," she replied with quiet emphasis. "I'm very grateful to you, Peter."

"This sounds intense," Gwen Johnson remarked, looking up from her conversation.

Abby smiled. "Not really. I'm just glad to have eaten smoked salmon sandwiches and seen some beautiful vases on a sunny day. That's all."

"You sound as if you're full of the joys of life," Linda Mendoza commented. "And on a Monday, too." Did she sound angry, as if she resented Abby's happiness?

"This week looks as if it might resolve one or two long-standing problems," Abby said with studied casualness. She caught Linda's gaze and held it defiantly. *Yes, Ms. Mendoza, I'm twitching your tail. If you're a tiger, I'm ready to fight.*

"That's a good reason for appearing cheerful." Linda Mendoza smiled. Suddenly she couldn't have looked more innocent. "Has the bank finally resolved those problems with Abigail's trust account, Gwen?"

"Yes, those problems have all been resolved," Gwen Johnson said with exaggerated patience. "That's what those papers we signed on Saturday were all about, Linda. Goodbye, Abigail. Nice to have seen you again.''

Peter escorted Abby to the front of his store. ''I'll try to set something up for late this afternoon. And Abigail, please show a little discretion. We're breaking the law, you know, and we're both state employees. For heaven's sake don't broadcast to the world where we're going. And not a word about what we plan to do.''

''No,'' she said. ''I won't tell a soul. It'll be our secret. Fix a time, Peter, and nobody will know about our date but the two of us.''

Chapter Nine

Abby was pleasantly surprised when Peter called less than an hour after her return to the Historical Society. Obviously nervous, and carefully avoiding specific names, he told her that "someone" in the Arapahoe County Registrar's office would arrange for Abby to be alone in the right room with the right material at four-thirty.

"She's promised me half an hour, and I had to swear that I would stay in the room with you. She's taking an enormous risk, Abigail. If anything happened to the county files, she could end up in jail."

"I'm more grateful than you can imagine." Abby understood why the clerk had imposed a time limit, but wished it hadn't been so strict. Discovering anything useful in thirty minutes would require a huge dollop of luck. "Peter, if I can ever return the favor, let me know."

"You can return it right now. Remember my friend's job is on the line, and don't tell anyone what you're doing. That's all I ask."

"You can rely on me. I understand what a risk your friend's taking. See you at the Arapahoe County Building at four-thirty."

"Wait! There's no point in two of us driving our cars all the way out to Littleton. Why don't you run by the store and pick me up? Or I can get you, whichever you prefer.''

''Makes more sense for you to get me, if you don't mind. I'm on the way, and you're not. Does three forty-five sound good?''

''Fine. We don't want to be late, otherwise my friend will have to shut up shop. The offices close at five. Can you be ready and waiting outside the Historical Society building for me?''

They agreed on a meeting place near the front entrance and hung up. Abby returned to work, determined to get through the papers remaining on her desk before leaving.

In giving Peter her promise not to tell anyone about their illicit search of the county records until after the event, Abby hadn't anticipated that Steve would call the office two minutes after she'd heard from Peter.

''How about an early dinner at Giovanni's?'' he suggested. ''We could drive to the restaurant straight from work and compare notes by candlelight. I've got lots to tell you. Including the fact that Linda Mendoza's middle initial is R. With no record anywhere in the bank of what the R stands for.'' His voice was heavy with significance.

Abby gave a quiet whistle. ''Did you tell Knudsen?''

''Yes, and he's going to check out her name with social security records. But he still wasn't much interested in our theories about Keith Bovery and your dad, and some old feud dating back to the Korean War. Knudsen isn't much of a man for speculating about thirty-five-year-old secrets. He's more interested in the fact that I finally turned up some practical evidence that suggests Howard Taylor was being framed for the bank embezzlements.''

''You did? That's great!'' Abby said. ''At least I think it is. What did you find?''

"I cross-checked the date and time of every theft with the dates of Howard's vacations, and discovered they didn't mesh. Howard was on his honeymoon when one of the thefts occurred. That discrepancy got me going, so I took his appointments calendar and compiled a rough schedule of days he was out of town for business meetings. He didn't travel much, but another theft occurred when Howard was giving a speech in Chicago. He physically couldn't have made the necessary computer entries for that particular theft."

"Can you cross-check Keith Bovery's vacations and out-of-town jaunts with the dates of the thefts?"

"I'm doing that now. Not just Keith's, but all the executives'. And if need be, tomorrow I'll compile the data for every clerk, secretary and teller employed by the bank. It's taken me the entire day to get the information and write the program, but I'm keying it into the computer now, and the cross-check should be complete before I leave. How about Giovanni's at six? That gives my program time to run."

An hour earlier, Abby would never have believed an invitation from Steve would make her squirm with misery. "I can't," she blurted out. "Steve, let me meet you in your apartment later this evening. I'm not quite sure what time I'll get out of here tonight."

"Abby..." Steve's voice was dark with suspicion. "Abby, I recognize every nuance in that throaty, desirable voice of yours. Right now you sound guilty and excited, all at the same time. That's one heck of a dangerous combination. What the blazes are you up to?"

"Nothing," she said breathlessly, then cursed silently. Even she could hear how unconvincing that particular lie sounded. "Honestly, Steve, it's nothing. Just some information I'm going to pick up."

"From where? About what? Abby, you aren't crazy enough to be planning to meet someone, are you? Where in the world did you get your reputation for being sensible? Sometimes I think Kate has more common sense than you do!"

"There's no need to insult my sister—"

"Oh no, kiddo. I'm not walking into that neat little trap. You're not going to fool me into changing the subject. Abby, tell me where you're going, or I swear I'll call Knudsen and ask him to send a squad car over to the Historical Society right now this second and arrest you."

"What for?" she demanded indignantly. "I'm not doing anything illeg—" Her protest died away abruptly; she realized that in fact, what she was about to do was highly illegal.

"Abby." Now Steve's voice sounded ominously threatening. "I have two phones in my office, and my fingers are poised over the dial of the other one. I'm starting to press in Knudsen's number right now—"

"All right! There's no need to dial Knudsen. If you must know, I'm going somewhere with Peter Graymont later on this afternoon. And that's all I'm telling you, Steve."

"Where are you going? To do what? It has to be something dubious, since you're so uptight at the mention of Knudsen."

"I'll see you tonight," Abby said with all the dignity she could muster. "At least, I'll see you tonight if you stop behaving like a . . . like a zookeeper. I'm your lover, you know, not your infant daughter or a pet monkey or something." She slammed down the phone with a gratifying bang. Nothing like losing your temper when you knew you were in the wrong.

"Well, well," said the director of the archives, peering over a huge carton of papers as she walked by. "Eavesdropping is getting more interesting around here all the time."

ABBY SHOULD HAVE KNOWN that Steve had given up far too easily. She arrived downstairs promptly at three-forty—and found him leaning against a lamppost, looking at ease with himself and the world.

"What are you doing here?" she demanded, furious because her stupid heart gave a little dance of pleasure at the mere sight of him, even though he was ruining her plans.

"Admiring the scenery," he replied blandly. "Great scenery in this part of town." He eyed her silk blouse appreciatively. "Of course, the scenery in your bedroom's better. Not to mention the totally terrific view from the living-room carpet."

Her cheeks flamed and her insides melted. "Go away," she said. "Go away right now this second. Steve, please, you don't understand—"

"I understand perfectly. A murderer is stalking you with intent to kill, and you're about to flit off on some assignation without telling anybody where you're going. Come on, Abby. Does that sound even halfway sensible to you?"

"I told you. I'm going with Peter Graymont."

"Right. That's reassuring. Did it ever occur to you that every time Peter came near your sister Kate, somebody shot at her or chased her or blew up a plane?"

"But Peter wasn't doing the shooting!" Abby exclaimed. "He was an innocent bystander who tried to keep Kate out of trouble!"

"And is that what he's doing for you? Keeping you out of trouble? Make sure he doesn't decide to keep you permanently trouble-free. On a slab in the morgue."

"You're being ridiculous," Abby said through clenched teeth. "Peter hasn't set me up for some dangerous assignation. *I* asked *him* for a favor. It's a big favor, and he's been very cooperative. Unlike some people I could mention."

At that moment a sleek, silver Accord drew up at the curbside. Peter's dark, equally sleek head peered out of the car window. "Abigail," he called. "Are you ready?"

"Yes," she said. She marched over to the car, ignoring Steve. "I *really* appreciate this, Peter," she murmured as she slid into the front passenger seat.

Steve straightened from his lamppost and strolled over to the curb. He thrust a hand under Peter Graymont's nose, beaming as if he had no doubt about his welcome. "Hi, I'm Steven Kramer, Abby's lover. I don't believe we've met, although I've heard *lots* about you. Shall I sit in the back? These imported cars aren't really designed for three in the front, are they?"

Without waiting for a reply from the dumbstruck Peter—Abby had passed beyond being dumbstruck, and was downright catatonic—Steve got into the car and buckled his seat belt. He smiled cheerily. "All set, Peter. Ready whenever you are."

Peter turned to Abby, his expression stricken. "How could you, Abigail? After all I said about the need for discretion. Obviously I'm going to have to call off our... little trip. I owe my friend that much. It's the least I can salvage. Thank God, I never mentioned her name to you."

Abby glared at her "lover." Steve smiled back sweetly. Lover, huh! At this particular moment, she would happily have strung him by the toes from the lamppost he had so recently vacated.

"I haven't told Steve *anything*," Abby said. "Peter, the fact is, he's afraid for my safety—although heaven knows why, since I'm with you, and clearly in no danger whatsoever."

Surprisingly, Peter's grim expression lightened somewhat. "Well, of course, I can understand that in view of the terrible attacks you've been experiencing lately, your fiancé feels the need to protect you...."

"Protect me! Him!" Abby just managed to refrain from snorting in indignation. Peter, at least, was gentleman enough to substitute the polite euphemism "fiancé" for Steve's totally impolite "lover." She couldn't imagine why Peter didn't simply turn around and toss Steve from the car. Although on second thought, comparing muscles, perhaps she understood all too well. She glanced at her watch. Four-thirty. If they didn't hurry up, the county offices were going to be closed. Damn Steve Kramer. At this moment he was, to put it succinctly, proving himself a royal pain.

She decided to stop worrying about Steve and start concentrating on more important matters. The certificates. That was what this trip was all about.

"Peter, if Steve stays in the car the whole time, could we please go where we planned to go? After all, if he does that, he can't pose any threat to your friend, can he? He won't even see her."

"I suppose not," Peter agreed grudgingly. He took his foot off the brake and spoke over his shoulder. "I want your word, Steven, that you're not going to get out of this car when we arrive at our destination."

"You have it," Steve said curtly. "Now would you mind telling me where we're going?"

Abby and Peter looked at each other. Finally Peter shrugged. "I suppose it doesn't matter if you know," he said. "We're going to the Arapahoe County Registrar's office in Littleton."

Abby was sure that Steve must have realized at once what she was looking for, but he chose not to fan the flames by mentioning the certificates, and merely nodded politely. Perhaps by now he also realized how unnecessary his rush to the rescue had been. Abby tried to smooth over the whole silly situation by talking to Peter about his reception at Golden Treasures, which seemed to have gone exceptionally well. Peter followed her lead and chatted knowledgeably about the ever-growing interest in oriental art, a surprising interest in the Rocky Mountain heartland. Steve didn't contribute to the discussion. He sat in the back of the car, seemingly absorbed in watching the flow of Denver's early-rush-hour traffic.

Suddenly he leaned forward and stared intently into the outside wing mirror, then unlatched his seat belt and swiveled around to stare out of the rear window.

"We're being followed," he said tersely. "Beige Buick. Old car. Driver's wearing dark clothes and some sort of cap." He squinted. "Sun's at the worst possible angle. I can't read the license plate."

"You must be imagining it," Peter said. "Why would anyone follow us?" He glanced sideways at Abby, then amended ruefully, "Silly question, I suppose, in view of what's been happening to you over the weekend." He drummed his fingers nervously on the steering wheel and peered several times into his rearview mirror. "I see the car, but are you sure it's following us? At this hour of the afternoon, everyone's driving south."

"Speed up and switch into the fast lane," Steve suggested.

Peter obliged. The Buick followed suit. It overtook two cars, cut in in front of a red Mustang, and settled down at a steady pace, four cars behind Peter's Accord.

"I guess that means he's following us," Abby said. The glow of happiness caused by Steve's lovemaking—a glow that had kept her feeling warm and secure all day—dissipated in a flash. Reality returned. *Somebody wanted to kill her.*

"How did they know where I was going?" she asked wearily. "I'm so tired of all this!"

Peter's dark eyes glowed with sympathy. "They must have been staking you out, I suppose."

Abby shivered, and Steve touched her lightly on the arm. "Hey, kiddo, they can't do much to us in the middle of a three-lane highway in broad daylight."

"How about run us off the road at high speed?" Abby suggested in a small voice.

"They'd never risk it. Too many witnesses, and too much traffic to guarantee a geta—"

"Don't worry," Peter interrupted. "I'll exit here at Evans and lose them." He didn't wait for approval of his suggestion. With surprising panache, he cut across the other three lanes of traffic and zoomed off I-25 with a screech of spinning tires.

"That'll fix 'em," he said with a pleased chuckle. "I'll circle around a few of these side streets, and then I'll go west on Evans. That's as good a route as any to the Arapahoe County Building."

Abby had always thought of Peter as a man who would react badly to the slightest hint of physical danger, but in fact he seemed energized by the brief car chase. He certainly drove far better than she'd ever anticipated. He tooled around several narrow residential streets with every appearance of good humor, despite the layer of rubber he'd left behind at the highway exit, then drove back onto Evans Avenue, which—although narrow—served as a major east-west thoroughfare in this part of the city.

"Four-fifteen," he said, consulting his watch. "We're going to be a couple of minutes late. Too much traffic."

"Will your friend wait?" Abby asked.

"For five minutes, I expect. No more. Too risky for her."

Steve cut in, his voice harsh. "The beige Buick's following us again."

"What!" Abby swung around. "How in the world did he find us?"

Peter didn't say anything. With considerable skill and a total disregard for legal technicalities, he spotted a gap in the flow of oncoming traffic and swung his car around in a dramatic U-turn. Without slowing down, he hung a hard right, and ended up once again in the quiet residential streets radiating north and south from Evans Avenue. He braked, bringing their speed down to the prescribed thirty.

"What the devil does the driver of the Buick expect to achieve?" he asked through clenched teeth. "Abigail, this is beyond a joke. I think I should stop right now and find a police officer. We're hopelessly late, anyway."

Abby's heart sank. "Peter, I really want to check out those certificates. You drove so well back there, we must have lost whoever's tailing us. Could we please go to the registrar's office first, and report this to the police afterwards?"

He shrugged. "It's up to you, I suppose. It's you they were chasing, not me." He peered out of the side window. "Where the heck are we, anyway? I've lost track."

"You're on Cedar," Steve said. "You need to take your first left to get back onto Evans."

"Cedar? I've been here before." Peter peered out of his side window again. "Yes, I can go south here and come out on Colorado Boulevard, which would be our quickest route." He backed his car into a convenient driveway and changed directions yet again. He had driven a hundred yards toward a small intersection and was slowing down for the stop sign, when a blur of beige came barreling out of a narrow service alleyway and headed straight for them.

Peter hauled hard on the steering wheel, trying valiantly to swing out of reach, but without success. The Buick was intent on inflicting damage. With a sickening crunch of metal, its right front grazed the left front of Peter's car. Headlights shattered, glass flew, and—for a second that stretched out longer than eternity—Abby waited for the roar of a rifle shot, the pain of a bullet. Nothing came. The Buick drove off as quickly as it had burst upon them, leaving Peter's Accord shattered and wounded at the edge of the intersection.

"Turn off the engine and unlock the doors," Steve said to Peter. "Quick, get out of the car. Both of you."

Peter stared dazedly ahead of him. "My new car," he murmured. "My poor new car. It's destroyed. A total write-off."

"Turn off the engine and unlock the doors," Steve repeated, raising his voice slightly. "Peter, turn off the damn engine! The car could catch fire any minute."

Peter gave no sign that he had heard, but must have responded to the note of command in Steve's voice, for he obediently turned off the ignition and pushed the electronic button that unlatched the doors. Steve leaped out, tugging open Abby's door as he ran around to the front of the car. Abby, shivering from fright as well as from the evening chill, slowly exited the passenger seat.

"It's not as bad as I thought," Steve said tersely when she joined him. "In fact, given that the Buick was heading toward us so purposefully, Peter's car is in pretty good shape. The left front end is smashed, but the bumper protected the front of the car, and the engine doesn't look as if it's been damaged."

Peter came and stood next to them, his face pale and pinched with anxiety. "It's going to cost a fortune to fix," he said gloomily.

"I'll pay anything the insurance company doesn't cover," Abby promised at once.

"You don't have to." Peter didn't protest very hard.

"I insist. None of this would have happened, if it hadn't been for me."

"Well, thanks. Anyway, the insurance should cover most of it." Peter's composure seemed marginally restored by the fact that his car was not, after all, a total write-off. He lifted the hood and glanced inside with reasonable calm. "Radiator's okay. Hoses all attached. Battery's not leaking. I guess we can drive it." He shut the hood, then looked again at the shattered light and crumpled, scratched left side. His eyes moistened and he reached into his pocket for a large handkerchief, blowing his nose fiercely.

"Sorry," he said in muffled explanation. "I only picked this car up last month. It was so new and shiny."

Guilt swept over Abby in consuming waves. "I'm really sorry," she said. "Peter, I'd never have asked for your help if I'd known anything like this would happen."

Peter made a visible effort to pull himself together. "Well, at least none of us is hurt, and that's something. But somebody horribly violent is out to get you, Abigail, that's obvious. I think it's time you treated these attacks a bit more seriously, and took some precautions regarding your own safety. Steven was quite right to feel worried about you. We're going to drive past a police station on the way home, I insist—"

A bright red Hyundai, loaded with teens drove up to the intersection. A young man stuck his head out of the window. "Need some help?" he shouted. "Want us to call a tow truck?"

"It's drivable, thanks," Peter replied. "But did you by any chance see a beige Buick on your way here? He did this to us, and then drove off without stopping."

"Sorry. We didn't notice a thing. Hope you catch the guy, that's for sure. Man, did he do a number on your front end." The young man whistled to emphasize his point. "If you don't need help, we'll be going." The young man withdrew his head and shot off toward the highway.

"Even if they'd noticed the Buick, they'd never have taken the number," Abby said.

"I saw the Buick's number." Steve's expression was thoughtful as he watched the teenagers drive off. "PBB 709."

"That's terrific, Steve!" Peter's face lighted up. "Now we'll be able to nail the bas—the, um, driver for sure."

"I doubt it," Steve said. "If he didn't bother to obscure the number, it probably means the car was stolen or hired from Rent-a-Wreck with a phony license."

Peter's face fell. "You think so?"

"This guy has to make a mistake sometime," Abby disagreed. "Every criminal does."

"Every criminal who gets caught makes a mistake," Steve corrected. He looked at his watch. "It's only a few minutes till five. I guess there's no point in going to the county building now."

"No," Peter admitted. "My friend will be long gone by the time we make it all the way over there."

"What's the betting the guy driving that Buick achieved his purpose, after all?" Steve murmured.

Peter looked at him in blank bewilderment. "What do you mean?"

"If the driver of the Buick wanted to stop us going to the registrar's office, he just succeeded, didn't he?"

"But he couldn't have known where we were going," Abby objected. "Nobody knew except Peter and me."

"That's true." Steve paused. "But then, maybe the driver of the Buick didn't need to know precisely where you were going. Maybe he simply wanted to stop you from getting there, wherever it was."

"That would be crazy," Peter said. "Look at the risk he took to achieve such a minimal goal."

Steve stared at the sun, setting in a purple blaze of glory beyond the mountains. "I think this guy enjoys taking risks," he said. "I think that's how he gets his highs."

Abby tucked her ice-cold hands into the sleeves of her linen jacket. Tiredness suddenly seemed to have eaten its way into her very bones. "Steve, if you don't mind, could we please go home."

She didn't wait for an answer, just went and sat in the car, fumbling with her seat belt for a long time before she managed to get it latched. Peter watched her sympathetically, then turned to Steve and spoke in a low voice.

"I don't want to butt in, Steven, and of course you can say it's none of my business, but if she were my fiancée, I'd hustle her out of town on the next available flight."

Steve smiled grimly. "You may have noticed, Peter, that Abigail is not the most pliant of human beings. But I'm taking her home right now and locking her in my apartment until she agrees to see reason. She can choose anywhere in the world, provided it's a minimum of five hundred miles from Denver."

"That seems like a wise move." Peter gave a last sad glance to his wounded car. "A very wise move. Abigail has obviously offended some violent people."

"They are violent," Steve said. "But I think 'frightened people' might be a more accurate description."

"Where criminals are concerned, maybe fear and violence are one and the same."

"I don't know," Steve said. "But I do know Abby isn't going to hang around in Denver to find out."

Chapter Ten

When Lieutenant Knudsen arrived at the Second District station house, summoned by Abby, the local police started to take Peter's report of deliberate assault and battery to his car more seriously. Knudsen swept off Abby and Steve for a private session of intensive questioning, leaving Peter to fill out reams of paperwork with the local duty officer.

After thirty minutes or so, the detective finally stopped asking questions. Neither Abby nor Steve could explain how the driver of the Buick had managed to pick up their tail three times, and their exhaustive retelling of the story was getting nobody anywhere.

Knudsen leaned back in the hard chair and rubbed wearily at the bridge of his nose. It was the closest Abby had ever seen him come to displaying normal human weakness. "Let's talk about something else," he said. "The lab in D.C. has promised me a preliminary report on those voice tapes tomorrow morning. I also had a chat with Linda Mendoza this afternoon. Seems the R in her name stands for Rainey, which was her maiden name. She showed me her birth certificate to prove it."

"Then I guess Linda Mendoza can't be Lynn Renquist," Abby said. "It was a wild theory, anyway." The news left her feeling neither surprised nor disapointed. It seemed as if she and Steve had done nothing for the past three days but come up with clever ideas and clues that ultimately led nowhere. She was beginning to suspect that when the report on the voice tapes finally came in, it would send them all speeding off on yet another wild-goose chase.

"I'm not convinced Linda Mendoza's in the clear," Knudsen said. "A couple of rather interesting facts emerged during our chat. Seems Mrs. Mendoza grew up in Alabama and trained as a nurse when she left school. She insists she was never in the armed forces, but she seemed very flustered when I asked her why she changed from nursing to secretarial work."

Abby thought that if she hadn't been so tired, she might have laughed at the irony of it all. "Have you noticed that's always the way things go with this case?" she asked Knudsen. "It's like an unsolved game of charades. Nothing is ever decided one way or the other. Everybody is always under a half cloud of suspicion." She stood up, pulling on her crumpled linen jacket with hands that shook slightly.

"I guess the car chase this afternoon served one useful purpose. You and Steven have made your point, Lieutenant. I'm tired of suspecting my own shadow and jumping out of my skin every time the phone rings. Knowing that somebody is lurking in the shadows, keeping me under constant surveillance, is the final straw. I give up. I'm leaving town tomorrow."

Steve gave her a quick hug. "You're doing the right thing, Abby."

"You certainly are." Knudsen was so delighted that he almost managed to crack a smile. "We're regular, ordinary people at the CBI, and believe it or not, Abigail, we don't like being summoned to clean up dead bodies. Particularly when we know the victim could have stayed alive by exercising a bit of common sense."

A knock at the door heralded the arrival of Peter and the police sergeant. "Mr. Graymont here would like to know how long you're likely to keep his friends, Lieutenant. He'd like to get home. He has an important appointment."

"Keith Bovery is coming to Golden Treasures at six-thirty," Peter explained. "He wants to discuss a price for all five of those Chinese vases for the bank lobby." He smiled wanly. "I never felt less like negotiating a deal, but this one is too important to leave to my store manager."

The digital clock showed 5:57—barely time for Peter to make his appointment with Keith Bovery, even if he left the police station immediately.

"I'll drive Mr. Kramer and Miss Deane back to their apartment building," the lieutenant volunteered. "You'll get back to your store quicker, Mr. Graymont. Not to mention that you're less likely to have cars springing out of alleys and attacking you, if the two of them are with me."

Peter didn't bother to disguise his relief. "That would be a big help, Lieutenant, thanks. Take care, Abigail." He grasped her hand. "I hope you're not going to spend the night alone?"

"Don't worry, I'm keeping her glued to my side," Steve said with a grim smile. "Siamese twins couldn't stay closer. You'll be pleased to hear she's agreed to leave town tomorrow, so we'll all be able to sleep a little easier after tonight." It was obvious that he disliked Peter Graymont intensely, which was odd Abby reflected, given his normally laid-back attitude to the rest of the world and its foibles.

"Great." Peter seemed impervious to the hostile undercurrents. "Good work, Steven. You're doing the smart thing, Abigail." He gave her hand one last vigorous squeeze and hurried off to reclaim his battered car.

Everyone seemed convinced she was behaving wisely, Abby reflected. So how come she felt totally wretched about her decision to fly off to safety? Was she the only person to have this horrible fear that she was putting her sisters in mortal danger by skipping town?

Knudsen, whose attitude had mellowed considerably now that Abby was on the point of leaving Denver, chatted amiably as he drove them to the parking lot near her office, where both she and Steve had left their cars. He then escorted them through the rapidly darkening streets to Larimer Square and their apartment building.

He continued his escort right to the elevator. "Oregon," he said to Abby in parting. "The Pinewood Lodge in Bretton Woods. You won't find a better place for a vacation in the entire U.S.A. I read Tolstoy's *War and Peace* the last time I was out there. Been meaning to read that book since I was a kid. Finally managed it at Pinewood Lodge. Peaceful. Trees and sky like you've never seen, not even here in the mountains. I'll give your Mr. Kramer a call when it's safe for you to come back to Denver. In the meantime, Abigail, enjoy your vacation."

Abby didn't have enough energy to ask why it was all right for Steve to stay in Denver, whereas she had to pack up and run. At that moment she didn't care if she was surrounded by male chauvinists, all determined to protect the little woman. She acknowledged defeat. The truth was that she no longer wanted to stay in Denver. She was scared. Scared right down to the marrow of her bones.

If she had ever thought about fear before, she would have said it was an intense emotion. Now she realized that fear could be intense enough to paralyze. She felt a weariness that invaded every pore of her body and numbed her curiosity. Was Keith Bovery trying to kill her? Was Linda Mendoza his accomplice? Abby just didn't care anymore.

She said goodbye to Knudsen, then followed Steve into the elevator and up to his apartment, relieved that she didn't need to take any decisions about where to go and what to do. Steve would take care of her tonight. Knudsen had told her to go to Oregon tomorrow. She was going to stop thinking and planning. Thinking and planning had gotten her precisely nowhere.

Once inside Steve's apartment, she stood irresolute in the center of the living room, waiting for instructions.

He brought her a Coke and gently propelled her onto the sofa. She leaned back against the comfortable quilted cushions and sipped obediently at her soda.

"Would you like me to make dinner, before we go down to your apartment to pack?" Steve asked.

"Okay."

Steve looked at her for a long minute and his gaze softened. He sat down beside her on the sofa, curling an arm lightly around her shoulders. "Sweetheart, we're going to find out who's doing this within the next couple of days. That's all it'll take, kiddo. A couple of days. Your sisters are going to be safe, I promise."

Something must have flickered in her expression, because he crooked a finger under her chin and forced her to meet his eyes. "Abby, your sisters aren't going to get hurt because you leave Denver."

"Aren't they?" She forced the question out of her parchment-dry throat.

Steve took the Coke can from her and set it on a side table. Then he gathered her into his arms and held her close. The comfort of his nearness relaxed her just enough for the numbness to vanish for a moment. Panic swept over her in a consuming wave, and she started to shiver. She clamped her teeth shut, holding her jaw rigid, fighting back the dangerous return of feeling. Numbness was definitely better than the black pit of fear and guilt that loomed at her feet.

"Abby, listen to me. As long as Knudsen and the CBI are actively pursuing this case, the killer is too busy covering his tracks here to go chasing off after your sisters. We're also talking about a very narrow time frame before things are resolved. I've sent for a full team of investigators to help me crunch numbers at the bank. They'll be arriving from New York tomorrow afternoon. Abby, this killer is reaching the end of his road."

"How can you bring in a full-fledged investigative team? Aren't you supposed to keep the embezzlements confidential?"

"It's too late for that now. We need to work fast. Besides, I want the killer to know he's in danger of being found out. That we're closing in on him."

"If the embezzler is Keith Bovery, he already knows he's in danger."

"If Keith Bovery is the man we're after, my whiz kids will turn up the heat under him. And I'm gonna watch real close to see if he dances to avoid getting burned. If Keith isn't our man, then my team should smoke the embezzler out of hiding and into action."

The phone rang, and Abby stiffened. "Relax, sweetheart." Steve kept his arm around her as he reached out to pick up the receiver. "This is my apartment, not yours, remember? Your anonymous caller has no idea you're here."

He held the phone with his chin, his hands continuing to stroke Abby's arm. "Hello?"

"Mr. Kramer?" asked a low but pleasant female voice. "This is Gwen Johnson from the First Denver Federal Bank."

Steve held out the receiver, so that Abby could hear that the conversation was nonthreatening. "Yes, Ms. Johnson. What can I do for you?"

"I'm sorry to interrupt your evening like this, but Mr. Bovery has been trying to reach you since late this afternoon, and there's been no reply."

"I only just got home. Peter Graymont and I were involved in a car accident. Some crazy driver plowed straight into Peter's car at an intersection."

"Oh dear, how dreadful for you both! You're all right, I hope? And Peter, too."

"Nobody was injured, thank God, but Peter was very upset about the damage to his new car."

"I'm sure he was. Still, the most important thing is that neither of you was hurt." Gwen Johnson paused for a moment, and then said, "It's really the strangest coincidence. Keith asked me to call because he had to rush off to an appointment at Golden Treasures with Peter Graymont."

"And he couldn't reach me because I was with Peter, filling out accident report forms at the local police station!"

"I didn't realize you knew Peter Graymont. He and I have been acquaintances for several years now. I've always enjoyed collecting antiques." Gwen Johnson paused again, perhaps feeling the exchange of pleasantries had gone on long enough. "Anyway, Mr. Kramer, to get back to business. Keith wanted to speak to you tonight in private about an urgent matter. He says it's not something that can be discussed over the phone, and he asked if you could be at his house by eight? He has, and I quote, 'some vitally important confidential information' to pass on to you. He asked me to say that he also needs your advice.''

"Do you know in what connection, Ms. Johnson?''

"I'm afraid Mr. Bovery didn't choose to take me into his confidence. I imagine it's something to do with the new computer system you're installing. I know your work is very hush-hush, for some reason.'' Ms. Johnson's tones became acidic. "Mr. Bovery believes in keeping a great deal of information confidential, I'm afraid, which sometimes leaves his senior executives floundering. Collegial management simply isn't his style.''

Keith Bovery's management style was obviously a long-standing grievance with Gwen Johnson, and Steve tactfully redirected the conversation. "It's already seven-thirty,'' he said. "But thanks for calling, Ms. Johnson. I'll grab a sandwich and do my best to get to Mr. Bovery's by eight o'clock.''

"Wonderful. Do you know his address?''

"Yes, I was at his home once before.''

"Good. Glad I finally managed to reach you. I'm just about to leave for a small party myself, and Keith really sounded anxious to be in touch. Good night, Mr. Kramer.''

"Good night.'' Steve hung up the phone and turned to Abby. "Well,'' he said slowly. "What do you think? Should we go?''

The prospect of gleaning sufficient information to put the killer behind bars sent a surge of adrenaline rushing through Abby's weary limbs. "We have to,'' she said. "Whatever Mr. Bovery has to tell us sounds important.''

"It might be a trap. Have you considered that?''

"But why would Keith Bovery try to trap you?"

"Perhaps he's decided I'm getting too close to un-masking the embezzler. And he would be right, of course."

"If Bovery is planning to murder you, would he ask Gwen Johnson to invite you to his house? That makes no sense at all."

"Gwen Johnson could be part of the conspiracy."

Abby drew in a sharp breath. "No!" she exclaimed. "For heaven's sake, Steve, let's not add another bizarre suspect to the list! We'll soon have accused half of Denver of being accomplices to embezzlement and murder." With heavy sarcasm she asked, "There's still a couple of people you've forgotten to accuse. How about Lieuten-ant Knudsen? Have you considered what an ideal suspect he'd make?"

Steve grinned. "Actually I have. But he has no access to the bank's computers, so I reluctantly crossed him from my list. Same goes for Peter Graymont, although he might have seduced some susceptible female at the bank into doing the dirty work for him. God knows, women seem to find him amazingly good-looking."

Abby made a brief, rude comment on what she thought of that idea. She discovered that her energy level was ris-ing by the minute. "Well, let's put in a call to Knudsen and tell him where we're going. Maybe he'll come with us."

Knudsen, of course, was not answering his phone, but the CBI operator promised to pass on Steve's message immediately. "Ask him to get in touch with me tonight without fail," Steve instructed. "It's extremely impor-tant."

"She seems to understand that we need to talk to Knudsen," he said, coming into the kitchen. Abby handed him a glass of milk. "Do we have time for a sandwich?" she asked.

He drained the glass. "No, let's get going. We can stop off for a late snack of spaghetti at Giovanni's after we've seen Keith Bovery. Perhaps by then we'll have something to celebrate. Like Knudsen arresting the murderer."

"Yes," Abby agreed. "Perhaps we will." *Provided this summons to Keith Bovery's house isn't a trap.* In which case, they might not be celebrating anything at Giovanni's—because they'd be dead.

THE LAMPS bordering Keith Bovery's semicircular driveway cast little crystalline pools of light into the darkness. Steve parked his Porsche directly outside the front door and cut the engine. He and Abby sat in the car, straining every nerve to detect something—anything—that might be out of place.

Night sounds drifted in through the open car windows. The breeze smelled of fall and carried a hint of mountain snow. In the distance they heard a horse whinny. Closer at hand, a gust of wind blew through an aspen tree, setting the leaves rustling. From the nearby lane came the hum of a car engine, the only man-made sound in this exclusive section of Cherry Hills village. Keith Bovery's house was a scant twenty minutes' drive from downtown Denver, but from its rural surroundings, could easily have been a hundred miles out into the country.

The porch light shone brightly upon the solid front door, illuminating the mock-Spanish carvings. Keith Bovery's house was familiar to Abby from a score of happy childhood visits, and suddenly it struck her as totally absurd that she was huddled in Steve's car, wondering if "Uncle Keith" was about to creep up and shoot her. Her sisters had been right, Abby thought. Keith Bovery and his wife had never shown the Deane family anything but affection and kindness. It was impossible to believe that all those Christmas visits, all those weekend picnics, all those chauvinistic but *loving* pieces of advice had really masked a diabolical hatred for Ronald Deane and his daughters.

"I've been a fool," she said abruptly, turning to Steve. "Keith Bovery never tried to kill me."

Startled, Steve looked around at her. "How did you reach that amazing conclusion?"

Abby's mouth twisted into a wry smile. "He and Helen always gave us chocolate Santas for Christmas. Great big ones. The biggest you could find."

Steve snorted. "Abby, it's great that you're deciding to hang a little looser these days, but this isn't the ideal moment for you to start turning into a clone of Kate."

"I'm not being irrational," Abby insisted stubbornly. "I can believe that maybe Keith embezzled funds from the bank. I guess we're all capable of stealing under the right circumstances. But he didn't try to kill me. If I'd been thinking straight, I'd have realized that days ago."

Steve opened the car door. "Great. I'm delighted to hear you've finally seen the light about good old Keith. Now, when we ring the doorbell, will you please humor my evil, suspicious nature and stand out of firing range, just like we agreed?"

They crunched over dead leaves on the driveway and climbed the small flight of stone steps leading to the front door. Abby was shivering when Steve rang the bell, but from cold, not from fright. From behind the front door she heard brisk footsteps ring out on the parquet floor of the long hallway, and her heart gave a little jump of excitement. She had a premonition that at last their questions were going to be answered.

Abby was thinking that Keith Bovery's house was a ridiculous architectural mélange of antebellum mansion and Mexican hacienda when she heard the bolt being drawn back and the latch unlocked. The door swung open and Peter Graymont peered out.

"Hello?"

"We've come to see Keith," Steve said. He sounded more than a touch aggressive, Abby thought.

"Why yes, of course, he's been expecting you." Peter held the front door open wider. "Abigail, how nice to see you again. Is Keith expecting you, too? He only mentioned Steve."

"No, he isn't expecting me," Abby said, trying without conspicuous success, she felt, to sound cool and self-possessed. "I'm an added bonus. What are you doing here, Peter? I thought your meeting with Keith was at Golden Treasures."

"It was, but Keith insisted on coming back here in case he missed his eight-o'clock meeting with Steven, so I came along to tie up the last few loose ends on our Chinese vase deal." Peter politely stood to one side, allowing them to pass. "Keith is in the study. Do you know where that is? Right-hand side, last room. I'll just come with you to say goodbye and then I'll be off."

"How are you going to get home?" Steve asked. "I didn't see your car."

"What? Oh, my car! Well, naturally it's in the repair shop. I've called for a cab. Should be here any minute. But I won't intrude on your meeting with Keith. It's a nice night, not too cold, and I'll wait outside on the front porch."

The door to the study was shut. Steve gave a light tap before pushing it open. He walked in, Abby hard on his heels.

The overhead light wasn't switched on, and the only illumination came from a gooseneck reading lamp pointed directly at the massive desk, a desk that had dominated this room ever since Abby could remember. Keith Bovery sat behind the desk in familiar fashion, but he didn't look up and smile a greeting. His head lay on the fancy blotter, so that the glow of the lamp highlighted the small halo of brilliant scarlet surrounding his head.

Abby's instincts absorbed the reality of the scene seconds before her intellect had the chance to analyze it.

"Steve! Don't come in!" She swung around and screamed out the warning—moments too late. Steve was already inside the study. She saw him slump, strangely quiescent, into the arms of a sinister, black-clad figure that had obviously stepped out from concealment behind the study door.

Her frantic gaze sought out Peter Graymont. Another scream died stillborn in her throat, when she saw the smile on his face and the gun in his hand—pointed straight at her stomach.

"Keith Bovery's dead," she said flatly.

"Very dead," Peter agreed.

"He didn't commit suicide."

"Why, whatever do you mean, Abigail?" Peter's voice, laced with laughter, openly mocked her. "Of course poor Keith committed suicide. Come a bit closer to the desk and you'll see."

"No, I don't want—"

Peter grabbed her by the scruff of the neck and dragged her over to the desk. "See, Abigail, my dear? The .38 Webley is in his hand. The famous .38 Webley that shot Douglas Brady and then Howard Taylor. The .38 Webley that everyone will conclude Keith brought home from

Korea. The police forensic team will even find powder burns on his finger where he pulled the trigger.''

"He didn't pull the trigger. Not unless you made him do it.''

Peter's gaze strayed to the silent, black figure on the other side of the room. "Did I? Well now, Abigail, that's a whole different story.''

"You'll never get away with it, Peter. You and your silent partner over there. Steve called Lieutenant Knudsen and told him where we were going. The police will be here at any minute.''

"My dear Abigail, give us credit for a little common sense. We're not planning to kill you here. You or Steven. Bodies are so damn difficult to dispose of in a cow town like Denver. No handy slums. No deep, dark rivers. No slime-oozing canals.''

The black figure spoke, its voice low, harsh and filled with hatred. "Do it now, Peter.''

"No!'' Abby flung herself sideways in a desperate attempt to evade Peter's bullets. But no shot came. Instead, Peter lunged forward and hitched up her dress with crude, groping fingers. Trapped by the desk behind her and Peter in front, she had nowhere to run.

My God, he's going to rape me, she thought. *And that revolting masked man is going to watch.* Bile rose into her throat, along with another strangled scream. Peter's body invading hers would truly be a fate worse than death. High on her thigh she felt a prick, then a sharp, burning sensation all along her leg. The ceiling slid down to meet the floor, enfolding her in darkness. Blackness. Nothing.

THE MURDERER slammed the door of the Golden Treasures delivery van on the two unconscious bodies. Stupid fools! People who thought they were smart always turned out to be the biggest fools of all. Pity these two had to be killed tomorrow night. It would have been fun to keep them locked up without food or water. To teach them a lesson. To let them die slowly in an agony of fear, before releasing them to death with a well-placed bullet.

The North Koreans had starved several of their prisoners to death, and tortured them as well. But not Keith Bovery or Ronald Deane. Their plane had gone down only a couple of weeks before the cease-fire on July 27, 1953. Two short weeks of captivity. Keith and Ronald had scarcely suffered, but they were welcomed home as heroes. The murderer, on the other hand, had come back as an outcast.

Well, that was all water under the bridge now. Life had had its bright moments over the past thirty-five years. Strange how everything had come together nine months ago, like the strands of a tapestry that had been half a lifetime in the weaving. Ronald Deane whispering his secrets, just at the time Helen Bovery was dying. The Confederate gold waiting to be claimed, just when the embezzlements at the bank had gotten out of hand.

Peter Graymont waited at the wheel of the truck, engine running. The Golden Treasures logo had been carefully obscured. No trace remained of their presence at Keith Bovery's house. This grand finale was going to be fun.

A familiar, heady rush of excitement gripped the murderer. Action. Danger. Living life on the edge. That was how things were meant to be.

"Ready?" Peter asked impatiently. "We have a long drive to Crystal Mine."

"Ready." The murderer was filled with another surge of elation as the truck drove out of Keith Bovery's driveway. Laughter echoed in the air.

"What is it?" Peter asked.

"I'm happy. I'm just thinking how pleased Steven Kramer's team of whiz kids are going to be when they finally unearth the culprit behind the embezzlements."

"When do you think they'll do that?"

"If there isn't too much confusion at the bank because of Keith's suicide, they might manage it tomorrow." The murderer laughed even harder. "Poor Keith. His reputation's going to be shot straight to hell when they discover that he framed poor Howard Taylor."

"At least he had the decency to kill himself in remorse," Peter commented. He looked at the murderer and winked.

Their laughter didn't stop until they turned off Hampden onto C-470, en route for the mountains.

"How long?" the murderer asked abruptly.

"An hour and a half should do it."

In twenty-four hours, Abby and Steve would be dead.

The murderer leaned back in the passenger seat and watched the passing scenery. It was a real pity that the pair of them couldn't be left in the mine to starve. Yes, a real pity. But the time for taking chances was over.

The murderer wanted Abby and Steve dead. Needed them dead. Dead like selfish, heartless Ronald Deane. Dead like useless, expendable Douglas Brady. Dead like fussy, inquisitive Howard Taylor. Dead like silly, trusting Keith Bovery. Dead. Dead. Dead.

A shooting star flared briefly behind a distant mountain peak. Beautiful. It had to be a favorable omen.

Sometimes, the murderer reflected, life was very good.

Chapter Eleven

Cold. Freezing cold. Bitter, freezing cold that convulsed her body in shivering spasms.

Darkness. Abby's hands moved in tentative exploration. She was lying on her stomach on a metal floor. She hurt.

She raised her head. The darkness dissolved into a blinding kaleidoscope of shifting colors. She closed her eyes and let her face fall back into her hands.

She was going to be sick.

What was that noise? Before she could drag herself into a sitting position, rough hands grabbed her shoulders and hauled her forward. She tried to resist, but her limbs flopped uselessly, and her leg scraped over a shard of jagged metal. Abby screamed as the metal sliced open her knee, but her captor paid no attention. Fierce pain mingled with nausea, blotting out thought.

A gust of icy wind knifed across her face and cooled the warm blood dripping down her shin. Fresh wind that smelled of pine. She had been inside somewhere. A truck? Yes, it must have been a truck. Now she was outside.

Her feet stumbled in an awkward step forward. Hands blocked her path. Two pairs of hands? She opened her eyes again. A mistake. A bad mistake. Dizziness spun her head in a sickening vortex.

"Walk to your right, on the path," a voice ordered. Harsh. Menacing. Peter's voice.

The hands let her go, but she couldn't run. Couldn't even walk. Abby collapsed onto her knees, retching hopelessly, nauseated beyond the point where she cared about dignity or defiance. Or even escape.

When the retching finally stopped, she crawled away and huddled her head into her lap. Grass, she realized. She was sitting on coarse mountain grass, frosted with snow. She risked another glance toward the horizon. This time the dizziness was less acute, and she was able to discern the angular shadows of mountain peaks against the blackness of the night sky.

She must be somewhere in the mountains. Peter and his accomplice had driven her out of Denver and up into the Rocky Mountains.

"Time to join lover boy." Peter's voice again. Mocking. Filled with hate. He dragged Abby to her feet and shoved her in the direction of a small wooden building. A cabin, she registered, with a shed or garage to one side. A simple A-frame cabin built for vacations.

A gloved black hand stretched out and pushed open the cabin door. Not Peter's hand. The other abductor. The man in black who'd somehow managed to knock out Steve with a single blow from behind. Was it the man who'd shot at her from the bushes in Boulder? It must be the same person. Abby wanted to turn around to look, but was afraid she would throw up again if she twisted her head.

"Get inside," Peter said.

The relative warmth of the cabin enfolded her like a benediction, although her shivers increased as her body tried desperately to raise its temperature. She had been led straight into a rustic, paneled living room, with a kitchen at one end. A kitchen with a sink.

"Water," Abby croaked. Her throat burned in anticipation. "Please, water."

She felt Peter's hesitation. "No." The voice spoke from behind her; low, grating, yet oddly triumphant. "No water."

"Whatever you say, boss." Peter jabbed Abby in the side. With a gun, she realized. Although he certainly didn't need a gun to ensure her obedience right at this moment. "Turn to your left, Abigail, my dear."

He pushed her into a bedroom that was little more than an alcove off the main living area. An old-fashioned brass bedstead, a single nightstand, and a small chest of drawers filled the cramped floor space to overflowing.

Steve lay on the brass bed, utterly still. His face was stark white, disfigured by the beginnings of a bruise that had been blotched with gruesome artistry along the line of his jaw. Abby's eyes weren't focusing too well, but she could detect no sign that he was breathing.

"Is he...?" She swallowed hard, choking back her despair. "Is he dead?"

"Not yet. At least I don't think so." Peter propelled her to the bedside. With sudden viciousness he lashed out, slapping Steve across the face. Without coming to, Steve moaned, his face contorting in pain.

"No," Peter said. "I guess he's not dead yet." His fingers traced the livid bruise on Steve's jaw. "The stupid fool tried to fight when we took him from the truck. I knocked him out."

"How *wonderfully* brave and macho of you."

"Tsk, tsk, Abigail, I don't know what's happened to your manners recently." Peter frowned mockingly. "Sarcasm is a most undesirable feminine trait. Not something I like to find in my female companions."

"That's good to know." Abby deliberately made the words sound as sarcastic as her thick tongue and woozy brain would allow.

Peter's mouth contorted with rage. With a brutal kick, he knocked her feet out from under her, flipping her backward onto the bed. The mattress was no more than a thin strip of foam, and the wooden bed frame jarred every bone in Abby's already aching body.

Peter leaned over her, leering. "Comfortable, my dear?"

Abby's strength returned just sufficiently for her to hit out at his smirking face with her fist. *God,* she prayed fervently, *Let my punch land square on his nose! Please.*

God apparently had better things to do than answer such an impious prayer. Peter caught her flailing hand with insulting ease. His gun, Abby noticed, was now tucked casually into his jacket pocket, as if he knew there was no danger of an attack from her. Unfortunately he was right. The remnants of whatever drug had been pumped into her system were still circulating with devastating effect.

The masked, black-clad figure of Peter's accomplice returned to the bedroom, carrying two lengths of thin cord.

"Tie her hands to the bed," he ordered gruffly, tossing a length of cord to Peter. "You take care of her, and I'll take care of lover boy."

Abby stared at the masked figure. "You *are* the man who called me!" she exclaimed. "The anonymous phone caller. I recognize your voice!"

The black-clad figure didn't answer, but Peter seemed to find Abby's statement amusing. "Yes, that's the man who called you. I'm afraid he has a long-standing grudge against your dear old dad. He really enjoyed making those calls.''

''But why does he hate *me*? And why are you helping him? Peter, for God's sake, what have I ever done to hurt either of you?''

This time neither Peter nor the man in black bothered to reply. The masked man lashed Steve's limp hands to two of the brass posts of the headboard with quick, economical movements. Peter followed his partner's example. He seized Abby's hands and wrenched them over her head, swiftly binding her wrists to the posts at the opposite end of the headboard.

Too weak and far too uncoordinated to resist effectively, Abby only managed to exhaust herself as she squirmed and wriggled beneath Peter's ministrations. He seemed to find her contortions amusing, swatting at her occasionally with no more urgency than he would have used against a gnat.

The black-clad figure gave a final test to both sets of bindings, then walked on silent feet to the small dresser. He opened the top drawer and returned, carrying two syringes.

''You do her, I'll do him.'' The masked man's voice had taken on a dreadful familiarity. Abby searched her memory. If only her brain weren't functioning with the clarity of cornmeal mush, she knew she would recognize that voice. She had met this man somewhere, heard his voice. Abby shivered again, this time not from the cold.

''I've increased the dose,'' the man in black said. ''Four hundred milligrams for her. Five hundred for him. That'll keep them out of trouble until tomorrow.''

"You're sure it won't kill them?" Peter sounded nervous. "We don't want any glitches on the autopsy report."

"There won't be an autopsy report, if I can help it. Besides, phenobarbital doesn't kill healthy people."

"Lover boy over there isn't looking too healthy right now."

"His constitution's strong."

Peter grunted an acknowledgment. Smiling, he turned back to Abby. "You heard what the doctor said, little girl. Time to take your medicine. Do what Uncle Peter tells you, and this won't hurt a bit."

Rage exploded inside Abby. Rage at her own weakness. Rage at her past blindness. Most of all, rage at Peter for taking such pleasure in humiliating her. Her brain wasn't functioning efficiently enough for her to formulate a conscious plan, but at some deep, subconscious level she knew that Peter and his masked accomplice would succeed in all they were planning, unless she could avoid this injection.

She shuddered as Peter eased up her torn and filthy skirt toward her hips. His fingers stroked with lascivious pleasure over her ice-cold flesh. Something told her that his actions weren't just routine debasements.

"Great legs you've got, Abigail. Spectacular, in fact." His hands explored the tops of her stockings. "Mmm...mmm... There's nothing I like better than a good old-fashioned garter belt and lacy panties."

"Peter!"

Abby had never expected to be so grateful for the sound of the masked man's grating voice. Peter's fingers stopped their invasion of her stockings. "Okay, okay," he muttered, shoving her skirt up to her waist in a single, quick sweep.

"Such a pity I don't have to time to stop and enjoy your—attributes," he said. "But we've got supplies to purchase and alibis to organize. Unfortunately, law-abiding citizens like my partner and myself don't have dynamite stashed conveniently in the garage."

"Dynamite!" Abby couldn't help the startled reaction. Was Peter going to blow up the cabin?

"I admit you really did catch us on the hop, Abigail, my dear. My partner and I couldn't believe it when we realized you'd discovered the significance of little Christopher's life and death. We *are* right in thinking you'd worked out that Douglas Brady was an impostor, aren't we?"

Abby didn't reply, but her expression must have betrayed her.

Peter sighed. "Yes," he said. "I knew our clever little scam with Douglas was about to come unraveled. I don't know how you did it, Abigail. My partner and I really thought we had the Christopher angle taken care of." Peter chuckled. "Anyway, I guess all's well that ends well. Thank goodness you came to me for help in finding the originals of those missing certificates. That was very considerate of you, Abigail. It was worth the sacrifice of my car to keep you away from the registrar's office. I'm afraid little Christopher Renquist's birth certificate really does reveal all."

Peter's hand traced a last, regretful sweep over her stomach, then picked up the syringe from the nightstand, where his partner had left it.

Abby didn't—couldn't—speak. She closed her eyes, and her whole body tensed, waiting for the prick of the needle. Waiting for just the right moment to twist away.

The tip of the disposable needle scratched against her skin. Abby sucked in her breath. Injections weren't her favorite form of recreation at the best of times. Peter pushed the needle deeper into the subcutaneous tissue. She waited for the telltale sensation that would indicate he had started to push in the plunger and that the drug had begun to flow.

Now! In a lightning move she twisted her hips, and jolted the thigh he was injecting sharply against the thin mattress. Peter's hand was crushed between her leg and the bed. Abby jerked upward, hard. Her heart gave a leap of joy when she heard the tiny ping of the snapping needle. Its point was still buried in her thigh, but from the wetness she could feel on her leg, it seemed likely that quite a lot of the drug had spilled onto the candlewick bedspread rather than into her body.

"Damn!" Peter elaborated his curse with a string of profanity. "She's broken the blasted syringe!" he yelled at his partner.

"Let me see." The man in black came around to Abby's side of the bed. Together he and Peter rolled her onto her back. Peter held her down.

The man stared at her leg, eyes glittering behind his woolen ski mask. "I don't have another dose with me. Phenobarbital isn't that easy to come by without a prescription. How much did you get into her?"

"Most of it, I think. Look, her eyes are closing. That's a good sign, isn't it?"

"Yes, it is."

The masked man grasped her wrist, searching for a pulse. Abby could feel the man staring down at her, and tried to let her limbs go flaccid. She prayed her eyelids wouldn't flutter. It seemed an eternity before he spoke again.

"Her pulse is slowing. She's going under."

Maybe it was a good thing that at least some of the phenobarbital had entered her system.

The voice continued. "She'll be out for six or seven hours, even if you only got two hundred milligrams into her. And lover boy's out for the next twelve. Besides, they're tied up to that headboard tighter than a pair of trussed turkeys, and the cabin's barred and bolted. Let's get out of here."

"Such a shame we have to get back to Denver before dawn." Peter leaned over Abby, cupping her breasts in his hands. She was supposed to be unconscious, so she forced herself not to cringe.

"Bye-bye, Abigail," he murmured. "Sweet dreams. See you tomorrow night."

"For heaven's sake, Peter, come on and let's get out of here." The angry instruction came from the doorway. The masked man's voice sounded impatient, weary. And colored with some other emotion that Abby couldn't name.

Abby listened as he walked to the door. A light switch clicked. Footsteps faded into the distance. The front door banged shut, and a few seconds later the engine of the truck fired. Tires squealed as the wheels skidded over snow-crusted gravel. Silence.

Abby let out her breath and opened her eyes. She and Steve were alone. Now all she had to do was fight off the effects of the phenobarbital. Escape from her bonds. Find a way out of the locked cabin. And hike a hundred or so miles back to Denver. Or at least a few miles to the nearest phone, so that she could call Knudsen.

Nothing to it, she told herself. Listen, kiddo, it's a piece of cake.

But if it wasn't, she and Steve would die.

Chapter Twelve

Abby twisted and turned and writhed for no more than fifteen minutes before the drug—and exhaustion—overcame desperation. She fell asleep. When she awoke, sunshine was seeping through the shuttered bedroom window with a brilliance that suggested the day was well advanced. Despite all her efforts, she seemed to have wasted as much as seven or eight hours on sleeping.

Her first coherent thought was that she would die of thirst. Her second, that Steve was already dead. His ice-cold body lay inert, his face bloodless, his lips blue. Staring at his chest with an intensity strong enough to will life back into him, she finally detected the shallow rise and fall of his breathing. Her relief was overwhelming, but she couldn't allow herself **the** luxury of celebration. As a mountaineer, she had enough experience in first aid to know that if she didn't find some way to warm him, Steve would die of hypothermia.

The narrow beams of sunshine provided light but no heat. Bitter mountain cold had overtaken the unheated cabin, chilling both Steve and herself, despite the fact that while she slept her legs had interwoven themselves with Steve's in an unconscious search for warmth.

How to get him warm again? Not to mention herself. Peter had tied her hands so that she could move the top half of her body vertically, but lateral movement was almost impossible.

Using her feet, Abby hitched up the overhang of the candlewick bedspread and successfully draped one corner over Steve's feet and ankles. Not much warmth in candlewick, but the cover was new and thick, so it was better than nothing. She then rubbed her feet up and down his legs with increasing speed, until she was finally rewarded with a faint sigh and the shifting of his hips. His face remained white and pinched with cold, but his lips gradually lost their terrifying blueness, as his circulation returned to a more normal rate.

Abby collapsed against the pillow, trying to ignore the stinging pain from the chafing of her wrists.

You're doing just great, she told herself. First you sleep all night, and now you've exhausted yourself reviving Steve. Presumably so that he can be alive this evening, when Peter and Partner return to kill us.

Her thoughts rambled. If only she were in the kitchen. Kitchens had knives and scissors. And water. Glorious water. Her throat was the one part of her that felt warm. It burned with longing. It was on fire with yearning. Right at this moment she would willingly have traded every penny she possessed for a tall glass of cool water. Two tall glasses of cool water. Three.

But you're not in the kitchen, and you're not going to get a sip of water until you move from this bed. Get moving, and get yourself out of those bindings.

Abby obediently tugged at the cords around her wrists. Alas, she had been right last night. The sturdy headboard was attached to the bed frame with solid, durable workmanship. She was never going to get loose by attempting to destroy the bed or pull the brass posts out of the headboard.

So you have no choice, she informed herself. You have to find some way to cut through the bonds. For which you will need a tool. And since you can't move from the bed, you don't have a very wide range of options.

Abby examined the dimly lighted bedroom with far sharper perception than she had been capable of exercising the night before. Her gaze paused on the nightstand. A possible treasure trove of scissors, knives and razors. But unfortunately she couldn't reach it until she'd cut the cords that still bound her wrists. At that point, of course, she wouldn't need the nightstand, or any scissors and razors it might contain. Abby hunched herself slightly sideways and stared at the nightstand. If she could just open the darn drawer...

Abby wasted half an hour trying to contort her body so that she could hook her toes under the handle and pull the drawer open. In the end she was forced to concede defeat. The angle between the bed and the nightstand simply made such a maneuver impossible. If only she could somehow turn onto her stomach and slide off the bed! Then she would be able to use her mouth to tug open the drawer. But her hands were lashed to the posts of the headboard in such a way that she was forced to lie on her back.

Abby stared at the ceiling, trying to see herself from the point of view of a fly on the wall. Gradually it came to her that if she could just turn her wrists inside the cords that bound them, she would be able to roll over onto her stomach and slide her knees to the floor. By twisting her head over her left shoulder, she might—possibly—be able to tug open the drawer with her teeth. At least the height of the nightstand was perfect for such an attempt.

There was only one snag. She would have to twist her wrists inside their bindings, deliberately rubbing her already raw, chafed flesh against the tight bindings. After a couple of seconds' thought, she shrugged. What had she got to lose other than another layer of skin? Her skin or her life. It wasn't a difficult choice.

Abby bunched her hands into fists, drew in a deep breath, and twisted as far onto her side as she could go without pain to her wrists. She paused, drew in another breath, then whipped her hands around, making the final quarter turn with her body at the same time.

The pain was worse than she had expected, but at least she was now facedown on the bed. Burying her face in the pillow, she panted for a few seconds to let the stinging of her wrists ease. After a couple of minutes, she slid her knees to the floor.

Her head swum dizzily, then elation took over. Her fly's eye view had been correct! The nightstand was pushed close to the bed and, since her hands were bound to the two outside posts of the headboard, she could twist her upper body so that her mouth reached the drawer pull with an inch to spare. Lifting the brass handle with her nose, she grasped the flap between her teeth and tugged. Hallelujah! The drawer slid open.

It was crammed full, seemingly with scrap paper and magazines. Not much use for cutting through nylon rope. Abby gritted her teeth, refusing to give up hope. People often kept nail scissors or nail files in bedside drawers. A pair of nail scissors could easily have slipped under all these magazines, she reasoned. Dipping her head into the drawer, she lifted the corner of a copy of *Vogue* with her teeth, hauled it over the edge and dropped it onto the floor. Odd choice of reading material, she thought vaguely. She would have expected to find copies of *Outdoor Life* or *Fishing and Hunting News*.

Abby repeated the same performance a half dozen more times, plopping copies of *People* and *Cosmopolitan* onto the floor alongside *Vogue*. As she picked up the very last magazine, a photograph fluttered to the floor, landing blank side up. No time to bother about pictures now. Abby stuck her head back into the drawer, nudged a few scraps of paper with her nose, and looked despairingly at what was left. A roll of peppermints, a pack of tissues, a flimsy emery board and a bottle of scarlet nail polish. Even she wasn't crazy enough to think an emery board would cut through nylon cord. All this effort for no purpose.

And then she saw it. Wedged into the far corner of the drawer was a letter opener. A businesslike implement with a sharp point and long, shiny steel blade.

Abby stared at the letter opener as if she had glimpsed paradise. The gleaming blade was surely the most beautiful piece of metal she had seen in nearly twenty-nine years of living. She hung the top part of her body over the drawer and nudged the handle of the knife with her nose. It slithered up the side of the drawer, then slithered back again before she could grasp it in her mouth. With infinite care she tried again, wedging her nose under the crossbar handle and coaxing the letter opener upward until she could grab the handle between her teeth. Success!

With a guttural croak of triumph, she twisted her head around and carried the knife across to the bed. A beam of sun bathed it in light, and she stared at the shiny blade lovingly as she regained her breath. After a couple of minutes, she bent over the knife and cautiously rubbed the end of her nose against the edge of the knife. The letter opener was wonderfully, blissfully sharp.

Once again Abby scooped the letter opener into her mouth and slithered her body up the bed, until she could drop the knife from her mouth into her right hand. Eagerly she aimed the blade toward the cord binding her left hand.

The twelve-inch space between the brass bedposts was too wide. The tip of the letter opener couldn't even scratch the surface of the cord, much less saw through the bindings.

"You're not going to defeat me now," Abby muttered, staring at the taut yellow twine. If she couldn't use her hand to cut the bindings, she would use her mouth. She took the letter opener back between her teeth and dug the point into the weave of the nylon cord. Stubbornly, obstinately, she sawed away, nodding her head back and forth in a patient rhythm. The blade was as sharp as she'd suspected, and the cord severed sooner than she had dared to hope. She wriggled her hand as the first loop of cord frayed open. Five more loops to go.

Abby refused to think about her cracked lips, her parched throat or her aching jaw. She refused to worry about the bleeding mess of grazed flesh where once there had been the smooth skin of her wrists. She simply concentrated all her attention on the strands of yellow nylon cord that were slowly springing apart beneath the blade of her letter opener. Fifteen minutes more, and she was going to celebrate her freedom with a drink of water! Water! The very thought of it was enough to inspire her with a fresh burst of energy.

In fact, it took only ten minutes to free her right hand, since the last two loops of cord simply fell away, once the other bindings had been cut. Freeing her left hand would have been a thirty-second job, except that her right was too numb to hold the letter opener, and she was forced to massage the circulation back into agonizingly painful operation before she could grasp the knife and slash through the last loops binding her left hand.

I did it! she thought with glee as the last strands of nylon cord fell onto the bed. But that was all the triumph she had time for as she dashed to the kitchen and stuck her head under the tap, sucking in great gulps of water until her stomach felt wonderfully bloated and her throat tingled from the cold.

Water had never tasted so heavenly. Eyes closed, mouth dripping, Abby leaned for a moment against the sink, relishing the sensation of well-being. Hoping against hope that there might be some hot water for washing, she reached a hand over the sink to adjust the faucet. The sight of her bloodied wrists pulled her up short, and for a moment her stomach threatened to regurgitate all the water she had just swallowed.

You don't have time to throw up, she warned herself. *You've got to revive Steve before Peter and Partner come back.*

Her stomach settled into reluctant quiescence. Abby couldn't generate any hot water from the tap, but the electric range worked, and she put a kettle of water on to boil. A hot drink would revive Steve, and they could both use some warm water for washing.

Scratching absently at the aggravating itch from the needle, she realized that the tip was still buried in her thigh, and she pulled it out. She rapidly searched the small cabin and found a phone in the living room. She snatched up the receiver. Nothing. The line was dead, but her disappointment was short-lived. She had never really expected Peter and Partner to leave her within reach of a functioning phone.

Waiting for the kettle to boil, Abby hurried into the bedroom and cut through Steve's bonds. His breathing was much stronger than it had been earlier, but her efforts to rouse him still met with no success. His skin felt dangerously chilled, so she wrapped him in a cocoon of blankets, stuck both pillows behind his head, and left him sleeping. She had no idea how much time they had before Peter and Partner would return, but Peter had muttered something about coming back "at night." The sun still shone outside the shutters, and her watch, now that she could see it again, said two-forty, so Abby figured she had at least a couple of hours to get Steve onto his feet.

And once Steve was revived, they would be home free. Abby tried not to let her optimism soar too high, but in comparison to what she'd already achieved, finding a way out of the locked cabin struck her as a mere nothing. One of the window shutters would surely break open, if it were banged hard enough with some kitchen implement. Abby didn't even waste time worrying about it.

She made two mugs of sweet, milky coffee with the supplies she found on a cupboard shelf, and left a can of tomato soup heating on the stove as she carried the coffee back into the bedroom. Judging from his appearance, waking Steve was likely to prove more difficult than getting out of the cabin.

She set the coffee on the nightstand and sat down on the bed, taking Steve into her arms. Not without some difficulty, she settled his head against her chest and patiently began trying to spoon the hot, reviving coffee into his mouth.

The first half-dozen times the coffee dribbled down his chin, she took tissues from the package in the nightstand

and gently wiped up the mess. The next few spoonfuls got no closer to being swallowed, and Abby felt the panic build inside her.

Dear God, what will I do if I can't get Steve to wake up? She wouldn't allow herself even to think the only sensible answer to her own question. There was no way she would leave Steve in the cabin while she made good her escape.

Half the coffee in one mug had now dribbled away down Steve's chin. Abby took a couple of swallows from the other one, letting the hot sweet liquid renew her energy level. With fingers that trembled slightly despite her best efforts, she pried his teeth apart, slipped the spoon into his mouth and gently tilted. For what seemed like the hundredth time, coffee trickled out of his mouth and rolled down his chin to soak into his sweater.

Abby's control snapped. "Wake up, you stupid, arrogant, good-for-nothing layabout!" she yelled, grabbing his shoulders and shaking for all she was worth. "What the blazes are you doing, lolling around in bed, when I'm beating my brains out trying to get us rescued? *Drink this damn coffee, you dumb klutz!*"

Steve's eyelids fluttered open. "Abby," he murmured in a husky tone of pleasure. "I heard your voice." His eyes drifted closed again. "Nobody has a sweeter voice than you."

"I'm not sweet! I'm mad!" Abby yelled. She burst into tears.

With an obvious effort, Steve forced his eyes open. "Why are you crying? Please don't cry." His voice faded to a mumble. "Sweetheart, I can't bear it when you cry."

"I'm not crying," she denied, blatantly disregarding all the evidence to the contrary. She sniffed. "Here, wake up and drink your dumb coffee. We've got to get out of here."

His expression dazed, Steve accepted the half-empty mug, holding it in both hands. He took several swallows as his gaze drifted vacantly around the bedroom. Suddenly he shook his head and pulled himself upright in the bed, grimacing with pain as his head moved.

"Where are we?" he asked tersely. "The last thing I remember is Keith Bovery lying dead across his desk."

"We were hijacked," Abby said. "By Peter Graymont and some mysterious accomplice."

"I walked into Keith's study, and somebody grabbed me around the throat. He pressed against the carotid artery. He knew exactly where to squeeze, or I'd never have passed out so fast."

"They also drugged you. Phenobarbital," Abby said. "Now we're in a cabin somewhere in the mountains. Peter Graymont and his partner are coming back tonight."

"How do you know all this?"

She explained as succinctly as she could all that she had learned while he was unconscious, downplaying her own achievement in avoiding the injection and escaping from her bonds. Steve lifted her hands, staring in horror at the raw grazes on her wrists.

"You have to find some medication," he insisted. "Isn't there anything in the bathroom?"

"I'll look later." Abby pulled a couple of tissues from the nightstand and used them as makeshift bandages. "Steve, we don't have time to worry about trivial details—"

"Like blood poisoning—"

"Steve, you don't seem to understand. Peter and his partner are planning to dynamite this cabin. Soon. Tonight."

"With us inside, I assume?"

"Very definitely with us inside."

"Then what are we waiting for? Let's get the hell out of here!" Steve swung his feet over the side of the bed, stood up, and immediately collapsed onto his hands and knees. He stared down at the square of floor where he had landed, muttering a string of profanities that was remarkable for its lack of repetition. Suddenly he stopped swearing.

"Where did this come from?" he asked, picking up a photo from the floor.

"What?" Abby knelt beside him. "Oh, I'd forgotten about that. It fell from a magazine I was taking out of the nightstand."

"Did you see who's in the picture?"

"Steve, is this the best moment to be looking at snapshots?" Abby peered over his shoulder. "It's my dad," she said with a touch of impatience. "My dad, with Keith Bovery and Lynn Renquist. Good grief, every time we turn around these days we seem to stumble over something connected to that woman. Come on, let's go." She put her arm around his waist. "Need some help getting up?"

"Thanks, I can manage." Steve stood up, then immediately sank back onto the bed. "Give me a couple of minutes, kiddo, and then I'll be ready to do handsprings or whatever else might be needed to break out of here."

Abby sat down again next to him, and together they stared down at the picture. Steve traced a forefinger over the black and white image of the woman in nurse's uniform.

"You know something, Abby? I'm beginning to think we've been incredibly blind. Aside from your father, who would be the one person most likely to know of the existence of birth and death certificates for baby Christopher?"

She considered the question. "Well, his mother, I suppose."

"In other words, Lynn Renquist. And who would know better than anybody else that Lynn had written letters to your father that might reveal some dangerous secret?"

"Lynn Renquist." This time Abby spoke more slowly.

"And who would know enough details about your father's past to set up a convincing impersonation of your supposed half brother?"

"Lynn Renquist." Abby shot out the name. "The only person who could be one hundred percent positive that my father's ex-mistress wasn't going to appear unexpectedly and blow Douglas Brady's impersonation out of the water."

"In fact, Lynn is the only person who could have guaranteed to Douglas that he wouldn't be denounced as a fraud," Steve pointed out.

Abby looked at the magazines scattered over the floor. Magazines a woman would choose to read, not a man. "There's something else, Steve. Lynn Renquist is far and away the most likely person to keep a photo like this in her nightstand. I don't know how she ties in with Peter Graymont, but what's the betting that we're locked up in her cabin?"

"I wouldn't bet against you." Steve's expression was grim. "More to the point, I think we've finally discovered the name of the person behind all these attempts to kill you. Her name's been staring us in the face for days."

Abby looked at the three smiling faces in the photograph and wondered sadly what had gone wrong with the tightly knit friendship. "Lynn Renquist," she said. "It's Lynn Renquist who's been trying to kill me. Although Lord knows why."

"For the reason we suspected all along, I expect. You're the keeper of the Deane family records. Once Douglas Brady failed in his attempt to steal the Confederate gold, she needed to get rid of you."

"Because I was the only person who had the documents to prove that Douglas was a fraud."

"Exactly. Documents that somehow threatened to involve her in the scandal. As long as you were rummaging around in your father's past, Lynn Renquist knew she was sitting on a powder keg that could blow up at any moment."

Abby stared long and hard at the photo. "She's got to be someone we know, but I don't recognize her, do you?"

"No," Steve said. "But I'm going to find her, and then I'm going to make sure that she gets put away for a hundred years." He swung his feet onto the floor and stood up, clenching his fist triumphantly when he didn't topple over.

"Superman returns," he said, flexing his biceps. He strode toward the window, but had to stop and clutch the chest of drawers when a wave of dizziness assailed him.

"Superman half returns," he amended, giving Abby a rueful grin. "Come on, my love, stop staring at that photo. Let's break open a window and get ourselves to a phone."

"Shouldn't we take a few extra minutes and search the cabin?" Abby suggested. "We could at least try to discover what Lynn Renquist calls herself now. I mean, she could be anyone. And how in the world did she persuade Peter Graymont and his masked sidekick to do all her dirty work?"

"Maybe she's paying them huge sums of money. The guy in black could be a paid killer. That would explain why he always wears a mask. He doesn't want to be identified, not even by Peter."

"Where did Lynn get enough money to bribe Peter and pay a professional hit man?"

"Probably embezzled it from the bank," Steve said. "That would explain the link to Howard Taylor, and why she had to persuade Peter and Partner to kill Keith Bovery."

"So Lynn Renquist is employed by First Denver. Is she Linda Mendoza, do you think? Were we right about that all along?"

Steve removed a screw from the window frame. "Honey, since Peter and his masked friend are likely to come marching in at any moment bearing sticks of dynamite, I'm not sure I care right at this moment what dear old Lynn calls herself, or how she fits into the overall picture. I vote we leave the sleuthing to Lieutenant Knudsen and get the hell out of here."

The hiss of food boiling over reminded Abby that she had left tomato soup simmering on the stove. She dashed for the kitchen and grabbed the saucepan. A memory flashed into her mind. It was so startling that she put the pan down again and sprinted back to the bedroom.

"Steve," she croaked. "I just realized something."

"What?" He was too busy with the window bolt to look around.

"Peter and his partner thought I was unconscious when they left this bedroom. But I wasn't. I was woozy, but not completely out. Peter's sidekick called to him from the doorway. Even then, something about his voice bothered me, and I've just realized what it was. It wasn't a man's voice. It was a woman's."

"*What?*" Steve dropped his screwdriver.

"Why are we assuming Lynn Renquist used other people to do her dirty work? Why couldn't she be the person who's trying to murder me? Herself. In person."

Steve recovered his calm. "Because the person who's been trying to kill you is a man. You've heard him on the phone. I saw him in Boulder."

"No. I heard a disguised voice over the telephone. You saw a figure in a ski mask. We all assumed that we'd seen and heard a man. But I don't believe he is. I think he's a woman."

She had finally captured Steve's full attention. "My God," he said. "I think you've got it. The person behind that black ski mask is Lynn Renquist."

Abby held up the snapshot, squinting to get a better view. "Wouldn't it be nice," she said, "if we knew what Lynn Renquist calls herself nowadays?"

Chapter Thirteen

Steve and Abby didn't have long to contemplate the ramifications of her great insight. A quick search of the cabin turned up no trace of any personal papers that might pinpoint Lynn's current identity. The lengthening shadows—reminders that Peter and Partner could return at any moment—soon sent Steve back to unscrewing his window bolts and Abby back to her smoking pan of soup.

She inspected the ruined remnants of what should have been their meal with a disgruntled eye, knowing that she and Steve would fare better in their trek down the mountain after some hot food. "I'll make us more coffee instead," she muttered, filling the kettle. "Cooking's too difficult."

Steve chose this inopportune moment to return to the kitchen. "Right," he agreed, laughter in his voice. "Heating soup would defeat almost anyone. Open can, add water, stir gently. Not a task for a novice."

She swung around to glare at him, but as soon as she saw his face, she forgot about the minor problem of burned soup. Frustration lay right behind his laughter. "What is it?" she asked. "The windows won't open?"

"Bad news, kiddo. The shutters are relatively easy to remove. But that's not going to do us a bit of good. The windows are secured from the outside with steel bars. Very efficient steel bars, riveted to the aluminum window frames. We'd need a blowtorch to cut through.''

She swallowed hard. "All of them?"

"I haven't checked here in the kitchen. But everywhere else. Including the bathroom."

"These kitchen windows are way too small for us to get through, anyway." Abby poured boiling water into the mugs, and handed a steaming cup of instant coffee to Steve. "Looks as if Peter and Partner have been planning our imprisonment for a good long while. They've had time to make the place very secure."

"I don't think the bars were put on the windows because of us," Steve said. "They look weather-beaten. I'd guess the cabin was secured against thieves and vandals when it was built. Lots of mountain property is protected by iron grillwork over the doors and windows. Particularly an isolated vacation cabin like this one."

The interior of the kitchen seemed to Abby to be darkening by the moment. She took another scalding gulp of hot, milky coffee, but it failed to warm her. Afternoon was fast fading into night, taking with it their hopes of an escape. Peter and his partner—Peter and Lynn?—would surely arrive at any moment. Of course there was a chance that she and Steve could overpower their captors. Not a very good chance, however, if Peter and pal walked into the cabin carrying loaded guns. Abby couldn't help thinking that while swift, flying kicks to the wrist might disarm the bad guys in a movie, in real life, she suspected that good guys who faced armed villains were depressingly likely to end up dead.

"Do we have time to dig a tunnel?" she asked, trying to joke so that she wouldn't cry.

"'Fraid not. No time and no shovel."

"We could try the front door again," Abby said. "Maybe we could unscrew the padlock? That shouldn't take too long." She pulled open one of the kitchen drawers. "Look, there are screwdrivers and wrenches in here. A hammer. All the basic tools."

Steve shook his head. "I'm sorry, sweetheart. You saw the chain on the front door. It's heavy-duty steel, and the padlock looks as if it was left over from San Quentin. We'd need hours of time to file through it. Or else an acetylene torch. That's why we decided to try the windows."

Abby's stomach knotted in fear and frustration. "Steve, this is crazy. We're not drugged, we're not injured. We're free to move around, we have tools, we have light. Dammit, we have to be able to get out of here!"

"Out of the chimney, maybe, if you can turn into Santa Claus or reduce yourself to the size of a small five-year-old." Steve took her hands into his. "Look, Abby, I don't think we have any other choice, so we'll have to try to overpower the pair of them when they come back. The situation isn't all in their favor. It'll be dark. They'll expect us to be bound and lying on—"

"Wait a minute! I just remembered the shed!" Abby interrupted, doing a little jig of excitement. "There's a shed or a garage or something attached to the side of the cabin. I'll bet it isn't as well protected as the main structure. Peter and pal certainly hadn't secured it with any padlocks or iron grillwork, at least as far as I could see when they brought me in. It just has a regular overhead door. And since the shed is built right up against the side of the house, maybe we could break into it through the kitchen wall."

Steve's face lighted up. "Better chance yet, through the utility room. The walls in there aren't likely to be paneled."

"The utility room's right here." Abby ran to the corner of the kitchen and flung open a door that led into the oversize closet housing the furnace, the water heater and the electric fuse box.

"Hallelujah!" she cried rapturously. "Look, Steve, the walls aren't even finished, let alone paneled."

Steve glanced at the flimsy plasterboard separating the closet from the garage, and hugged her in delight. "Abby, my sweet, you're a total and complete genius. No wonder I'm so desperately in love with you." As if surprised by his own words, he stopped, then grinned. "I guess the truth is out, kiddo. I can't hide it any longer. I lust after your delectable feminine mind."

Abby's heart gave a little leap that had nothing to do with their prospects of escape. Steve had spoken in his usual teasing tone, but she was finally beginning to understand that his laid-back manner didn't necessarily mean that his feelings were as lighthearted as his voice. Abby didn't fool herself with the hope that Steve Kramer, bachelor par excellence, was ready to make the sort of lifetime commitment she secretly yearned for. But at this moment she didn't need a lifetime commitment from him. She simply needed to know that he truly cared. During their brief marriage, Greg had taught Abby the bitter lesson that entrusting your happiness to another human being was a high-risk procedure. For the past six years, after the pain of Greg's multiple betrayals, she had taken care never to expose herself to even minimal risk. She could continue to protect herself in familiar fashion simply by answering Steve with a sassy remark.

Or she could risk displaying her vulnerability, and maybe learn the truth about his feelings.

Abby looked at Steve intently, trying to read his expression in the dusky half-light of the shuttered kitchen. It suddenly seemed intolerable that she should face imminent death, while lacking enough courage to ask him a simple question.

"Did you mean what you just said, Steve?" she asked quietly. "Are you really *desperately in love* with me?"

His body tensed. He paused in his search through the tool drawer and swung around to face her, his stance oddly defensive. The kitchen was wrapped in silence for a second or so. Then he shrugged, laughing in wry self-mockery.

"Do you really need to ask?" he said. "I've been in love with you for years, Abby. I decided my case was terminal six months ago."

"When you bought the penthouse apartment in my building."

"Right." Not quite achieving his usual flippant tone, he added, "I had some crazy idea that nearness might make your heart grow fonder. And not only for my cooking."

Abby finally understood what it felt like to tingle with happiness. "It wasn't a crazy idea," she said softly. She leaned her head against his chest. "I think I've loved you forever, Steve. Since the moment I first saw you walking toward me across campus. It just took me a bit longer than most women to recognize the truth about my own feelings."

"Sweetheart, think nothing of it. What's a mere ten years?"

"A lot of wasted time," she whispered, linking her hands behind his head and raising her face to his kiss.

His head bent slowly toward her mouth. "I love you," he said; his mouth crushed hers in a kiss that heated her blood and warmed her soul.

"I love you, too." Her reply was lost in the passion of their embrace.

Reality returned far too soon, and they drew apart. He tucked a stray wisp of her hair behind her ear. "Abby, my sweet, much as I would like to carry you into the bedroom and spend the next few hours making love, the truth is, we don't have time for any of this."

"No more deep, meaningful conversations?"

He shook his head. Abby took his hand and rubbed his knuckles across her cheek in a caress that ached with unexpressed tenderness. "Get us out of here, Steve," she murmured.

He drew in a sharp breath. "I plan on it, kiddo."

"Great. So let's get cracking." With determined briskness, she lifted a hammer and knife from the drawer and gave them to him with hands that shook slightly. "Chisel us out a nice big escape hole, okay? This definitely isn't the right place for our great love affair to end."

"Nowhere is right until I've made love to you again. A few hundred more times." He pressed a final hard kiss upon her mouth, then lifted his head and gave her a familiar grin. "In our next incarnation, do you think you could notice that I'm crazy about you *before* some homicidal maniac starts using the pair of us for target practise?"

"I'll try," she promised.

"Great. Now I can look forward to all my future lives with renewed confidence." He gave her an affectionate pat. "Get busy, kiddo. See if you can find us a couple of sweaters, will you? We're going to need them."

Steve squeezed between the furnace and the water heater, starting to pry a sheet of plasterboard from its wooden supports before Abby had even left the kitchen. She noticed that neither of them had mentioned the possibility that they might break through to the garage, only to find their exit barred every bit as efficiently as in the main cabin. Some things, she acknowledged, were better not discussed.

"There's only one sweater in this entire cabin, but at least I found some sneakers and woolly socks," she said on returning to the utility closet ten minutes later. Darkness had encroached so rapidly that it was almost impossible to see, and she flipped on the kitchen light without stopping to think.

"Don't!" Steve ordered sharply. "Switch it off, Abby! Remember Peter and pal expect us to be tied up on the bed."

Abby couldn't help thinking that if Peter and pal returned before she and Steve broke free of the cabin, the kitchen light was going to be the least of their problems. But she obediently flipped off the switch and rummaged through the tool drawer where she had earlier noticed a small, compact flashlight, not much bigger than a pack of cigarettes. She found the gadget and directed the narrow, high-intensity beam toward the closet. The light bounced off Steve's exuberant smile and white, dust-covered hair.

"Your escape route awaits, m'lady." He gestured to a jagged hole, almost four feet by three, that he had chiseled out of the plasterboard. "One step down, and you're in the garage."

Abby gave a little crow of laughter. Passage into the shed was going to be more than easy. It would be a piece of cake. Hadn't she promised herself that all along?

"I'll hold the flashlight," Steve said. "You put on the sweater." When she tried to protest, he simply yanked the garment over her head. "Sweetheart, we don't have time to argue. You've had all the good ideas so far. Let me be macho and freeze, okay?"

The storage shed cum garage was windowless and so dark that it made the kitchen they had just left seem bright by comparison. A deafening hum from one corner marked the presence of an electric generator, but apart from that the shed seemed to be empty.

The lack of clutter made their search easy. With the help of the flashlight, it took them mere seconds to locate the door, which was a typical overhead, garage type. It was secured against burglars and vandals by two massive steel bars that acted as oversize bolts. The bars, however, were designed to keep thieves out, not prisoners in, and unbolting the door was literally child's play. They had the two huge steel levers lifted from the locked position in less than a minute.

Panting slightly, they looked at each other, eyes gleaming with anticipation. "This is it," Abby breathed.

"We're gonna make it." Steve gave her the thumbs-up sign, and she ran to the far side of the garage.

"Ready, set, go!" He yelled the instruction over the noise of the generator. They pushed upward on the steel handle grips that were helpfully provided at either end, and the garage door creaked and rattled open on squeaky hinges.

They stepped out into the crystal-clear, ice-cold mountain night. Fresh air had never smelled so magnificent.

"We did it!" Abby exulted. "We escaped!"

Behind them, the garage door crashed noisily shut, as if emphasizing their successful exit. They both laughed. Against all the odds they had succeeded. Abby grabbed

Steve's hand, and he pulled her close in a swift, triumphant hug.

"Race you to a phone!" he teased. They started running toward the road. Toward safety and freedom. Toward the endless possibilities of their future.

They had traveled scarcely twenty feet along the path when Abby registered that the sound she still heard wasn't the thrum of the generator, but the revving of a truck engine. Steve must have come to the same realization at the same instant, for they both stopped in midflight, searching frantically for cover.

My God, Abby thought, head twisting from left to right and back again like a mesmerized rabbit. *We're trapped between the locked cabin at our backs and the roadway ahead.* The cabin had been built in a natural, rock-strewn clearing. Apart from a couple of ponderosa pines framing the entrance, there wasn't so much as a single tree trunk for twenty yards in any direction. And the rocks that decoratively lined the pathway were barely large enough to provide cover for a squirrel.

Their frantic scanning of the terrain couldn't have lasted longer than ten seconds. To Abby, those seconds felt like an eternity. Worse, she seemed paralyzed by the sudden swing of her mood from reckless hope to mind-numbing terror.

"Run to your left," Steve ordered, his voice cool, crisp and allowing no room for refusal. "Make for the stand of trees behind the cabin. Quick!"

The van rounded a final corner in the road, automatically spearing them in the powerful beam of its headlights as it turned toward the cabin.

"Go! Now."

Steve swung her around, literally pointing her body toward the small copse of trees to the rear of the cabin.

Obediently she started running. The night air tore her
breath from her lungs and chilled the last vestige of hope
in her heart. Where was Steve? She couldn't hear him behind her. With a sickening rush of despair, Abby realized
he must have run in the opposite direction, hoping to at-
tract the full attention of their pursuers. He couldn't avoid
being seen. His capture was certain.

If he was sacrificing so much, it was imperative that she
should make the sacrifice worthwhile. Abby put on a final, almost superhuman burst of speed and dodged to the
rear of the cabin. The beam of the van headlights didn't
reach this far, and she felt a split second's flash of hope,
a hope that she might yet be able to hide herself in the
trees and the darkness.

She slipped deeper into the small stand of trees. No
point in running, or she would simply emerge into the
open again. Should she try to climb a tree? No, that would
only draw attention to her position. At this moment, utter stillness offered her the best chance of remaining un-
discovered. Feet frozen within her borrowed sneakers,
teeth chattering, Abby tucked her hands into the shelter
of her sweater and waited. She heard the slam of the van
door, the sound of feet racing across the frosty grass. And
then an explosion that was all too easy to identify. Gun-
shot.

Tears froze on Abby's cheeks. Over the pounding of her
heart she heard Peter's voice.

"That was a friendly warning, Kramer. Stop running.
Turn around and put your hands over your head. Unless
you want a bullet in your back."

Abby sagged against the trunk of the concealing pine
tree, trying to bury herself in its protective shadow.
Everything now depended upon her. Steve had deliberately sacrificed himself by running into the open. Deso-

lation crept along her limbs, chilling her blood more effectively than the bitter night wind. Even if she managed by some miracle to escape, how in the world was she going to save Steve? His life could probably be measured in minutes.

She strained to decipher the tangle of sounds. Peter's voice, issuing a command, and Steve's reply. She recognized the defiance of Steve's tone, although she couldn't distinguish the words. At least he wasn't wounded so badly that he was unconscious. Perhaps Peter's shot really had been fired only in warning. Perhaps Steve wasn't wounded.

Abby heard the twig crack behind her a split second before a gloved hand was clapped over her mouth. Something round, cold and hard was pressed into the small of her back. Something easily identifiable. A gun.

Her captor leaned so close that Abby could feel the woolen ski mask rubbing against the side of her face. Nausea churned in her stomach. The intimate scratch of the wool and the warm breath of her captor on her skin seemed a worse violation than the gun threatening her back.

"You and lover boy are beginning to annoy me," a familiar voice rasped into her ear. "I don't enjoy all this scrambling about through the snow."

Abby's captor spoke in a semiwhisper—a gruff, low whisper that could easily have been male. The arm circling Abby's neck was wiry and muscled, strong enough to belong to a man. But the perfume the murderer wore was unmistakably feminine, a delicate floral scent that hinted incongruously at tea parties and silken nightgowns. Almost choking on the smell of roses, Abby felt herself gag.

"Why are you doing this, Lynn?" she asked. "What have I ever done to make you want to kill me?"

Silence. The gun was stroked slowly along Abby's spine, as if Lynn couldn't decide whether to pull the trigger or give her an answer.

"So you guessed who I am," Lynn said at last, still in the same harsh murmur. "Maybe it's better this way. I'd like you to die knowing the truth."

"What is the truth?" Abby asked desperately.

"That you're alive," Lynn said slowly. "You and your sisters. All three of you are alive, but my poor little baby died."

"Christopher was your son." Abby forced herself to add the rest. "Your son and my father's."

"Our son and your half brother. When I first told your father I was pregnant, he tried to pretend the baby wasn't his. But in the end, even he had to admit that Christopher was his son. His only son. Poor little bastard."

"He didn't . . . my father didn't send you any money?"

Lynn's harsh laughter held a lifetime of bitterness. "Oh, he sent money, all right. Not enough, but enough to buy off his conscience. What good was money in those days? I needed marriage. A husband. Respectability."

"He . . . he couldn't marry you. He was married already."

"He should have thought of that when he came back from his combat missions, always so damned eager to hop into bed. Him and Keith Bovery. A pair of conniving lechers, that's what they were. Neither of them told me they were married until after they'd seduced me."

"You had a relationship with Keith Bovery as well as with my father?"

Lynn didn't answer that question. "I scarcely dared to eat when I got home from Korea, trying to stay thin so that nobody would realize I was pregnant. Have you any idea what it was like being an unmarried mother in Alabama in the 1950s?''

''It must have been—difficult.''

''My little boy only weighed five pounds when he was born.'' The low, rasping voice was laced with remembered pain. ''All eyes in a tiny pink face. He caught a cold, and that was it. Two days of fever. The end. Your father had never even been to see him, although I wrote, begging him to come.''

''I'm...sorry,'' Abby whispered. Impossibly, illogically, it was true. She was about to die, and she felt sorry for the woman who planned to kill her.

''I don't want your pity. I don't need it.'' Lynn tightened her grip around Abby's neck. ''If I didn't want you to suffer, I'd kill you now. But I want you and lover boy to be wide-awake when the big bang comes. Wide-awake and scared.''

''I'm scared now.'' Abby spoke nothing but the truth. She was terrified.

''Good. Now you know how I felt for nine long months.'' The gun was jabbed with painful force into Abby's spine. ''Walk, Abigail. Time's a-wasting.''

Lynn had been careful to keep her voice pitched at little more than a whisper. Muffled by the ski mask, Abby found it impossible to identify the speaker. ''Who are you, Lynn?'' she asked, the ache of frustrated curiosity in her voice entirely genuine.

''Lynn Renquist, your father's discarded mistress. The instrument of your death.'' The whispered words resonated with hatred. ''Walk, Abigail. My dear friend Peter doesn't like to be kept waiting.''

Chapter Fourteen

The gun at her back, and Lynn's hatred a tangible presence thickening the crisp night air, Abby stumbled over the coarse grass. To her surprise, Lynn didn't push her toward the cabin. Instead she was prodded in the direction of the truck, parked by the side of the road with its headlights still blazing.

Peter lounged against the hood, twirling his gun around one index finger and blowing curls of frosted breath into the beam of light. As Abby approached, she could see that his handsome face was wreathed in a smiling parody of welcome.

"My dear Abigail, I'm so glad my partner found you! How amazingly resourceful you are. We thought we had you both tied up nice and tight, but obviously we were badly mistaken. Still, all's well that end's well. I seem to be saying that much too often these past few days, don't I? My partner keeps leaving me to clean up her little messes. *Her* messes. Oh, naughty me! Have I betrayed a secret?"

"They know I'm Lynn Renquist." The harsh whisper came from behind Abby's back.

"What busy little detectives you and Steve have been." Peter still smiled, but his tone had grown venomous.

Abby tilted her chin defiantly. "Where's Steve? What have you done to him?"

"Why nothing at all, Abigail. Steve did it all to himself. He was only too willing to cooperate. So noble of him to sacrifice himself in the hope that you'd get away! Foolish, but noble."

"You're a slug, Peter, did you know that?"

His smile was switched off, and he hauled her tight against his body, rubbing his gun over her hips with a repelling suggestiveness. "Little girls aren't supposed to be rude," he said. "And they're supposed to lie still when their elders and betters tie them up."

"I'm not a little girl." Her voice shook infuriatingly despite her best efforts. She drew in a steadying breath and looked over her shoulder at Lynn. "I want to see Steve."

Both ignored her request. Peter drew his gun slowly across her body and nestled it between her breasts.

"How cute you look, Abigail, my dear. My gun suits you. Seeing you like this, I might even be persuaded to forgive your silly attempt to escape." His brown eyes glazed with malicious pleasure. "I don't *only* like little girls, you know. Sometimes, if they're *real* nice to me, I like mature women, too."

"Drop dead, Peter."

He twisted her arms behind her back and thrust his chest hard against her breasts, his horrible smile returning. Thank God, the thick down parka he wore made the contact less repulsive than it might have been. "No, my dear, I don't think I'm going to die. Life is sweet right now. Real sweet." Peter put one knee between Abby's legs and his free hand on her breasts, flicking his gaze derisively toward Lynn.

With sudden understanding, Abby realized that his lecherous behavior was directed as much at Lynn as at herself. Peter was simply using her as a weapon in some ongoing private battle. She didn't doubt that Peter would be capable of raping her as part of a power play, without expending an atom of emotion on the transaction, but the knowledge that he felt no genuine desire for her somehow made his advances easier to tolerate.

She closed her eyes, forcing herself to show no other reaction when Peter crooked a hand under her chin and dragged her toward the beam of the headlights.

"Tut, tut, Abigail. You've made yourself all dirty. And look at your poor sore wrists! Dear, dear, I don't like the look of those rope burns at all. If you'd done as you were told, and stayed neatly tied up on the bed, you wouldn't be in this nasty mess."

"You're right. We'd probably be dead of hypothermia. Where's Steve?"

Lynn finally spoke, answering Abby's question in her usual rough whisper. "Your lover is in the truck. And you're about to join him. Enough of this, Peter."

"Whatever you say, Lynn dearest."

Gun at the ready, Lynn moved out from behind Abby. Peter finally gave up playing with his gun and directed it toward Abby's stomach with businesslike intent. Looking at the taut stance of her two captors, Abby hadn't the slightest doubt that both Lynn and Peter would fire if she twitched the wrong muscle. The serious business of murder was about to begin.

Peter jerked his head toward the rear of the truck. "Move that cute little tush, Abigail. We don't have all night to get you two to the mine."

"To the mine? Which mine? You're not going to kill us here? Right now?"

Abby belatedly clamped her mouth shut. *Great going, kid,* she told herself. *Nothing like encouraging a couple of killers to get right down to business.*

Peter fondled the barrel of his gun without disturbing its deadly aim. "Oh no, Abigail, we're not going to dispose of you here. Why in the world would we draw attention to my friend's cabin? That would be a sure way to get ourselves arrested. We're taking you to Crystal Mine."

Dear God, they're going to dynamite the mine. Their plan was far more clever than Abby had envisioned. Blowing up the mine would inevitably set off a rock slide that would bury the entrance, along with the unwanted bodies of Steve and herself. The contours of the land would be radically changed by the explosion, making it almost impossible to find the original site of the mine, even if someone came looking. Which they probably wouldn't.

With a sickening lurch of her stomach, Abby realized that her two captors had a better than excellent chance of getting away with murder. Two more killings, achieved without a breath of suspicion clinging to either of their names. Fury, all the worse because it was so impotent, clawed at Abby's gut. She was tired of triumphing against the odds, only to have her victory transformed into the cold ashes of defeat.

"Why take us to the mine?" she asked. No point in letting on to her captors that she understood their plans. "There's no gold left in there, you know. It was all converted into regular currency weeks ago."

"We're not expecting to find gold," Lynn said bitterly. "Your sister Kate ruined that for us. She and that damned interfering do-gooder, RJ."

"You should be flattered, Abigail." Peter sounded cheery. "My partner and I plan to do you and Steve proud—an exit scene to remember. Our ultimate salute to all those lost millions in Confederate gold. The grand finale for Crystal Mine. What a pity we'll have such a small audience."

"You're insane," Abby said softly.

"Not at all." Peter's eyes narrowed. "There isn't an insane bone in my body. I'm merely greedy. You see, I acknowledge the truth about myself. A man who's going to work on the wrong side of the law needs to understand his own character, don't you think?"

"I wouldn't know."

"Take it from a pro. I can assure you that the successful criminal needs to know where he's coming from, as well as where he's going. I was born poor, Abigail, and growing up poor isn't much fun, although that's something you wouldn't understand. I like money, Abigail. Lots of it. And your family has managed to deprive me of several lovely millions that I'd earned. I don't screw fifty-year-old women just for the fun of it, you know."

"You bastard!" The agonized exclamation came from Lynn Renquist.

Peter gave her a cruel smile. "Don't take it to heart, sugar pie. You were almost an exception."

His hand shot out and grabbed Abby by the throat. "Into the truck, Abigail. This conversation is beginning to bore me."

Peter dragged her over the few feet of snow-covered ground to the rear of the truck. She saw Steve as soon as Lynn swung open the doors. He sat hunched on the floor, hemmed in by two wooden crates, and handcuffed to a steel bar running the length of the interior panel. Surgical tape stuck crisscross over his mouth formed an effective gag. Above the gag, his green eyes blazed in impotent fury. He looked away as Abby was pushed into the truck and locked into another pair of handcuffs on the opposite side of the van. Abby understood how he was feeling. He couldn't bear to give his captors the satisfaction of seeing his rage. Or his despair.

While Peter kept his gun trained purposefully on Abby's stomach, Lynn walked to the front of the van and took the seat behind the wheel. She then turned around, holding her gun to Abby's temple, while Peter slammed the doors and clambered into the passenger seat. Lynn and Peter were taking their guard duties seriously, although Abby had no idea how they expected either of their prisoners to escape from metal cuffs and a locked truck. She wished she could think of some even halfway viable escape plan.

They jolted along without speaking for several miles, the hum of the engine and the rushing of the wind loud in Abby's ears. Because of the way she was handcuffed, she couldn't see out of the front of the van, and the side panels had no windows. But she assumed they weren't too far away from Crystal Mine, since Peter and Lynn presumably planned to finish their killing and complete the two-hour drive back to Denver long before dawn.

Abby tried to think herself into Lynn and Peter's shoes. Precisely what were the two of them planning? Obviously she and Steve were going to be shut up inside the mine. But would they be shot first? Or was there any hope at all that the two criminals might stash them in the mine in a state of reasonable physical fitness?

The faintest whisper of hope began stirring at the edge of Abby's mind. If their adversaries hadn't already planted the dynamite, they would need at least half an hour to set up the explosion. Dynamiting the mine was going to need skill and care. Lynn and Peter had lived in Colorado for years, and must know that carelessly ignited dynamite could set off an avalanche of falling rocks that would bury everything in its path. Including the people planting the dynamite.

But she and Steve would need more than time to effect an escape. Peter seemed to be in a mood to shoot out their kneecaps, just for the sport of it, and crippled prisoners weren't going to make it anywhere. Then they would need a light, and Steve might not have the flashlight from the cabin anymore. Even if he still had it, its batteries might give out too soon. So many contingencies. *Too darn many.* She shouldn't allow herself to hope.

The truck jolted over a deep rut in the mountain road, and the metal handcuffs cut with sickening force into Abby's wrists. Unable to help herself, she screamed, and for a moment blacked out with the pain. When she came to again, she knew that she had been thinking something important, something about their escape, but couldn't quite recapture the thread of her thoughts. Hoping to minimize the impact of future bumps, she braced herself against the side of the truck, and her gaze traveled woozily to Steve, instinctively seeking his support.

He had been watching her all along, Abby realized, and his eyes met hers in a look of such unmistakable love, regret and apology that she literally felt her heart contract. Indifferent to Peter's and Lynn's presence, uncaring if they saw what she was doing, she quietly mouthed the words, *I love you, Steven Kramer.*

The pain and the regret disappeared from his eyes for an instant, and nothing was left save the love. Though his mouth was still covered with surgical tape, she didn't need to see his lips to know what he was saying. Love and longing were written in every line of his body.

Peter's mocking voice shattered their precious few seconds of understanding.

"What a pair of lovebirds! Such a sweet, silent ex-change between the two of you. Young love is very pre-cious, don't you agree?" Peter ignored Steve's scathing frown and Abby's ostentatiously turned shoulder and continued his monologue.

"You know, my friend Lynn and I have really done all you Deane girls a favor, when you come to think about it. Look at it this way. Linsey and Kate would never have met their husbands, if they hadn't been chasing around trying to protect that wagon load of Confederate gold. And you, Abigail, dearest. Well, I'm sure you've seen dear Steven here in a whole new light since my friend Lynn started taking potshots at you."

"And missing me. Don't forget that part of the story." Abby hadn't meant to respond, but she couldn't resist the chance to sow a little discord between her two captors.

Peter's voice hardened. "She's missed for the last time."

"If you say so," Abby said politely. "Not that I want to teach a lifelong criminal like you his business, Peter, but you don't seem to have done a very good job of choosing your colleagues."

Peter's veneer of good humor vanished. "Unfortu-nately I have to work with what's available," he snapped.

"I can't believe there was nothing better in the crimi-nal marketplace than Douglas Brady. A man who couldn't keep his mouth shut in a bar, and then, when you and Lynn had pulled him out of the disaster he made of your original scam, he sold you out to a bunch of Las Vegas gangsters! If you hadn't relied on Douglas, you'd be five million dollars richer right at this moment."

Peter's face darkened with fury. He started to shout an angry reply, but Lynn turned to him with a single author-itative command. "Shut up, Peter."

Obediently he fell silent, reinforcing Abby's conviction that although Peter might act as spokesman for the duo, Lynn was the person in charge.

Lynn's fingers drummed out a restless tattoo on the steering wheel. She didn't seem much happier than Peter with Abby's recounting of their failures. "Tell our friends in the back about our latest success story," she said, turning to Peter. "Tell them about the discovery of poor Mr. Bovery's suicide. And how shocked everyone is at learning what he'd done with the First Denver Federal sleeper accounts."

"Why certainly, Lynn, that would be my pleasure." Peter grinned, his good humor entirely restored. "Poor Mr. Bovery was discovered at ten-thirty last night by Lieutenant Knudsen and another detective. He'd shot himself with a .38 Webley that the police think he must have brought back from Korea. The very same gun that had been used to shoot Douglas Brady and Howard Taylor. Isn't that amazing? The lieutenant was very shocked when he came to see me. My manager and I both assured him that Keith had seemed in the best of spirits when he left my store, chatting about his purchase of the Chinese vases as if he didn't have a worry on his mind. Knudsen was kind enough to say that we shouldn't blame ourselves for not detecting his mood. He said that when criminals have suicide on their minds, they often conceal it amazingly well. Still, Knudsen had a few questions at first as to whether Keith's death might not have been murder, didn't he, Lynn?"

"Oh, indeed he did." Lynn chuckled gleefully. "At first he didn't want to believe that Keith had committed suicide, but the evidence at the scene of the…er…event was so convincing, he soon changed his mind."

"The news from the bank clinched it," Peter added. "We have you to thank for that, Mr. Kramer. Your associates arrived at the bank this morning—your whiz kids, I believe you call them—and guess what they discovered? You'll be shocked to hear this, Abigail, but that naughty Mr. Bovery had been embezzling money from his own bank."

Lynn gave a rasping laugh. "And then he framed poor Howard Taylor, so that we all thought Howard was the guilty party. Wasn't that wicked of Keith? What poor Helen would have said about all this, I can't imagine."

For the first time, Steve couldn't control his need to speak. He made a few inarticulate sounds behind his gag, but quickly fell silent again when Lynn and Peter stared at him in derision.

"Everything can't be quite such plain sailing for you two," Abby said heatedly. "Hasn't the lieutenant noticed that Steve and I are missing? After all, I assume it was our message to the CBI that sent him around to Keith's house in the first place."

Peter chuckled. "Fortunately, the message from Steven was very garbled by the time it reached our hardworking lieutenant. He decided you'd found Mr. Bovery's body and then left at once for the airport, shattered by this final discovery."

"Surely he'll expect us to call again."

"But Steven has called again," Peter said. "He called today and left another message with the CBI switchboard operator. He explained that you were utterly devastated by all that had happened here in Colorado, so he'd decided to fly out of town with you, Abigail, and keep an eye on you. According to Steven, your nerves are all shot to pieces, and you're not behaving very rationally right now."

"Didn't the lieutenant insist on speaking with Steve in person?"

"My partner and I are not fools, Abigail, as I keep reminding you. Naturally 'Steven' called when we knew for sure that the lieutenant was otherwise engaged. Interviewing people at the bank, as it happens."

"The most wonderful part of all this," Lynn interjected, "is that we won't even need to provide a precise alibi for the time of your murder. 'Steven' hinted to the operator at the CBI that you'd decided to soak up the sun in Acapulco, and that you wouldn't be coming back to the States for at least two weeks."

"It's really clever, don't you agree?" Peter smiled. "By the time people start seriously wondering where you are, you'll have been dead for weeks. And then they'll start trying to trace you in all the wrong places. Your car's been parked at the airport, of course, so they'll have no reason to doubt you left town. They'll waste days searching through the hotels in Acapulco. Then they'll wonder if the operator misunderstood, and 'Steven' really said somewhere else in Mexico."

"And in the meantime, we've made sure that no inconvenient bodies will turn up in Denver," Lynn said—and giggled, for the first time sounding like a woman. "This really is a good plan, Abigail. Foolproof. Absolutely foolproof."

Abby wondered why the thought of dying was so much worse when you knew your murderers were unlikely to be brought to justice. Unfortunately, she had to admit that Peter and Lynn were correct in their assessment. If she and Steve died inside the Crystal Mine, it could be another hundred years before their bodies were discovered. Maybe another thousand. They would end up in some thirtieth-century natural history museum as examples of the primitive body type of Early Man.

She swiveled around to stare at the back of Lynn's head. The woman still wore the concealing ski mask, in spite of the warmth blasting out from the powerful truck heater. "Who are you, Lynn?" she asked. "Why is it so important to you to keep your identity secret, even though Steve and I are going to be killed? Why don't you let us see your face? We'll never be able to tell anyone what we've seen."

Lynn gazed straight ahead. Only the tightening of her gloved hands on the steering wheel betrayed the fact that she had heard the question. "Ronald Deane never acknowledged my existence while he was alive," she said at last. "Even after his wife died, he never attempted to make amends. He never saw me socially, never introduced me to his precious daughters. So now his precious daughters will die without knowing who I am. That's justice, Abigail Deane. Finally justice for me and my baby."

Lynn's words fell like stones into Abby's heart. *His precious daughters.* "Daughters" in the plural. Somehow Abby had known all along that the killing wasn't going to stop with herself. She had been the most threatening of the Deane sisters, because she kept the family records. Though Peter's motive for murder might be straightforward fear of discovery, Lynn's was much more complex. She didn't only fear discovery. She wallowed in hate. Hate that had been thirty-five years in the growing. With a sinking feeling in her stomach, Abby accepted the fact that unless she and Steve could stop Lynn's fanatic killing spree, Kate and Linsey were going to be in deadly danger.

Abby wanted to scream with frustration. Rage boiled inside her. And—horribly—mixed in with the rage, pity for Lynn still lingered. Abby had always considered her father a kind and honorable man. But from the seeds he had so carelessly sowed in Korea, his surviving children were now reaping a bitter, poisonous whirlwind. Abby sadly acknowledged that her admiration for Ronald Deane had fallen victim to Lynn's lethal bitterness. She would always love his memory and cherish the happy, carefree childhood he had given her. But from her perspective as an adult woman, Abby couldn't help thinking that her happy childhood had been bought at a terrible price.

The truck drew to a bumpy halt. "Time to get out," Peter chirruped. "Let's take this real slow and easy, shall we? I'm sure neither of you wants a bullet in your spine to spoil your last few minutes on earth."

Lynn got out of the truck and came around to the rear, flinging open the double doors. "I'm considered an expert marksman," she murmured, leaning forward, gun in her left hand, while she used her right hand to unlock the cuffs chaining Abby to the truck. "Don't try to jump me."

She straightened and ordered Abby out of the truck. As soon as Abby's feet touched the ground, Lynn clasped an arm around Abby's neck and stuck the gun to her head. She cocked the trigger. The small sound reverberated explosively in the isolation of the mountains.

"You can unlock lover boy's wrists now," she said to Peter. "I don't think he's going to try anything brave and daring, while I'm holding Abigail like this."

Steve slid out of the truck and scrambled to his feet. He gave a quick glance around and immediately stood still. Abby wasn't surprised. One quick glance was all that was needed for anybody to see quite clearly that escape was impossible; Lynn and Peter had stationed themselves for maximum control. Lynn had her gun to Abby's head, and Peter stood five feet from Steven, too close to miss, too far away for Steve to knock the gun from Peter's grasp, even with a well-aimed kick.

"Walk," Lynn commanded. "Into the mine."

"You can walk in of your own free will, or you can resist and we'll put a bullet in each of you," Peter said. He sounded cheery enough to have been inviting them to a birthday party.

The threads of Abby's earlier hope, threads that had been temporarily severed when she lost consciousness in the van, began to knit together again. Lynn and Peter had assumed that the chain link gate across the front entrance was the only possible way in or out of the mine.

Abby's frustration gave way to an all-consuming fear. Her biggest worry now was that Steve would adopt some desperate, self-sacrificing tactic that would fail—and leave the pair of them inside the mine, wounded or even dead. At this moment their very best bet was to pretend submission and terror. But how in the world was she going to convey to Steve the message that heroics were dangerous and unnecessary? Could eyes really speak volumes to the one you loved?

She turned to him, trying by her body language to convey a warning. "We'll walk. We won't resist," she said, letting her breath catch on a smothered sob, strictly for the benefit of Lynn and Peter. She tried to give subtle emphasis to the word *we*.

"Wh-what's going to happen to us? You aren't going to leave us to starve in the mine, are you?" she asked, feigning terror.

"I wish we could." Lynn's gun prodded Abby forward. From the corner of her eye, she saw Steve start to move in the same direction. His footsteps weren't eager, but at least he wasn't offering overt resistance.

Abby let out a full-scale sob. "Don't leave us to starve," she pleaded. "I couldn't bear that. Alone in the dark...I'm *terrified* of the dark." She hoped Steve would remember from countless climbing expeditions that she wasn't in the least worried by darkness.

"We're not leaving you to starve," Lynn said with obvious regret. "We have to take care of killing you tonight."

"Let's tell them what we're going to do," Peter said excitedly. "Please, Lynn, I want them to know. I got the dynamite," he added petulantly. "It's my right to tell them."

"If you must."

"We're going to blow you up." Peter sounded as excited as a kid on the Fourth of July with a bumper supply of rockets. "We've found a fault line in the rock opposite the mouth of the mine, and we're going to create a major rock slide. Kaboom! The mine will be buried forever. You probably won't suffer at all. The inside of the mine is so old that the structure will never withstand the force of the slide. We estimate the interior will collapse thirty seconds or so after the slide hits."

She and Steve would be trapped in a collapsed mine tunnel, but not necessarily dead. *Kaboom* summed up the situation pretty accurately, Abby thought wryly. She gulped. Being buried alive didn't sound all that much more attractive than starving to death. By the time they arrived at the entrance to the mine, her teeth were chattering noisily, not only from the biting cold. Dear God, suppose her memory of the map was incorrect? Or what if she and Steve couldn't make the climb?

The sturdy chain link gate that Abby herself had ordered two months earlier to keep out curiosity hunters and thrill seekers gleamed silver in the beam of the powerful kerosene lantern that Lynn had placed on the roof of the truck. Abby had searched Denver to make sure that she bought the best, and the gate looked ominously solid. An impenetrable barrier to prevent their escape, bought and paid for by the victim. Somehow Abby couldn't quite appreciate the subtle irony of the situation.

"H-how will you get us inside? The gate's padlocked." The closer she got to the mine, the less sure she became that her escape plan would work. The quaver in her voice was all too genuine. How long would it take Peter and Lynn to plant a few sticks of dynamite? Not very long, even if they exercised proper care. Probably not as long as she and Steve would need.

"Getting you in is simple." Lynn dragged Abby up close to the gate, leaned around her body, aimed her gun and fired twice. The huge padlock shattered, swinging uselessly at the end of its chain.

"And in case you get any bright ideas, I have the replacement right here in my pocket." Peter held up a lock and chain, jangling them to show their weight and strength. "Now, my dear captives, into the mine with you. Abigail, you get over here by lover boy. Lynn, honey will you do the honors?"

Lynn swung open the heavy iron gate, while Peter kept Steve and Abby immobilised at gunpoint. The gate opened inward from the center, and latched onto a steel hook thoughtfully provided by the installers. *When you supervise a job, you sure take care that it's done right,* Abby reflected despairingly. *Every convenience to assist your murderers.*

"Bring them in!" Lynn called, straightening from her task.

"You heard the lady." Peter aimed his gun, and with lightning speed fired off a shot. The bullet exploded into the ground about two inches from Steve's heel. Unable to prevent the reaction, Abby smothered a scream with her hand.

Peter smiled and stroked his gun. "Yes, sir. I guess when you grow up poor enough to have to shoot your dinner, you never quite lose the touch. What do you think, Steven, old buddy?"

Steve stared stonily ahead, and Peter's eyes narrowed in anger. He struck out at Steve's head with the butt of his gun. "Move, you arrogant fool!"

Steve started to walk forward, and with an inner sigh of relief Abby followed suit. A few feet ahead of her, Steve stumbled on the rocky path, toppling so clumsily that he had to touch the ground in order to right himself.

Abby was beside him in an instant, pretending to help. "Don't resist," she hissed urgently. "Cooperate."

There was no time to say more. No time to explain that she wasn't giving up, merely preserving their strength for the final battle. Peter dragged Steve to his feet. Abby could only hope that Steve knew her well enough to realize that she would never ask him to cooperate with their killers unless she was working on an escape plan. She and Steve had been friends for years, but she hadn't really seen him for the man he was until a few days ago. Was she being unreasonable to hope that Steve was more perceptive? That he knew and understood the real Abigail Deane?

Steve didn't glance in her direction, didn't indicate by so much as the twitch of an eyebrow that he'd heard her whispered command, but a few feet further on, she saw his fist unclench. The rock he had picked up when he supposedly stumbled rolled quietly to the ground.

Thank you, God! Abby breathed. Steve had understood.

The interior of the mine was pitch-black, black with an intensity that seemed not just an absence of light, but an actual presence of darkness. Lynn and Peter switched on the flashlights they carried strapped to their waists, but the beams did no more than cast a feeble gray glow over the dank, dusty interior of the mine.

"This is it, boys and girls. Have a lovely death!" Gun steady, Peter backed toward the entrance of the mine. When he reached the gate, he unhooked it, holding it open just far enough for his fellow murderer to pass through. "Ready to start planting dynamite whenever you are, Lynn, honey!"

Lynn gave one final, scornful look at Abby and Steve, huddled together in the middle of the cave that formed the entrance to Crystal Mine.

"Don't try to follow me out," she said coldly. "I would take real pleasure in shooting you somewhere excruciatingly painful. In fact, maybe I could take out your kneecaps...."

Abby held her breath, sure that her heart had stopped beating until the husky voice spoke again. "No, I guess I can't risk the bullets. There's always the faint possibility that somebody may discover your bodies in the next couple of years or so." Her teeth gleamed in a brief smile behind the mask. "Thank your lucky stars that I'm such a cautious killer. I really would have liked to see you suffer a bit more."

The flickering beam of the flashlight retreated toward Peter and the gate. Abby heard the rip of tape leaving skin as Steve tore off his gag. Lynn called out her final fare-well.

"Goodbye, Abigail Deane. May you and your no-good father rot in hell. I'll send your sisters to join you as soon as I can."

The gate clanged shut. Darkness descended, a totally enveloping shroud.

Steve spoke, his voice warm with rueful laughter. And love. How in the world had she ever missed the love? "Abby, my sweet, I sure as hell hope you have a wonderful plan for getting us out of here."

Abby discovered she was shaking. She curled her fingers tightly within Steve's grasp, needing the reassurance of his touch.

"I finally recognized Lynn Renquist's voice," she said. Her words sounded hollow. From shock? From the acoustics of the cave? Abby wasn't sure. She leaned closer to Steve, seeking the solid strength of his muscled body.

He wrapped his arms tightly around her, offering comfort and support. "Who is it?" he asked softly. "Not Linda Mendoza. The body shape is all wrong."

"No, not Linda. It's Gwen Johnson. My God, all this time, all this killing, it's been Gwen Johnson."

Her words echoed around the cave, dying away on a final eerie whisper. *It's been Gwen Johnson.*

Chapter Fifteen

"Gwen Johnson," Steve repeated slowly. "Full name Gwendolynn. Nickname Lynn." He let the idea sink in for a few seconds, then said, "She doesn't look much like her pictures from Korea, does she?"

"Her hairstyle's completely different, and her face has aged, of course. But she still has the same thin, angular sort of body. She's tall for a woman, at least five foot nine. And in those photos we found, if you remember, Lynn was almost the same height as Keith Bovery."

"Poor Keith," Steve said. "Who of course didn't embezzle any money from the bank."

"You think Gwen Johnson is the embezzler, too?"

"I'm sure of it. She's our gal, and she set me up perfectly. I thought I was so clever not believing that obvious trail leading to Howard Taylor. But she was ahead of me every step of the way. She never expected me to accept Howard as the embezzler. She was setting up Keith Bovery all along."

"For revenge," Abby said. "I'm sure that was her form of revenge, because Keith didn't marry her when they got home from Korea."

"I should have suspected her," Steve muttered. "Good grief, she's the VP of customer service. Nobody would know better than Gwen Johnson which accounts were safe to tamper with.''

"And if anybody did discover money missing from their account, they'd probably end up being seen by Gwen. Who would apologize profusely and immediately put things right, so that the chain of discovery always stopped with her.''

"Brisk, efficient, no-nonsense Ms. Johnson. Robbing the bank blind for the last year at least.''

Abby shivered in the darkness. "Why did she do it, Steve? After thirty-five years, and with a successful life behind her, why did she suddenly allow old wounds to open and start bleeding? Why does she need to kill me and my sisters now, when she doesn't seem to have given us a moment's thought in the past thirty years?''

"Sweetheart, much as I would love to stand here, cuddling you and psychoanalyzing Gwen Johnson, I feel obliged to remind you that Peter and Gwen are out there on the mountain, busily planting a crop of dynamite. Which they will ignite at any moment. Could we get the hell out of here first and psychoanalyze later?'' He kissed her swiftly. "Much later, after we've taken care of the cuddling.''

"You seem darn sure that I have an escape plan.''

"As soon as you hissed that warning at me, I realized that the Abigail Deane I know and love couldn't possibly own an old gold mine without having at least a dozen comprehensive maps of the interior filed away in her records. You're about to tell me that we simply need to take three brisk turns to the left, and we'll come out at the rear exit.''

Abby laughed softly, although the situation wasn't nearly as simple as Steve suggested. Within the circle of his arms, however, life seemed very precious and the possibility of death impossibly remote. "It isn't quite that easy," she said.

He sighed. "Now why doesn't that surprise me?" he murmured. "Tell me the worst."

"There's no rear exit. The tunnels leading out from this main entrance chamber all burrow directly downward. But there are a couple of sinkholes, and one's quite close. First tunnel on the left, only about twenty feet along, if my memory serves me correctly."

Steve's body tensed, and he cleared his throat. "Abby, my sweet, it's not that I want to complain about your great escape plan, and I'm sure you have the map of the mine memorized perfectly. But has it crossed your mind that sinkholes tend to be vertical shafts? As in straight up and down, with no hand- or footholds?"

"We're expert climbers," Abby suggested meekly.

"There's expert and expert," Steve said darkly. "My sweet, climbing out of a sinkhole is what might euphemistically be called *challenging*—translation: death-defying—even with lots of light and top-notch equipment. And we don't even have a rope."

"I hoped you might still have the flashlight from the cabin," Abby said meekly.

"I do. Peter never bothered to search me. He was feeling much too pleased with himself." Steve reached under his sweater and produced the miniature light. In grim silence he flipped it on. The high-intensity beam, which had seemed so powerful in the confined space of the cabin's utility closet, illuminated a circle no more than four feet in diameter. Without comment, Steve switched off the light to preserve its batteries and replaced it in his pocket.

"I never claimed it would be easy," Abby said. "But we're both expert rock climbers."

A muffled boom echoed through the chamber, dislodging small pieces of rock and shale that clattered to the ground in a noisy shower of dust and debris.

"I think they just set off their test explosion," Abby commented in a small voice.

"Right." Steve carried her hands to his face and kissed each palm swiftly. "I'll tell you what, kiddo, that sinkhole is sounding better by the second. Who needs ropes and pitons? Hell, they're just for sissies."

Abby did her best to think macho, although her stomach felt decidedly sissy. "The entrance to this chamber faces due west, which should help to orient us," she said, pleased by her matter-of-fact tone.

They squinted toward the entrance, which was distinguishable more by a slight absence of darkness than by any real presence of light. The chain link gate was a ghostly gray glow in the surrounding blackness.

"Okay, not too difficult," Steve said. "We need to walk straight back from the entrance and take the first left-hand tunnel. Right?"

"Right."

Steve switched on the flashlight and directed its beam carefully toward the rear of the cave. The chamber in which they stood, Abby knew, had been cleaned so thoroughly after the Confederate gold was stolen by Douglas Brady that no obvious debris remained. There were no old wagon wheels or discarded tools to impede their progress into the tunnels radiating from the far side of the chamber. The natural unevenness of the ground would be their biggest hurdle.

As far as keeping their sense of direction was concerned, the task would be fairly simple. The faint light at the entrance would provide a consistent point of orientation. Finding the tunnel itself would be no more than a question of trailing along the left-hand side wall of the cave until they came to the gap that would indicate the start of the mining tunnel.

Steve took her hand, and they walked over to the left-hand side of the chamber. "Let's go, kiddo." He rubbed his stubbled face against her cheek. "Here's to great escapes and growing old together."

The walls ran with moisture, and although Abby wasn't scared of the darkness, she had a hearty dislike of creepy-crawlies, not to mention an even stronger dislike of bats, rats and miscellaneous reptiles likely to go slithering away into the night. She licked her suddenly dry lips.

"Do you think there are snakes in here?" she asked, trying to sound casual.

"No snakes," he said. "Too dark, too cold, and nothing for them to eat."

"Maybe they go outside to eat. Snakes only need a mouse every month or so to be in peak condition." She jerked her hand away from the wall. "Oh, my God, what's that? I've been bitten!"

Steve swiftly turned on the flashlight, and Abby stared in silent embarrassment at the fragile skeleton of a dead bat, which clearly hadn't bitten anything in several years.

"Well, it felt like it had bitten me," she murmured.

Steve squeezed her hand and tactfully directed the beam of the flashlight ahead. "Looks like the tunnel's only about six feet farther on," he said, dousing the light once more. "I'm sorry, kiddo, but we need to keep touching the wall, because in this degree of darkness we could get disoriented inside about ten seconds flat."

Abby had thought darkness couldn't possibly become more intense than what they had experienced in the entrance chamber of the mine. Once they turned into the tunnel, however, she realized how great had been the psychological effect of the pale moonlight glimmering around the entrance. No wonder primitive cave dwellers had worshiped fire and the sun as gods, she thought. Anything that dispelled this stygian gloom would seem miraculous.

"I'll have to switch on the flashlight," Steve said, after they had groped their way a couple of yards into the tunnel. "We'll have to risk the batteries. We don't have time to find our way by touch."

Abby was only too happy to agree. The tunnel bore consistently left and downward, but the rock-strewn floor was quite easy to navigate with the help of the flashlight, and they took less than five minutes to round the final curve in the tunnel and confront the sinkhole.

"Great map reading, kiddo!" Steve circled the light over the sides of the sinkhole, finally pointing straight up. "We're in luck," he said, his cool tone contrasting with his words. "Look, the top of the hole is open. We can see the sky."

"That is lucky," Abby agreed. With many sinkholes, nature quickly took over and spread a thick layer of grass and lichen over the opening. Without a knife, she and Steve could have found it extremely difficult to break through a "lid" of grass. She kept her gaze trained studiously upward. "And I guess it's not more than fifteen feet to the top. That's less than I expected."

"Yes." Steve finally lowered the beam of the flashlight and allowed it to play one more time over the bottom reaches of the sinkhole. The light bounced off smooth rock that was dampened by trickles of running water.

He and Abby stared at each other in a weighted silence. With special equipment the climb was feasible, relatively easy for climbers of their skill. With plenty of light and hours of time to search out minuscule hand- and footholds, the climb might even be feasible without special equipment. Unfortunately they had neither time nor equipment, and their light was grossly inadequate.

It was Abby who found her voice first. "You win a gold star when you get to the top, Kramer."

Steve turned around and tucked the flashlight into his belt. He cupped her face in his hands and gazed down at her. Abby knew she must appear filthy and dust-streaked. Steve stared at her as if he had never in his life seen any woman as beautiful. Then he smiled. "I'd rather win you," he said simply.

Her lips parted into an answering smile as her body leaned into his in an instinctive movement of response. Steve closed the tiny gap between them, his mouth hot and seeking as he touched her lips. His kiss burned with all the passion that there was no time to express. Her body ached with love.

They drew apart without speaking again, since there was nothing either of them needed to say. They were both experienced climbers. They had both seen at a single glance that the sides of the sinkhole were appallingly smooth. If they made it to the top, this would be the climb of their lives.

Steve spotted a small piece of rotted wooden support beam that had collapsed into the tunnel, and dragged it over to the foot of the sinkhole, thus providing them with a stepping-stone about two feet high. Two feet might not seem like much, but on this climb, every inch saved would be a help.

Abby debated whether or not to discard her tight linen skirt. In the end she decided that its warmth, once she reached the top, was well worth the inconvenience of climbing with it hitched up around her waist. In this re-gard Steve was far better off, since he was wearing comfortable slacks, whereas she was still dressed in the same clothes she'd worn to the office two days earlier. Thank heaven she'd found sneakers in the cabin! In her high-heeled patent leather pumps the climb would have been literally impossible.

"How are we doing on time?" she asked, tucking her skirt and underslip into her panties.

"Fine," he said, stepping onto the wooden beam and getting ready to swing into his first hold. The careful neutrality of his reply warned her that in reality, time was slipping by much too fast.

Toes still perched on the step and clinging to the sides of the sinkhole with his other hand, he half twisted toward her, holding out the flashlight. "You'd better take this," he said. "I'll scout up a couple of feet and see which is the best route to take."

A second before she stepped forward to take the flashlight, the muffled boom of a massive explosion reverberated inside the tunnel. The ground rocked beneath her feet; the movement feeling twice as frightening in the pitch blackness. Then a rumble from deep inside the tunnel warned her that some of the rotted support beams were too fragile to support the weight of the tunnel's roof. Her instincts all screamed at her to run, but since she was blinded by the dark, there was no direction more logical to run toward than any other. She had no choice but to stand frozen in the middle of the tunnel, straining her ears to detect the sounds of falling rocks and timber.

The explosion, like passing thunder, gradually rumbled into silence. "Steve, are you okay?" she called, groping toward the sinkhole. She stumbled over an obstacle that hadn't been there five minutes earlier, sending pain shooting along her toes. "Steve, switch on the flashlight! I think a couple of beams have collapsed."

"In—a—minute."

His words were so clipped that she was instantly fearful. "Steve, were you hit?"

She heard the sound of a light, sure-footed jump, which reassured her considerably. The beam of the flashlight pierced the inky blackness, revealing a tunnel blocked by shattered beams and crumbling lumps of rock and earth. Steve leaned against the side of the tunnel, dusting assorted debris from his hair and shirt.

"My God, you were hit!"

"Nothing to waste time worrying about. I was scared stiff of dropping the flashlight, though."

He directed the flashlight beam upward. "Sinkhole looks just the same as it did before. At least the top didn't get covered by a falling boulder."

His voice sounded—off-key, Abby decided. She walked over to him. "Steve, are you sure you're all right?"

He grinned. "All present and correct, ma'am." He raised one hand in mock salute. "Abby, we don't have time to talk. We can't count on that one explosion being their last effort. The next one could collapse the tunnel system." He tucked the flashlight into his belt. "Help me move this beam, will you? Look, I think we can wedge it next to the other one at the base of the sinkhole and give ourselves almost a five-foot leg up on the climb."

She hefted one end of the beam and they carried it across to the sinkhole. Steve stumbled as they bent down to wedge the beam in place.

"Sorry," he grunted. "Rock on the ground. I wasn't paying attention."

Was it her imagination, or did his face look ghastly pale in the flickering light? She clambered across the beam toward him. "Steve—"

"Start climbing," he said sharply. "Abby, for God's sake, we can't hang around."

"I thought you were going first."

"I . . . changed my mind. Better if I come behind and direct the light for both of us. Besides, if you miss your footing, I'm strong enough to catch you."

"Okay, Mr. Macho." She kissed her grimy fingertips and pressed the kiss against his mouth. "Make damn sure you get to the top, Steven Kramer, because I'm planning to marry you as soon as we get back to Denver."

"Good grief, what a dilemma," he muttered. "A lifetime with Abigail Deane or death in a discarded mine tunnel. Damned if I know which one to choose."

She was smiling as she swung around to face the sheer rock face and take the first step of her climb. *We have to get out of here safely,* she thought, *just so that I can say thank-you for all the hours of laughter Steve's brought into my life.*

In fact, the first few feet of the climb were the worst. About halfway up the shaft, the rock surface became much rougher, with ledges five and six inches wide to serve as resting places. Abby soon realized that the biting cold was going to be her worst enemy. The closer she got to the top of the shaft, the colder the air became. Her hands and feet first grew stiff, then numb, making the chance of a slip that much greater. At least the numbness prevented her feeling the blood that was no doubt seeping from her bruised and battered toes into her sneakers, she reflected.

She slowed her pace a little—and realized that Steve was less than halfway up the shaft. The light she'd been utilizing had come from the moon and the stars, not from Steve's flashlight. Cautiously she turned around.

"Steve?" she called.

"Get—the—hell—out—of—this—shaft."

"You're hurt. Dear God, you were hit by that falling beam!"

"Get—the—hell—out—of—here."

Fear added wings to her feet as she scrambled up the last three or four feet. Scarcely noticing the frozen crystals of snow riming the grass, she lay flat on her stomach and stared down into the darkness she had just left. Steve, she saw, with a shudder of stark horror, was using only one arm to climb. His left shoulder was hunched at an awkward angle, and his left hand dangled uselessly at his side. So much for wanting to catch her if she fell! The idiotic bozo had chosen to climb second because he was afraid of slipping and knocking her from her perch!

"Can you hear me down there, Steve Kramer?" She leaned over the hole and yelled. "You'd better make it to the top, or I'm going to . . ." *Die of a broken heart?* Abby gulped down a sob. "I'm going to sue you for breach of promise!"

No reply. Just the grim echo of his panting breath, and the thunk of his foot successfully finding a new ledge to rest on.

"You only have five more feet to go. You can make it." She prayed that she was speaking the truth. Wedging her feet behind a boulder, she stretched both her hands down into the shaft and grabbed his good arm. "Hold on to me. I'll help pull you upward."

Together they struggled to lever his body up the last couple of feet and out onto the grass. Steve smiled at her weakly. "Gosh, lady, you sure are anxious to catch your man."

He keeled over in a dead faint at her feet.

Chapter Sixteen

The entire left side of Steve's upper body was puffy and swollen. Terrifying blue lines of contusion ran along the veins and were already darkening into a massive, body-sized bruise. A falling beam had obviously broken his collarbone, Abby decided, if not his entire shoulder, and the climb had made the gruesome injury a hundred times worse.

Abby wondered how many more disasters could befall Steve and herself before they finally gave up and acknowledged defeat. Against all odds they had escaped from the mine, but how in the world were they going to travel fifteen miles across mountain trails to Crystal Lakes, the nearest town? Given the freezing temperatures and their fatigue, the hike would have been difficult in any event, but with Steve barely able to stand, and no access to even the most primitive first-aid supplies, the fifteen miles might as well have been a thousand.

Ripping off her skirt and wrapping it around Steve's head in an effort to prevent further heat loss, Abby tried to visualize every map she had ever seen of the area surrounding Crystal Mine. She mentally drove up the gravel road from Crystal Lakes and over Cottonwood Pass, then followed the dirt trail around the meandering curves of the creek to the small lake, set among blue spruce and tall ponderosa pines, which lay just east of the mine. Unfortunately no human habitation sprang to mind. And the phone company, with a deplorable lack of foresight, had seen no reason to install phone booths in this pristine stretch of wilderness.

But there are cabins at the foot of Cottonwood Pass, Abby thought, sighing with relief as her mental image of the countryside came into sharper focus. And thanks to the clear sky and bright moon, she and Steve could realistically hope to follow the creek to the pass and reach the cabins in an hour. Always provided, of course, that he could remain conscious long enough to complete the walk.

Steve could do it, she told herself. Any man stubborn enough to climb out of a vertical sinkhole with a broken shoulder could certainly manage to stumble over a few rough miles to the warmth and safety of the cabins.

Now all she needed was to find shelter somewhere that was dry and out of the wind and to watch over Steve until he regained consciousness. And in fact, finding temporary shelter might not be too much of a problem. Gwen and Peter, in setting off their murderous avalanche, had conveniently provided all the dry rocks she would need to construct a windbreak.

Steve's eyes flickered open. Contorting his face, he immediately levered himself onto his right elbow. His good hand went to his head, and when he felt the skirt, his mouth sketched an attempt at a smile.

"Stamping me with your brand of possession, huh?" He unwound the skirt and held it out to Abby. "Thanks for the loan, kiddo."

"Steve, you need to keep warm—"

"Put it on, sweetheart, and please don't argue. I'm too weak to argue back."

Complying seemed less threatening to Steve's health than continuing the discussion. Abby stepped into the wreckage of her skirt and tugged up the zipper, a somewhat wasted gesture, she realized, since the side seam had been ripped open almost to the waist.

Steve tried to produce another smile and almost succeeded. "An interesting fashion statement, kiddo. If you would give me a hand up, we can start walking to the nearest phone. I won't slow you down, I promise."

"Maybe we should rest another few minutes." It was a relief that Steve had come out of his faint so swiftly, but Abby was secretly horrified by the pallor of his face and the clammy sweat beading his forehead. She could think of only a couple of reasons why he might be sweating when the temperature was well below freezing, and she didn't like either of them.

Steve dragged himself onto one knee. "Sweetheart, lying around on snowy grass isn't going to make me feel one bit better." He put his hand into hers and staggered to his feet, swallowing a grunt of pain so fast that Abby almost didn't hear it.

"Where are we headed?" he asked, when he managed to catch his breath again. "Cottonwood Pass?"

"I thought that seemed our best bet," Abby agreed. "We need to cross over the trail and meet up with the creek that leads to Cottonwood Pass. The first few hundred yards will be the most difficult part of the hike. We'll have to clamber up to the top of a pretty steep bank opposite the mine, and there's almost certain to be a lot of loose shale from the explosion Gwen and Peter set off. Think you can make it?"

"Easy as falling off a log," he said lightly.

One glance at the rigid line of his mouth was enough to convince Abby that any more discussion was useless. Steve was not going to admit that every step he took was an excruciating exercise in willpower. He would keep going at full speed until he keeled over again. Besides, in her heart of hearts, she knew Steve was right to insist on standing up and moving about. He could either walk out of here with her or stay alone on the mountainside. And they both knew that if he waited, he courted almost certain death from exposure.

The sinkhole emerged about two hundred yards southeast of the mine entrance, they discovered, but at a considerably lower level, since the old tunnel had followed the downward slope of the land. Conserving their strength, neither Steve nor Abby spoke as they trudged up the rocky incline and around the northern side of the mine back toward the entrance.

They rounded the final bend and came out onto the dusty dirt road that fronted the mine entrance. They both saw the paneled truck at the same moment, parked directly in front of them, the kerosene lamp still burning from its perch on the hood.

Abby gasped and instinctively flung herself back against the rocky exterior of the mine. "Good grief, they're still here!"

Steve crouched next to her, putting a finger against his lips to warn her to keep her voice down. "Gwen's up there," he said softly, nodding toward the crest of the small hill directly opposite the mine. "Looks as if she's planting more dynamite."

Abby followed the direction of Steve's pointing finger and saw the black-clad figure squat, apparently digging. Digging, moreover, in the middle of the route she and Steve needed to take in order to reach Cottonwood Pass.

Why hadn't Gwen and Peter gone back to Denver? Abby glanced to her left. A hollow in the hillside indicated that the main chamber of the mine had partially collapsed, but the mine entrance itself was not completely blocked by shale and boulders. In fact, the top half of the chain link gate was still clearly visible. Either Gwen and Peter hadn't created a big enough explosion the first time, or they had miscalculated the angle of the slide. From the huge piles of rock she saw lying south of the mine entrance, Abby guessed the latter. She had no doubt that the miscalculation had saved both Steve's and her own life.

"They didn't manage to seal the entrance with the first explosion," she murmured. "No wonder the tunnel we were in didn't collapse. They had their stress lines calculated wrongly." She scanned the hillside. "Where's Peter?"

"I don't see him." Steve lowered his voice another notch. "Maybe he's inside the truck."

Abby's heart thumped hard against her ribs. If Peter was in the truck, she and Steve were standing in a highly exposed position. A glance out of the truck window would be enough to reveal their presence. On the other hand, if she and Steve could somehow overpower Peter, they could steal the truck and save themselves a long, chilly walk to a telephone.

"Do you think we could manage to take Peter by surprise?" she asked wistfully. "Knock him on the head or something? Right now, I'd love to be climbing behind the wheel of that nice warm truck."

Steve snorted. "Sorry, kiddo, I left my Superman cape down at the bottom of the sinkhole. Given that Peter and Gwen are both armed with loaded guns and dry dynamite, not to mention fully functioning shoulders, I vote we let them keep their truck."

"It's going to be so darn cold sitting on a rock, waiting for the pair of them to move out," Abby complained mournfully.

"Better cold than bullet-ridden." Steve started to move backward on soundless feet, hugging the dark shadows of the mine's exterior overhang. "Come on, Abby, you can play the heroine another day."

Abby gave the truck a final, regretful look as she turned to follow Steve. At that very instant, she heard the sound of someone jumping out of the back of the truck. She squeezed deep into the shadows, watching as Peter, arms loaded with sticks of dynamite, started the long trudge up the hill to join Gwen. After a few seconds, he passed out of Abby's line of sight, but she stayed absolutely rigid until his footsteps faded completely into the distance.

"Steve!" Abby hissed his name, but he was too far away to hear and she didn't dare to raise her voice. Sound carried in both directions on the crystal clarity of the mountain air. The fact that Steve hadn't come back for her served to confirm Abby's suspicion that walking was such a tremendous effort for him that he simply had no energy to spare for keeping track of her precise whereabouts.

"Steve!" She risked saying his name a fraction louder. Still no reply. Abby stared at the unguarded truck, trying to calculate the degree of danger she would face in stealing it. If she knew for sure that the keys were in the ignition, the danger would be slight. The second she got behind the wheel, she could start driving, giving herself a tremendous advantage over Gwen and Peter who would be on foot, stuck halfway up a hill.

But since the engine wasn't running, she had no way of knowing for certain. There was at least a fifty-fifty chance that Gwen or Peter would have them in one of their pockets. And climbing into the truck without any certainty of being able to set it in motion would be an invitation to disaster.

With a weary sigh, Abby acknowledged that Steve was right. It was crazy of her to be standing here, working out ways to storm the truck. If she hadn't been so chilled and tired, not to mention worried about his broken shoulder, she would never have wasted valuable time on a project so unlikely to bring success.

Abby heard a tiny noise. She whirled around. Gwen stood not two feet away, gun aimed directly at Abby's heart. Dear heaven, when had Gwen come down from the hill? *How could I have been so careless?*

Gwen appeared almost as horrified as Abby. "You're supposed to be dead." She spoke the words in a guttural whisper. "My God, you're supposed to be dead! Dead with your father. Why do you keep coming back to haunt me?"

Abby was so furious with herself—and so frightened—that she almost missed the rising note of panic in Gwen's voice.

"I'm not easy to kill," she said, suddenly realizing that Gwen's panic represented her only hope of survival.

The gun wavered, then steadied in Gwen's hands. "Where's lover boy? The brave and noble Steven Kramer?"

"In the mine," Abby lied. "You killed him. You killed the man I loved and wanted to marry."

"I guess that's something to be thankful for," Gwen muttered. "What the hell am I going to do with you? How am I going to get you back inside the mine?" In a fit of clearly uncontrollable rage, she lashed out and struck Abby across the face. "I didn't want to use bullets!" she screamed. "Now I'll have to shoot you, and bullets can easily be traced."

"You didn't worry about bullets when you killed Howard Taylor and Douglas Brady."

"Oh, that." Gwen seemed to recover a measure of calm. "I stole Keith's .38 Webley a couple of years ago. I always knew if that gun was ever traced, it would only throw more suspicion on Keith." She prodded Abby toward the truck. "Get moving," she muttered. "It'll have to be a rifle shot. Peter has a rifle in the truck. That's almost impossible to trace."

"But even if you shoot me, you won't be able to get me back inside the mine," Abby pointed out. "What are you going to do with my body?"

Steve, she prayed silently. *If telepathy works, this would be a great moment to prove it. Please come dashing to the rescue. Anytime now would be ideal.*

"If you just toss me into a ravine, you know some hiker's going to find me," Abby persisted. "That's what this whole elaborate setup with the rock slides was all about, remember? You didn't want anyone to find my body."

Gwen hesitated, and for a moment her eyes darted distractedly back and forth. Abby stood poised on her toes, ready to spring for the gun, but before she could launch herself forward, Gwen's attention steadied, and her hands firmed once again around the revolver.

"I'll have to kill you right in front of the entrance to the mine," Gwen said, her voice appallingly matter-of-fact. "Peter's getting ready to detonate such a huge explosion that no one will ever find you. It's true your body will be outside the mine, but it will be deeply buried, and I'll be quite safe from discovery, Abigail. You needn't worry."

"Actually I was more worried about myself."

Abby's sarcasm was entirely lost on Gwen, who stepped forward abruptly, jerking Abby away from the truck. "I've decided not to bother with the rifle. Too difficult to get it from the crate without you jumping me."

Abby's disappointment must have shown fleetingly in her face.

"Aha, Abigail," Gwen cackled. "I'm not as silly as you think. I know you're planning to take this gun from me the minute I come too close. But I'm too smart for that. We're old friends, this gun and I. Smith and Wesson at their very best."

Gwen jerked her head toward the mine. "I want you to walk straight to the mine entrance, Abigail. Peter's anxious to set off the explosion, so that the two of us can get back to Denver at a reasonable hour, and I don't want to keep him waiting. All this nighttime activity is exhausting, you know. Peter and I both have demanding jobs to get to in the morning."

"Especially you, Ms. Johnson, isn't that right? And you always pride yourself on your punctuality at the bank, don't you? I'm sure you wouldn't want to tarnish your sterling reputation for the sake of a little chore like murder."

Abby could feel the ensuing silence as an almost physical presence. "So you know who I am," Gwen Johnson said at last. "Perhaps it's better this way. You'll go to your death with my name on your lips and in your heart. That's good. And I'm perfectly safe, since dead women can't talk, except to other dead people."

"You'll be caught eventually, Gwen. Crazy people like you always are."

Gwen chuckled. "What was that meant to provoke, Abigail? A storm of argument from me, protesting that I'm not crazy? I'm much too sane to waste time arguing with you. All I have to decide right now is where I should shoot you first. Before I blow your brains out. Your stomach, maybe? Your kneecaps? The North Koreans used to favor the groin, but then men have such a hangup about the groin, don't they? I'm sure you've noticed that, Abigail."

Abby shuddered, as much at the undiluted hatred of Gwen's attitude as at the actual threat of death and torture. "Why, Gwen? Why are you doing this? I know my father treated you badly—"

"Treated me badly!" Gwen's entire body vibrated with the intensity of her scorn. "The English language doesn't have words to describe the way that man mistreated me. He sweet-talked his way into my bed without ever telling me he was married. And when I told him I was pregnant, he said 'You're a nurse, Lynn, sweetie. You ought to know how to take care of the situation.'"

Abby felt sick, mainly because Gwen's angry words carried the bitter ring of truth. But she had to keep asking questions, both because she desperately needed to know the answers, and also because Gwen forgot to propel her toward the mine entrance when she was talking.

"I understand why you feel so bitter," Abby said. "But I don't understand why you're taking your revenge now. Why not thirty-five years ago, when all this first happened?"

Gwen didn't answer for a moment, then she slowly reached up and pulled off her ski mask, shaking out the soft curls of hair that had become flattened against her head.

"Thirty-five years ago I was young and pretty and I still had hope," she said. "I married Ed Johnson, thinking maybe we could make a life together." She choked off a gasp of laughter. "I should have known better. Ed taught me everything about how rotten men are that your father and Keith Bovery didn't have time to show me. After Ed, I didn't bother with love anymore. I started buying the men I wanted. And you know what, Abigail? A woman can buy herself a damn sight better lover than she can ever earn by offering her heart.''

If she hadn't been so scared, Abby knew she would have been feeling pity again. ''You . . . pay Peter to be your lover?''

Gwen's mouth twisted in a sour smile. ''Why not? He's great to look at, terrific in bed, and he likes the good life as much as I do. Unfortunately, Peter is an expensive luxury. He knows he's a great sexual athlete, and he likes to be rewarded accordingly. I started stealing from the bank to support him, and one day I woke up to realize that I'd taken more than a half million dollars from First Denver.''

''It seems to me you should be mad at Peter Graymont, not at me or my family.''

''You still don't understand, do you? I loved your father, damn his soul. *I loved him*. For thirty years I worked here in Denver, hoping that he'd notice me. When your mother died I thought, *This is it. Now he'll turn to me*. He never did. And last year I learned he was planning to get married again. Not to me, mind you, but to some homespun *Hausfrau* he kept stashed away in the mountains.''

''Gwen, my father couldn't possibly have known you still cared about him—''

''He called and ask me to come and see him, you know.'' Gwen hardly seemed to have heard Abby's remark. ''When he was in the hospital. Said he wanted to tie up some of the loose ends in his life.'' She laughed, a painful hacking laugh that tore at Abby's gut. ''That's all I was to your father, Abigail. Me and my little baby. Two annoying loose ends that needed to be tied off before your father went to meet his Maker. He gave me the snapshots he'd taken of the Confederate gold wagon and the entrance to this mine. Said he was working on a treasure hunt for his girls, and wanted me to be the one to set the whole game in motion as soon as he died. Said he wanted to think of his 'sweet daughters' working on one last family game after he was gone." Gwen's voice hardened. "At least I made sure the games you all played were deadly."

"I'm sure my father didn't mean to offend y—"

Gwen interrupted. "You know what your dear old dad sent me after I'd visited him in the hospital?" she demanded. "He sent me a letter, thanking me for my trouble. And he enclosed a golden bracelet as a 'measure of his esteem.' A gold bracelet worth maybe five hundred dollars, and you girls were going to collect five million by the time the treasure hunt was over! How I *hated* your father and all you girls when I opened that package and saw his damn gold bracelet!"

Gwen had long since stopped pushing Abby toward the mine entrance. Her back was turned to the hillside where Peter was working, and both Gwen and Abby were obscured from Peter's line of sight by the pile of rubble created by the first landslide. Looking over Gwen's shoulder, Abby could see Peter rise to his feet, apparently satisfied with his final check on the positioning of the dynamite. Casually dusting off his pants, he retreated to the side of the hill, unrolling ignition cables as he walked. Abby glanced back at Gwen, who seemed to have forgotten all about Peter and the impending explosion.

Abby realized that in fact, Gwen was no longer entirely in control of herself. The years of resentment against all the men who had betrayed her had built into an explosive, mind-blowing state of anger, as she spewed forth her litany of hatred. The gun wobbled in her hands, but her eyes remained fixed on Abby, burning with the flaming residue of her hatred for Ronald Deane.

Abby cautiously moved back a step. Gwen didn't seem to notice. Abby glanced up at the hillside. Peter's tall, wiry body was silhouetted against the moonlit sky; like a scene from an old black and white movie. In a movie, the cavalry would be poised in the wings, ready to come riding to the rescue on galloping hooves. The hero would snatch the plunger from the villain's hands mere seconds before he set in motion his scheme to kill the innocent, virginal heroine.

But this, regrettably, wasn't the movies. Steve had probably passed out somewhere on the mountainside and was likely dying of his injuries. He needed Abby's help in order to survive. Small as her chances of success might be, Abby would have to rescue herself.

She risked a second backward step, and then another. Gwen continued to scream abuse, her eyes fixed on Abby in an unseeing glare. Abby suspected the woman's vision was filled with torrid, angry scenes from the long-ago past. The present, at this moment, had little reality for Gwen.

Up on the hill, Peter had stopped his walk about thirty yards away from the stash of dynamite. He flashed a powerful signal lamp in a series of light pulses. A warning, Abby realized, to alert Gwen to stand clear of the mine entrance. Would he come down the hill looking for Gwen, if she didn't answer the signal? If so, Abby had better make damn sure she seized control of Gwen's gun in the next few seconds.

A horn tooted inside the truck. Abby jumped in astonishment, watching in delight when Peter waved his hand in acknowledgment. Naturally he thought Gwen was inside the truck, since he had no idea that Abby and Steve weren't already lying dead—or at least gravely injured—inside the mine.

Still babbling, Gwen looked around dazedly, as if not quite sure what the sound of the horn could mean. She blinked. Belatedly she swung around to look up to the crest of the hillside—just in time to see Peter press the plunger that would set off the explosion.

Abby didn't wait to see Gwen's reaction. She ran as fast as her shaky legs would carry her toward the safety of the truck, where Steve must surely be sitting. Who else could have beeped the horn? Panting, expecting at any moment to feel the sting of Gwen's bullet in her back, she dragged open the truck door and tumbled inside.

Steve was sitting behind the wheel, holding a rifle.

"You are the most beautiful sight," Abby breathed. "When did you get here?"

He leaned across the stick shift and dropped a brief, hard kiss upon her mouth. "About two seconds before Peter flashed his warning light. I had my finger on the trigger, ready to fire at Gwen, when I saw his signal." Steve gave Abby another kiss. "Great to see you safe, kiddo. Be back soon...." He scrambled awkwardly out of the truck, his useless left arm pressed close to his body.

"Steve, where are you going?" Abby yelled, but her question was drowned in the sudden, earsplitting crash of tumbling rocks and rolling boulders. Something had gone wrong, Abby thought dazedly, staring out of the truck window. Peter couldn't have planned to set half a mountain in motion, which was what seemed to be happening. The entire front of the hill was peeling off and sliding down toward the mine entrance.

Gwen had, it seemed, finally realized the extent of her danger. She started to move, but instead of running toward the truck and safety, she spun on her heel and dashed toward the pile of rubble left by the last explosion. What was she planning to do? Abby wondered. Climb the rock pile? Was she rational enough at this point to be planning anything?

The thunderous avalanche of rock, uprooted bushes and soil tumbled down the hillside, slowly at first, then gathering speed as it traveled. Mesmerized, Abby watched as Gwen tried to scramble up the pile of rubble to safety. Halfway to the top, she lost her footing and slithered back down, landing in a crumpled heap on the rock-strewn ground. For a moment she lay still. Then, hunching onto her knees, Gwen struggled to her feet.

Abby's last sight of the woman who had tried so hard to kill her was that of a black figure, thin to the point of fragility, angry fists raised to the sky, mouth contorted into a scream of rage—of grief?—as the boiling river of rocks and dirt washed over her, enveloping her pain and hatred in a ten-foot shroud of crushed stone.

The night seemed peculiarly silent in the aftermath of the slide. Abby discovered that her cheeks were wet with tears—tears that wouldn't stop flowing. She scrubbed at her eyes with her knuckles, wondering whether she cried because her own life was saved, or because Gwen's life had been so spectacularly wasted. Perhaps, she decided, for both reasons.

A huge clod of earth bounced to the ground in front of the truck, and was followed by a hail of pebbles that struck the windshield in a shattering shower.

Hastily Abby slid behind the wheel. This was obviously not the ideal moment either for tears or for philosophical speculation. The keys, thank God, were in the ignition. She turned on the motor and reversed the truck away from the last rumbling remnants of the explosion. The silence closed in on her. Where was Peter? Much more to the point, where was Steve?

Galvanized into action by the realization that Steve had put himself in deadly danger by pursuing Peter, Abby got out of the truck and scanned what was left of the hillside. On its new, much lower crest, she spotted two figures, gray shadows against the night sky: Peter and Steve. Each held one arm clutched awkwardly against his body, but Steve, walking in the rear, still held the rifle.

Not quite able to believe this final miracle, Abby leaned against the truck, waiting for the two men to join her. Peter, dripping blood where Steve had shot his gun out of his hand, appeared dazed. His face was almost as white and dirt-streaked as Steve's.

"Tie him up, Abby," Steve said, his voice hoarse with weariness. "Let's shovel him into the truck and get the hell out of here."

Peter stood numb and unprotesting as Abby staunched the bleeding in his arm with the surgical tape left over from Steve's gag. She then finished off the reel of tape by strapping his arms to his body. Peter didn't attempt to escape. As he turned to climb into the truck, he gazed sadly at the stone hill he had created. The stone hill that now covered Gwen.

"I never meant to hurt her," he said, his voice dull, apathetic. "She was good to me. I didn't want to kill her."

Peter was feeling very sorry for himself, but Abby discovered that her sympathy level had reached its limit.

"No," she said bitingly. "You didn't mean to kill Gwen. She was your ticket to the good life. But you meant to kill Steve and me. And you didn't care how painfully we died. Get in the truck, Peter. You make me sick."

"You're wrong, Abigail. I didn't mean to kill anybody," Peter insisted. "I'm a believer in nonviolence."

"Right. You just locked me and Steve in the mine so that we could have a fun night climbing."

"All I wanted was to have a share in that Confederate gold. You didn't need the money, damn it. Your father left you rich, quite apart from that gold. When Douglas Brady double-crossed us, Gwen went a little crazy, and after that, everything kind of snowballed. She made me help her. She threatened me. I didn't want to do any of this."

"Sure, Peter. And if the jury believes your story, you shouldn't get a day over a hundred years. The way they calculate sentences these days, you'll be eligible for parole at least two weeks before you're eighty."

Steve slammed the doors of the truck. He walked around to the front and slumped into the passenger seat. "My shoulder," he said succinctly, "is killing me."

Abby leaned over and kissed him. He tasted of grit and sweat and smoke. He tasted *alive*. She wanted the kiss to last forever.

When they finally came up for air, the pain lines around Steve's mouth seemed less deeply etched. He pushed a strand of hair out of her eyes with gentle fingers. "A few more kisses like that, Abigail Deane, and you might discover how many unexpected things a one-armed man can accomplish."

"I can't wait to find out." Abby reversed the truck and pointed it in the direction of Crystal Lakes. Civilization lay ahead. Phones, doctors, food and hot steaming baths. Life suddenly seemed very good. She looked at Steve and smiled.

"As soon as you've seen a doctor, Steven Kramer, I'm going to demand a demonstration. A hundred ways to pleasure a woman by the world's leading one-armed expert.''

He grinned, the grin that always made her heart turn over with love. "A thousand ways, Abby, my sweet. I'm sure I can find at least a thousand.''

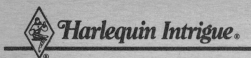

Harlequin Intrigue

High adventure and romance— with three sisters on a search . . .

Now that you've seen Abigail save the Deane family fortune, see how it all began with the hunt for the golden treasure. Share Linsey's danger-filled #120 *Treasure Hunt* by Leona Karr (August 1989) and go along with Kate on her mad chase after the lost gold in #122 *Hide and Seek* by Cassie Miles (September 1989). Don't miss any of the books in THE DEANE TRILOGY.

Indulge a Little, Give a Lot

To receive your free gift send us the required number of proofs-of-purchase from any specially marked "Indulge A Little" Harlequin or Silhouette book with the Offer Certificate properly completed, plus a cheque or money order (do not send cash) to cover postage and handling payable to Harlequin/Silhouette "Indulge A Little, Give A Lot" Offer. We will send you the specified gift.

Mail-in-Offer

	OFFER CERTIFICATE			
Item	A Collector's Doll	B Soaps in a Basket	C Potpourri Sachet	D Scented Hangers
# of Proofs-of -Purchase	18	12	6	4
Postage & Handling	$3.25	$2.75	$2.25	$2.00
Check One				

Name _____

Address _____ Apt # _____

City _____ State _____ Zip _____

ONE PROOF OF PURCHASE

To collect your free gift by mail you must include the necessary number of proofs-of-purchase plus postage and handling with offer certificate.

HI-1

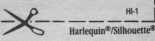

Harlequin®/Silhouette®

Mail this certificate, designated number of proofs-of-purchase and check or money order for postage and handling to

INDULGE A LITTLE
P.O. Box 9055 Buffalo, N.Y. 14269-9055